GONE FERAL

GONE FERAL

Gwen Moffat

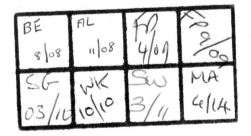

CHIVERS

British Library Cataloguing in Publication Data available

This Large Print edition published by BBC Audiobooks Ltd, Bath, 2008.
Published by arrangement with Constable & Robinson Ltd.

U.K. Hardcover ISBN 978 1 405 64490 7
U.K. Softcover ISBN 978 1 405 64491 4

Printed and bound in Great Britain by
Antony Rowe Ltd., Chippenham, Wiltshire

Chapter One

'Look—' Exasperated, Sophie Daynes tried again: 'Think of him like an injured cat: he comes to your door crying, you'd take him in, wouldn't you?'

'He's healthy, he can be charming—' and any injuries are of his own making, Marjorie Neville thought grimly. Aloud she added, 'You're not a doormat.' It was a warning.

'You don't mean that.'

'No. What I mean is—' Marjorie checked. Don't interfere, she told herself; you don't tell your god-daughter that her husband is a freeloader, she'd said enough already, and not for the first time. 'It was you who likened him to an animal looking for a home,' she pointed out.

'You never married.' It was meant as a fact and sounded like a jibe. In full flight Sophie didn't think to moderate her tone. 'You don't know what that kind of bond is like. You've never shared a home.'

'I have cats.'

'It's not the same.' Of course it wasn't, Sophie was thinking of shared sex but her godmother's mind was on companionship.

'We're back where we started. Forget it. Let me freshen your drink.' Marjorie poured the Talisker with a lavish hand.

1

'I'll be drunk!'

'You're not driving, girl. And what harm can you come to in my woods—or the neighbours' come to that? Grizzly bears? Man traps? Now what have I said?'

'Nothing.'

'You flinched. This is the Lake District, not the Rockies or the Dark Ages.'

Sophie shrugged. 'Well, sprained ankles, a broken leg? You can die of hypothermia at relatively high temperatures. Who'd look after Michael?' She smiled ruefully.

Marjorie refused to accept it as a joke. 'You're positively neurotic today. What's eating you?'

'Michael.' The younger woman stared gloomily at the fells on the far side of the lake. 'He wants to go to Iraq.' She sounded like a condemned prisoner.

'To join the Army!'

'As a reporter. It *is* his job.' The tone was reproving.

'Er—yes.' It wasn't the moment, if it ever was, to point out that he'd left his last newspaper job under a cloud. 'It's dangerous,' Marjorie said.

'That's what bothers me: the situation there.'

'Don't worry. What I mean is it's so dangerous I'm pretty certain that pressmen will be very carefully screened before they're allowed to go. Michael hasn't the necessary

2

experience.'

'You reckon. Are you sure? I suppose you'd know.'

Marjorie wrote short stories nowadays but in her thirties she'd done some freelance journalism. Now she elaborated on just why Michael Daynes wouldn't make it to Iraq, forbearing to mention that she thought it merely another of his attention-seeking ploys, or indeed that he was blacklisted, information she'd caught on the media grapevine. It had to do with his claiming expenses for reports that he'd concocted at home. Michael maintained to family and friends that he had been unfairly dismissed but he'd made no attempt at redress and since his last job he'd taken time out: writing a book, he said vaguely. It could be competent; his writing, however artificial, was colourful.

Sophie left after her second whisky, citing supper to prepare, going down the lawn to the wild garden and the woods, and the path that would take her along the lake shore to the Boathouse. From the terrace Marjorie watched her go, a frown deepening to a scowl as she pondered the girl's situation. Girl? She was a woman in her forties and should be well able to take care of herself—and did except for this one blind spot. Marjorie's thoughts rambled. Took after her mother, that was the trouble. They'd been at school together: Marjorie and Frances Maynard, friends till the end. Frances had even bought the Boathouse as a holiday retreat, and widowed, retired to live there for the few years left to her before the cancer was diagnosed. She'd been a fierce, passionate woman and here was her only child inheriting those genes and employing them in the wrong direction: passionately in love with a sponger, a Walter Mitty character, and fiercely protective, loyal to a fault despite the flaws. Marjorie, literate if not romantic, thought of Ruth in the alien corn: 'whither thou goest I will go . . .' and the Book of Common Prayer. That had a lot to answer for: till death do us part indeed. She grimaced at the water beyond the spring-green foliage; she'd opt for cats any time: no malice. She cast around and located Sharkey supine in the shade of the oak bench and thought wryly that he wouldn't miss her if she died tonight. Patchouli would; here she was: walking backwards up the lawn dragging a large rabbit. Marjorie softened to jelly: a dumpy old lady descending her terrace steps to receive a gift most proudly presented by a tortie-and-white queen.

* * *

Sophie moved quietly through the woods, telling herself she was looking for deer but knowing she was watching for what Michael called her stalker. She'd glimpsed him only once—him because who ever heard of women poachers—and that was what she assumed he was: a poacher familiarizing himself with the territory in the daylight. The woods were private and full of roe, occasionally red deer too came down off the fell. Michael's teasing was superficial, in reality he was uneasy about intruders. He had never liked the isolation of the Boathouse; it nestled deep in trees, open only to the water, the mansion it had belonged to razed long ago, its crumbled ruins taken over by wild plants and animals. Michael would put the Boathouse on the market and move to Manchester but Sophie gloried in this shabby Victorian cottage she had inherited. She cherished it like an animal, scraping and painting inside and out, taking cuttings from old rose bushes in the ruins, bringing them home to her garden: new life for neglected beauties. She loved the silence of her home, the fact that you could see no neighbours' lights at night, only faint pinpricks across the water, and the fairy lights of the steamer passing on summer evenings, chartered for parties, music coming across the lake. Once they were playing Mozart under the moon.

She didn't see the stalker this May evening. She had meant to tell Marjorie but had chickened out, aware that her godmother watched her carefully, never actually saying she was neurotic until tonight, not being as close as Michael. They could be right; the fellow was trespassing but he could be a naturalist, a fungus gatherer—no mushrooms in May—a bird watcher then. Michael said she'd make a drama out of a dead pigeon, that she should be writing the book. She might at that, her life was full of little excitements—and now it was spring. Spring was always thrilling, even more so at the moment when, between jobs, she had the weekend free to work in the garden and to go up to the ruins and see how the stoat family were getting on. There'd be time for Michael too, they could take the boat out. There was no hurry, she'd start looking for work on Monday.

Michael didn't like her working, he said they should keep goats and hens then they'd have meat and eggs; at the moment all they had was vegetables and fruit in season, they had to buy meat. But if she ran a small-holding she'd still have to find part-time work, animal feed cost the earth. Michael said goats ate grass and hens could be fed on kitchen scraps; he was a townie, not a clue about country life. Actually she'd been surprised that he should suggest they keep animals, he wasn't an animal person, even allergic to cats. He never visited Marjorie. It wasn't only the cats; when she came to the Boathouse, and that was seldom, there was a certain coolness.

He was sitting on the deck when she approached, coming up the steps from the slip. He was relaxed, a glass in his hand, and she observed him fondly for a moment before he realized she was there. Now turned forty he was starting to show his age, the blond hair thinning, the mouth less full; could men lose their chiselled lips as women do in middle age? But his eyes would always be grey, not fading as blue eyes do. He was at his best when sitting, he'd lost the lissom grace of youth but then: forty-one, Sophie's heart bled for him. She was forty-five and thought she was in her prime: tough, powerful, not an ounce of fat. To her, hair was something you brushed in the morning and then forgot about, you washed your face when it was sticky. She had good bones but the flesh had sagged and the eyes were too deep in their sockets. She looked what she was: a worker who might be striking if the face filled out. The passionate nature was mostly hidden but at the moment, and after two whiskies, her eyes approved him as she climbed the steps. Flawed, she thought; like I said: an injured cat but I love him, thank God he stays home, I'd kill him if he ran after women.

He regarded her warily. 'Where were you?'

'At Marjorie's.'

'Ha! You've been at her Scotch.'

'Malt actually, but how did you guess?'

'You look soft. Hard shell, soft centre. Sit down, take the weight off your feet.'

He got up stiffly, revealing a bottle by his chair: Glenfiddich, his favourite. She licked her lips, trying to suppress the obvious question. Maybe he'd sold something, she mustn't ask but it would look odd if she didn't say anything. Shortly after they were married she'd started to miss the odd pound coin from her purse, or thought she had, then an occasional ten-pound note when she'd been to the bank and splurged on shopping and didn't know how much she should have left. She was careless about money. Had been. Now she never kept more than two notes in her wallet and hid the rest like a squirrel. But Glenfiddich cost the earth. She had never told Marjorie of course but the awareness that her husband was a petty thief affected her relationship with her godmother and made for misunderstanding and confusion, like the silly exchange this evening.

Michael returned to the deck with a tumbler, a few drops of water in the bottom. He knew how she liked it. 'How can we run to a single malt?' she asked, all innocence.

'I sold a story.'

'Oh, that's great!' Such relief. 'Who to?'

'A Norwegian magazine.'

'Really. How did you do that? Don't you have to go through an agent?'

'I sent it direct.' He didn't question her surprise at his success. 'Sam sells stories to them; he gave me the editor's name and address.' Sam Lewthwaite was a newspaper colleague working in Lancaster.

'You'll have to send them more. What did

they pay you?'

He looked along the shore. 'There's a diver off the point, must be from that boat. What? How much did they pay? A hundred.'

She blinked. 'It doesn't sound much.'

'It's a start.' He seemed abstracted. She said nothing, pondering his lack of enthusiasm at a sale. He turned to her suddenly; they were sitting side by side, touching, convivial. 'See your stalker in the woods?' he asked, grinning.

She shook her head. 'He could be quite innocent.'

'No trespassers are innocent.'

'I mean innocent of anything other than trespass, and that's hardly a major crime.'

'If there are intruders on private property they're most likely watching houses to see who lives alone, who keeps dogs and so on.'

'Michael, you're paranoid!'

'Rubbish. I'm sensible, that's all. And now with the season getting into swing, not that we don't have a drugs problem any time of the year . . . Most burglaries are drug-related.'

'At least we have nothing worth stealing.'

'And what happens when they break in and find nothing? They turn on the occupant.'

'We're becoming obsessed with this,' Sophie said, a shrill note creeping in. *She* wasn't obsessed. 'This is the Lake District, not Manchester. I'm going for a swim.'

'Don't go near that diver.'

'Why not?'

'He might be the lookout for your stalker—'
He stopped, catching her furious eye; he'd
gone too far and his face lightened. 'Just
joking, love. Go and enjoy your swim. I'll do a
bolognese.'

She was on her feet but she paused in the
doorway, staring back at the lake. The little
boat was moored off the point, one figure in it,
in a wetsuit. The other diver had disappeared.
Sun gilded the water, thrushes were singing
their hearts out, the fells slumbered like plump
grey cats. It was a gorgeous May evening, for
her to be disturbed by a black blob in the water
(he had just surfaced) was ridiculous. Paranoia
was infectious. She went indoors to change.

*   *   *

'I was wondering about divers . . .' Sophie's
tone was suspiciously casual. 'How far towards
the water does the private land extend?'

'Towards the water?' Marjorie barked, on
edge because the call had come just as she'd
settled to watch elephants in Namibia. 'The
lake's public, the banks are private, at least
around here. You know that.'

'Suppose they found something. Who owns
it?'

'Such as?'

'Well, what *are* divers looking for? This isn't
the sea with interesting rock formations and
fish and things. What are they after in a lake?

10

There's two off the point now.'

'Can't be, there's no access. They're illegal. Call the cops.'

'They've got a boat.'

'Then they're not illegal, they've come along from an access point.' On the screen, muted, cumbersome elephants slithered down a sandbank; on the opposite side of a shallow river crocodiles shifted nervously. Sophie was rambling on . . . The camera focused on a tiny elephant, surely not long born, the cameraman panned to an enormous croc. '. . . so vulnerable,' Sophie was saying, 'they can see our lights, yours too—from the other side. All they have to do is launch a little boat at night, no one would know. And burglaries go wrong. Anything could happen.'

'Sophie, have you been drinking—since you left here?'

She heard a giggle. 'Not that much. Michael had a bottle of Glenfiddich.' Quickly, forestalling unwelcome comment: 'He sold a story. Isn't that great?'

'Good.' Marjorie's relief was heartfelt but directed at the screen as the crocodiles backed off in the face of a towering matriarch. 'Where'd he sell it?' she asked, once a professional, always—'And how much?' Wondering what kind of price a blacklisted writer could command.

'It was to a Norwegian magazine and they pay, they paid a hundred. He says the price

11

will go up in time.'

'I would hope so. If that's *Hjemmets* I've sent them the odd story myself.' She didn't add that she'd take nothing less than three hundred. And Michael wouldn't be blacklisted in Norway. Or was this a ploy and he was paving the way for a jaunt to Scandinavia? But Michael didn't have the money for foreign travel, in fact he didn't have the cash for single malt . . . Marjorie brought the conversation to an end, dismissing her god-daughter's notion of forays across the lake as melodrama, making scant effort to mask her derision. They were used to each other and she appreciated that Sophie often turned to her deliberately because she was pragmatic and scornful of flights of fancy, or fantasy. And here, this evening, Marjorie was less concerned with divers close to the shore on this side of the lake than with Michael's claim to have bought expensive whisky out of the meagre proceeds of a sale to a Norwegian magazine. It didn't ring true.

The Red Baron came in the kitchen, sat down, glared at her and howled for food. She glared back. Despite the long hair, somewhere in his disreputable ancestry (like the others he was a Rescue cat) there had been a Burmese or a Siamese, something ethnic; he had a voice like a stag belling. Absently she reached for the Go-Cat, thinking that Michael was devious, the Norwegian rigmarole could be

12

just that: an elaborate screen to cover the acquisition of enough cash for a bottle of single malt. 'She should look in her wallet,' she told the Baron, 'count her notes. I wonder now, does she always know where her credit cards are? I trust that fellow as far as I'd trust a crocodile.'

She went back over the recent conversation. Was the girl really worried about divers or nocturnal villains from across the water, or was she fretting over some problem with her own husband? She grunted, angry with herself, it wasn't her business. She'd feed the cats, go back to watching television and forget the telephone call. It could be no more than idle chat, how people kept in touch nowadays. In touch? Sophie had been here only this afternoon . . . She went out to the terrace, wondering where Sharkey and Patchouli were, calling, reminding herself that there was nothing here to hurt a cat: no traps, the relationship with foxes was mutually circumspect . . . and here they came prancing up the lawn. She'd gut the rabbit tomorrow, must remember to bury the skin, she'd learned her lesson the first time she'd presented a skin to Sharkey and he'd taken it to bed with him. Her bed. She observed them critically as they crouched over their food bowls, then returned to the sitting room, but the elephants had given way to a game show. She stood at the window and the question came back like a nagging terrier, intensified. If Sophie rang to chat what was the purpose of the chat? Michael? Money? I'll go to the Boathouse in the morning, she thought; the girl rang for a reason and if there was a coded message there I didn't get it. I shall tomorrow.

*   *   *

There was a cat crying to come in. She opened the door and it was a stranger: an old tabby with a big head, a tom with a torn ear, one eye closed and weeping pus. Something light as a butterfly brushed her hair, the call was not a tom's but a tiny kitten cry, inquiring, concerned . . . She heard the thrush singing, she smelled lilac and with a gentle blooming everything was real again, Sharkey pawing her shoulder from the back of the sofa. 'I was dreaming about one of you,' she said, stretching carefully, relieved that she didn't have an animal here in pain, and then wondering whom she had been dreaming about, remembering Sophie telling her to think of Michael as a cat, injured and homeless: 'You'd take him in, wouldn't you?'

Light dawned, a shaft of light only because beyond it the depths were darker than before. She hadn't remarked it at the time but now it seemed bizarre that the girl should have likened her husband to someone injured, crying out for succour. Was something wrong

14

with Michael? *That* had been the message: some illness, a condition—cancer?

Chapter Two

It was eleven by the time Marjorie came down the drive to the Boathouse, swearing as she tried to avoid the potholes in her new Peugeot. She was in a bad mood already, held up by the mail and the obligation to compose a letter of condolence. So many falling off the perch as one aged—and then there were the obituaries, the need to read them, today a request to write one. And Michael was only in his forties, why should he succumb? Her concern for her god-daughter outweighed her common sense; she had wakened this morning convinced that he'd been diagnosed with something terminal.

He was on the telephone, visible through the kitchen window as she approached the back door—actually the main door but occupants of lakeshore houses called the aspect that faced the water the front. He smiled and waved to her to come in, replacing the phone as she entered. She had brought eggs from her hens.

'Brown eggs!' He beamed. 'Lovely. She's away shopping.'

'She shops on Tuesday.' Marjorie was irritated.

'I sent her specially.' He paused, preparing her. 'We're in the money. I sold a story.'

'You'd expect to. You're a writer. Didn't know you went in for fiction though.'

'It's where the money is: America, Scandinavia.'

'It pays better than journalism?' She was sceptical.

'You don't stand a chance as a freelance nowadays; on the other hand Americans love English short stories, there are magazines publishing nothing else in the States. It's a gold mine.'

'Really. So who are you selling to?'

He hesitated. 'Norway at the moment.'

'So do I. Who are you with?'

'I didn't know—' She'd shaken him and he didn't believe her but he couldn't retract. 'It's called *Hjemmets*, if that's how you pronounce it.' He had it right.

'Snap. Yes, they pay quite well.' She waited but he didn't rise to that one.

'She'll be back shortly,' he assured her. 'Let's have coffee while we wait, and you can tell me about—chickens. She's thinking we could use some.'

He was making conversation. She studied him as he busied himself with a cafetière; he appeared quite healthy, thickening round the middle but that was to be expected at his age, and he wasn't keen on exercise. There was loose skin at the throat rather than the start of

16

a double chin; he wasn't a young man any longer but nor was he one heading for the knacker's yard, not to show it anyway.

'Keeping well?' she asked brightly.

'Of course.' She'd startled him again. 'Did you hear something to the contrary?'

'Neighbourly inquiry. I haven't seen you for a while.'

There was no reply to that except the truth: that they didn't visit, and Michael was not about to be rude. He was wary of her but covering it well, the awkwardness was on her side. She was no good at disguising her feelings and was relieved when their familiar green Mini appeared in the yard. Michael went out to help his wife with the shopping.

Sophie, striking in shades and a fetching straw hat, was bubbling with enthusiasm as she unpacked what she evidently regarded as trophies. Marjorie watched in amazement as the goods were set out on the kitchen table: scallops, king prawns, avocados, a mango, saffron bread. There was Glenfiddich and two bottles of white burgundy.

'You'll stay and eat with us.' It was a command, and Sophie was smug. Her godmother had to share in her husband's triumph. 'We're eating early,' she explained, 'because then Michael can go back to work this afternoon and produce another story so's we can eat like this next month.' The joke had the slightest element of threat behind it (he'd better keep it up) but the look she gave him was playful.

'It's fortunate you don't have a mortgage to find.' Marjorie was churlish, calculating that much of the cheque was already spent—if there had been a cheque. She declined the invitation, pleading business in town, annoyed that she'd wasted time coming here, meaning to speak to Sophie on her own and getting lumbered with the husband instead. Not that he was overtly hostile but his manners were not innate, they were a mask he donned at will or when occasion demanded. His attitude had changed with the arrival of his wife; any stiffness evaporated and as she unpacked the delicacies he looked on with the kind of indulgence that he might have accorded her had she been responsible for the cost of providing them herself.

Sophie said, fingering an avocado, 'This would be too rich, I think, before scallops in a cream sauce. You like guacamole—' to Michael, 'tell you what, we'll have a party this evening; Marjorie can come down for drinks.'

She couldn't refuse the second invitation, that would be gauche despite Sophie's being well accustomed to her foibles; she said she'd come along after she'd shut up her fowls. Foxes were a problem along the lake, owners forced to secure their birds well before dusk.

They stood on the step as she trudged out to her car, Michael's arm round his wife's shoulders: an odd gesture in the circumstances, lending an air of importance to her departure that seemed unwarranted, out of place, as if she were a house guest who'd spent a long weekend with them. As she switched on the ignition she saw to her increased amazement that Sophie's arm was round his waist. Marjorie was not a demonstrative woman herself, revealing her feelings in speech but never in physical contact, except with cats. Nor was she given to self-analysis so, finding the couple's obvious display of affection mystifying, she was annoyed at her own reaction. It was perfectly natural, she told herself, this was spring, all animals were in a high state of excitement and these two, being human animals, were no different. All the same she wished Sophie had found a *steadier* man, she couldn't help wondering if there were too much of the physical side in this marriage.

As the Peugeot disappeared Sophie couldn't wait to get him upstairs. He protested that the food would spoil, you had to be careful with shellfish. She rushed back and threw the fresh stuff in the refrigerator then, as an afterthought, she put the burgundy in there to chill.

He was standing by the window in their bedroom, looking across the water. He turned to her, smiling, and moved to unbutton his shirt. She fumbled with his belt. 'You're like an animal,' he told her, 'a fierce, rutting bitch.'

'I'll take that as a compliment.'

'A good idea,' he said.

She would remember the exchange for a long time.

*   *   *

She left him sleeping, exhausted, showing his age. She wondered if anyone ever looked really ugly in deep sleep; it must be the absence of tension. With their muscles relaxed and the lines smoothed out, lovers became as vulnerable as babies. She sniffed wryly as she went downstairs, reflecting that this would have been just the kind of frenzied moment to conceive, but she wouldn't. Never had and, since they were usually broke, or had been until this week, she had never consulted a doctor. Children were expensive. Some women were infertile and that was that; she had plenty on her plate without a baby to look after. A husband was enough.

The Glenfiddich stood on the table, unopened and alluring. She poured herself a good measure, added a drop of water and went out on the deck. Ripples lapped the pilings and the surface of the lake held a silver sheen. Woods on the far side were still in tender foliage, a foil to copper beeches and the spires of exotic conifers. The steamer dawdled past, a full complement of tourists on her deck. They waved. Full of geniality she waved back, amused, knowing that in a foul mood she would have glared. Chuckling, she returned to the kitchen and reached for a recipe book.

She had set the table with her mother's crystal glasses and what was left of the Royal Worcester, was about to add the cream sauce to the prawns when the telephone rang. She swore and started to panic, thinking that it would wake Michael, but then that could be a good thing, she'd just called him and got no response. She pulled two pans off the hobs, glanced at the asparagus, stepped to the phone—and the pinger went.

She grabbed the phone off the wall, shouted, 'Hang on,' and left it dangling. She wrenched open the oven door, retrieved the scallops, placed them on a warm hob and turned off the heat under the asparagus.

'OK,' she said to the caller, 'bad moment there. Who is it?'

'It's your husband I want.'

She grimaced. Strange voice. A man. Young. 'He's not here,' she lied, now acting haughty. 'Who's speaking? I'll tell him you called.'

'I'll call back.'

'You won't. He's away.'

'I know.' So why—? rose to her lips but he hadn't finished. 'He's with my fiancée,' he said.

'What was that?' Her attention was on the stove.

'He's with my girl. They've gone off,

together. Don't tell me you didn't know.' He was jeering: drunk, drinking anyway, but he could enunciate clearly. 'You didn't know,' he stated into her silence, and now he was cold, accusing. 'No more did I but she told me today, now, an hour since. She's pregnant. Why didn't you see it, for fuck's sake? You *must* have known.' His voice climbed, he was losing it.

'No,' she said firmly, taking a grip on herself. She could hear Michael moving about upstairs. 'You've got the wrong man. My husband isn't with your girl, he's here, with me, in our house. Someone's played a joke—a trick on you, it's a case of mistaken identity.'

'Put him on.'

'What?'

'If he's there he'll talk to me.'

She was furious. They were about to *eat* . . .

'Michael!' she bellowed, going to the foot of the stairs, shouting up. He appeared, looking wary.

'Don't scream,' he murmured. 'I'm here.'

'There's a drunk—' She lowered her voice, whispered fiercely, 'A man who's been drinking, says his girl ran off with a fellow. Says it's you. Wouldn't give a name. She's pregnant and he's beside himself. Get rid of him, love, but don't be hostile, he's distraught. Hurry, I'm dishing up.'

He stared at her, shocked, every vestige of vulnerability gone: a different man, thin-lipped and vicious. She stepped back, appalled. 'He's *drunk*, Michael.' It was a warning.

He brushed past her and out of the back door. She went to call him, his name on her lips, but she made no sound. She went back to the kitchen and picked up the phone. 'He's gone out,' she said without expression.

'I know. He's not there. You better put your house in order, lady, I'm not going to stand for this.'

She replaced the receiver gently. After a moment she poured whisky into her empty tumbler. Then she dialled 1471. The robot voice gave her a number. She didn't recognize it but the code was local.

The scallops were cooling and a thick skin had formed on the cream sauce. Resentfully she started things going again, her mood exacerbated by Michael's stalking out like that, leaving her to cope with an hysterical drunk, trying to prepare a very special lunch at the same time. She poured more whisky, stirring the sauce one-handed, spilling the malt, giggling at the waste, licking the counter.

'What the hell are you doing?' Michael was in the doorway, wide-eyed.

'I spilled whisky. Where did you go?' She was suddenly raging. 'You left me—on my own—' She was spluttering.

He threw up his hands in submission, and he was beaming. 'Sorry, sorry, sorry! You surprised me. I was on cloud nine, only half awake, smelling the cooking, then you screamed—'

'I did not scream, I was—'

'OK, shouting for me, but you were so—frantic—I thought you'd cut yourself, a burn, something . . . And then you tell me there's a drunk on the phone. Hell, love, I switched off. For God's sake, you can handle a nuisance call, that's how I saw it. I forgot all about the meal, I mean: you hate being interrupted in the middle of cooking. Of course you'd be mad if you were distracted, and by a wrong number just.'

She gaped at him. 'A wrong number! I never thought of that! Why didn't I? It's the normal reaction—but then, he seemed to know us, he gave the impression . . . coincidence of course. Here was me telling him he'd got the wrong man, or someone was playing a trick on him, and all the time it was a wrong number! Stupid of me.' She added, smiling, 'I was dreaming too, I wasn't with it at all, enjoying preparing the meal, boozing—'

'I can see that.' The level had sunk alarmingly in the bottle. 'So when are we eating?'

'Now. Open the wine, will you? It's in the fridge.'

He said the scallops were delicious. She didn't contradict him, they should have been eaten straight from the oven and they were a trifle rubbery but redeemed by prawns and mushrooms in the sauce. The asparagus was flaccid but he didn't comment. The burgundy was good; she couldn't appreciate it after the malt but Michael accounted for most of a bottle.

They had a mango fool for pudding and it wasn't until she was serving coffee and he was clearing the table that he saw the note on the counter.

'What's this?'

'Oh, that. I dialled 1471 after the wrong number and that's his. Does it mean anything to you?'

'Nothing,' He crumpled the paper and dropped it in the pedal bin.

They washed up and she said she must go to the village and replenish supplies against Marjorie's visit this evening; after the amount she'd had to drink she couldn't risk driving to town. The village was only at the end of the lake. She rather hoped Michael would offer but he said he'd take the boat out and get some fresh air. She didn't remind him that the plan had been for him to work on a short story that afternoon. Things were a little fraught since the unpleasant call.

She was in the bedroom retrieving a couple of banknotes from the toe of one of her winter boots when she heard the soft clonk of wood on wood. She looked out at the slip as Michael stepped into the boat. Something flashed and struck a thwart. He grabbed at it, rocking the boat, and slipped it in his shirt pocket. Not a wallet, that wouldn't make a sound, it must be his mobile phone. She frowned, watching him putter away from the slip, coming round to make for the point. She wondered if the stress of making love (stress?), of rich food and rather a lot of wine had been too much for him; the purposeful departure had an air of escape. Did she—could she be smothering him?

She went slowly downstairs, her thoughts reverting to telephones, to mobiles and wrong numbers. She looked in the pedal bin. She'd removed a full bag before lunch. The new bin liner was empty. The note had gone.

The telephone rang as she was about to leave. She recognized the voice immediately: a southern accent with a veneer of refinement. He said, without preamble, 'Do you know where they are?' The question was cool and clear, which was a surprise; assuming he had continued to drink, he should be comatose by now.

She asked coldly, 'Who is this?'

'That's not the issue.'

'You must have picked up the wrong number. I'm not talking to someone I don't know. If you were genuine—'

'I'm Andrew Lambourne and I'm the receptionist at Marten House. Your husband's Michael Daynes and he's gone off with my fiancée, Mary Spence. I know where you live.'

She felt very cold. 'It's been going on for months,' he continued, and now there was a trace of gloating in the tone. Over what or whom? At that moment it didn't occur to her that she was being baited. She was in shock. She hung up the receiver as he was speaking.

She walked out of the house, down the steps to the slip and, taking the path that led through the woods parallel to the shore, she ran fast to the back of the point. It wasn't far, only about half a mile. The headland was a little crag some thirty feet high crowned with scrubby oaks, and beyond it was a secluded bay where people landed illegally and picnicked. There were no tourists today, only the boat stationary on the water, Michael hunched in the stern, a phone clapped to his ear.

Chapter Three

'You haven't been long,' she observed when Michael came home. 'You spoke to Andrew Lambourne.' It was the flattest of statements.

'Who's—You're back already?'

'We're full of surprises today.' She smiled but her eyes were blazing. 'Andrew Lambourne? At Marten House?'

He licked his lips. 'What exactly are you on about?' He glanced towards the sitting room. 'Isn't Marjorie here?'

'I put her off. You lied to me. You've been lying all along. You've been *living* a lie! For months and months and months!' It was strained and harsh but not loud, and the more scathing for that.

He was frightened, backing off. 'If you're going to go on like this, not explaining, I'm walking out.'

'To her? When are you meeting her? You phoned her, that's why you took the boat out. Who is she?'

'Look, love—'

'Don't you dare call me love, don't you dare—'

'I never lied to you.' It was level and heavy.

'*What?* This afternoon: here in this room, you said—' She checked, groping, trying to remember what he had said. 'You told me the phone number meant nothing to you.'

'It didn't. I had no idea.' He glanced at the pedal bin. 'How did you find out?'

'Lambourne told me everything.'

'Where did you get the number? Of course I took it; I needed to find out who was calling us, making a nuisance of himself. But how did you know where to phone?'

'There you are! You do know Lambourne.'

He shook his head. They stared, each gauging the other's reactions. 'I do know it's the number of Marten House,' he conceded, 'because that's how my call was answered. I asked who I was speaking to and some guy said

I was through to Reception.'

'Then what? Did you tell him who you were?'

'No, I needed time to think about it. I cut the connection. Was I speaking to this Lambourne fellow?'

'Are you saying you don't know him?'

'Never heard of him.'

'He's the receptionist at Marten House and he's Mary Spence's partner.'

'Ah-h.' It was drawn out. She watched him in pyrrhic triumph, the injury so deep that she felt no pain. Now, as if the situation had eased, he pulled out a chair and sat down. His eyes wandered, he could have been looking for a drink but equally he could be avoiding her relentless stare. 'Back in the winter,' he began, 'one time when you were spending the evening at Marjorie's, I met a girl in the Packhorse and gave her a lift home. To her home, I mean. I was rather under the weather and she came on heavy . . . nothing much I could do about it.' He shrugged, embarrassed. 'It didn't mean anything, I would have forgotten—I mean, drunk, one does forget, right? But she's been a bit of a pest since.'

'So it's been going on since the winter.'

'Nothing's going on!' It was explosive. 'She calls me: that's it.' He hesitated. 'She's not very intelligent, in fact she's neurotic, lives in a dream world . . . she's been in therapy . . . she's convinced herself she's going to go away with me.'

Sophie said sweetly, 'It didn't occur to you that you might be taking advantage of a girl who was mentally challenged?' Dangerously reasonable she went on, 'So Lambourne had it right. Where were you to meet? And when?'

He sighed. 'I said, it's all in her mind. She's had a tiff with the boyfriend and has thrown my name in the chap's face: taunted him. Now she's walked out and he assumes she's speaking the truth. Maybe she is and she has gone off to join a lover, another one; she came on like a nymphomaniac. The girl needs treatment.'

'You said she'd had treatment. She told you that?'

'It came out in conversation.'

'The night you drove her home.' He said nothing. 'She calls you here?' Sophie glanced at the phone. 'I don't remember speaking to a strange—and demented woman.'

'She calls me on my mobile.'

'What was in your mind when you gave her your mobile number?'

'I didn't. She must have got hold of it when I was drunk.'

'What did she have to say today when you told her the balloon had gone up?'

His jaw dropped. 'I—haven't spoken to her for weeks.'

'You said she calls you constantly—'

'I don't answer.'

30

'Who were you phoning from the boat?'

'You were spying on me?' There was a flash of fury but it vanished in the face of her amazement at his daring to accuse her of misconduct. 'I called Marten House—to find out who might have it in for me.'

'You'll have to watch your back. He says he knows where you live.'

'Figure of speech. His girlfriend's nothing to me.'

'Incidentally, where does she live?'

'I've no idea.'

'You took her home.'

'I was dead drunk. All those places look the same at night.'

'What places? Sink estates? Institutional housing?'

'You've every right to be upset, love, but honestly, it was just one stupid mistake, virtually rape on her side; why, I hardly knew where I was.'

'You were able to drive to Kelleth.'

After a moment he said, 'Was it Kelleth? I can't even remember whether it was Kelleth or Kendal.'

* * *

At Marten House Andrew Lambourne said quickly, 'I'll call you back,' replaced the receiver and smiled politely at the couple who came in from the terrace, placing empty glasses on the hall table.

'The midges are starting to bite,' the woman said, rubbing her arm.

'They come earlier each year,' Lambourne told her. 'It's global warming. But they don't go on the tops. You had a good day on the hill?' This was his first season in the Lakes but he was picking up the speech patterns.

'We saw the deer!' Deer came in the night to feed on the hotel's roses but he didn't disabuse her; middle age and Gucci accessories commanded respect. 'How exciting,' he breathed as the telephone started to ring.

He waited until they'd gone into the dining room and only then did he snatch up the receiver. 'Yes?' he snapped. He relaxed as he listened and collected himself. 'I'm so sorry, yes, this is Marten House. How can I help you?'

Mrs Foley came through from the kitchen as he was ending the call. 'Andrew, will you get on to the plumber, ask him to come out first thing tomorrow; that sink's clogged up again. And one of the taps in number seven is running much too slowly; it's nothing to do with the pressure, the other taps are functioning properly. What's wrong? You look peaky.'

'Nothing's wrong, Mrs F., but I need to make a call myself. Would you stand in for me for just a few minutes?'

'Andrew! You're on duty.'

They faced up to each other: the manageress, large and plain, a woman of considerable presence, confronting her darkly handsome and usually respectful receptionist.

'It's a family emergency,' he said, producing it like an ultimatum.

'Tell me.' And that was Mrs Foley, who hadn't risen to manage a three-star hotel in Lakeland without acquiring authority.

He grimaced. 'Mary—my fiancée—she's missing.'

'What d'you mean, missing?'

'Disappeared.' He threw a glance towards the dining room. 'I can't say more here. Afterwards?' He was pleading. 'I was talking to her brother when the Staffords walked in, I promised to call him back. He'll be waiting.'

'Five minutes then. I'll call the plumber.' Andrew was a well-mannered boy, good at his job. If it was only a telephone call . . . Mrs Foley squeezed behind the desk and pulled out the list of service numbers.

In his room Lambourne lit a cigarette and dialled Keith Weston on his mobile. No way was he going to use the land line with the old cow listening in downstairs.

'What kept you?' Weston spoke with an East Anglian accent. There was no warmth in it, at least not at the moment.

'Guests.' Lambourne snapped. 'This is a hotel.'

'You work there?'

'I'm the receptionist. That's not important. If she isn't with you or her parents, has she been in touch?'

'No, she hasn't. How long's she been gone?'

'She left at lunchtime.'

'It's only seven, man! Can't the woman go off on her own for a few hours? Are you living together?'

'No. She has her own place in Kelleth—'

'I know that—'

'Then why d'you ask—'

'I meant she's got her own life to lead. You're not married to her, what's the urgency? Why call me?'

'Because,' Lambourne said through gritted teeth, 'she told me she's going away with another guy and they've been having it off for months: a married man.'

There was a smothered exclamation then: 'What d'you expect me to do about it?'

'I don't expect anything.' Lambourne was running out of steam. 'I'm serious about her and she's your sister. I hoped you'd help.'

'Stepsister. Did you call her place?'

'There was no reply. I'll go there once I come off duty.'

'You do that. Let me know how you get on.' There was a pause. 'Did you have a row?'

'Yes.' Lambourne was tight-lipped.

'There you are then. She'll be back. I mean, if she's serious too. If not, I guess you'll just have to do what everyone else does in the circumstances: take it on the chin. But call me back. Speak to her neighbour, Barbara something, she could know where Mary is.'

* * *

'Stop being so fidgety,' Barbara Howard said. 'The car's hidden, he doesn't even know I have a garage, and if you keep your blinds down there's no way he can know you're inside the flat.'

Mary Spence said, 'I'm not bothered about Andrew.' Her tone changed. 'But I can't keep still, I'm too excited, can't relax. I adore Michael, all I want to do is spend the rest of my life with him.'

Mary wouldn't normally have been taken for a beauty; she was on the thin side, her hair was unremarkable: worn loose and unshaped; basically she was an ordinary girl who was artful with make-up, only now, imbued with delight and anticipation, she had the air of a bride, the inner glow that turns people's heads. She frightened Barbara.

'When are you meeting him?' The older woman was concerned about Andrew's reaction; when he came here, as surely he would, she'd become involved herself. They lived in flats, the Howards above Mary, in one of Kelleth's gentrified yards: a jumble of eighteenth-century cottages, some whitewashed, others in granite or rosy sandstone, and all blazing with flowers in pots and window boxes, their flights of steps festooned with vines and creepers.

Barbara was a sharp little mouse of a woman, married to a long-distance lorry driver who was now somewhere in Eastern Europe. Mary had come upstairs ostensibly to ask her to water her plants while she was gone but there was no way she could keep her excitement to herself; she maintained she had burned her bridges, had come clean with Andrew and left him to join up with her lover. Andrew was a nice boy but there was no depth to their relationship, it had become like a marriage; Andrew was the old husband, Michael the new lover. The ages were the wrong way round but she didn't dwell on that, it was immaterial.

Barbara, who was forty and contentedly married, asked about Michael's wife, but this was a subject that didn't concern Mary who was so overwhelmed ('I realize now that I've never been in love before. Isn't that amazing?') there was no room for anyone in her life other than the lover. Andrew was a discard, something left behind.

She had begged to put her car in Barbara's garage so that when Andrew came looking for her he wouldn't know she was here; she did take him into consideration but only as a potential hazard, nuisance value. In a confrontation with Michael Andrew would come off worst; all the same, if there were any possibility of a problem, however small, it had to be crushed in advance, so her car was hidden.

'Michael will call me when he can get away,' she said as they drank Riesling in Barbara's living room, the window open wide above the yard where people passed slowly, exclaiming at the quaintness of this little backwater, taking pictures.

'What's keeping him?' Barbara asked, curious but practical with it.

'His wife's being difficult.'

'All the more reason—what? You mean, she knows?' This was a surprise; until now Barbara had thought it a clandestine affair, and that telling Andrew had been the first move towards exposure.

Mary drew rings on the table with her wine glass. She looked shifty. 'Andrew called her.'

'He called Michael's wife? And told her you were having an affair with her husband! How could he do that?'

'He was mad—furious.'

Barbara sighed in exasperation at men's stupidity. Actually she felt rather sorry for this woman whom she'd never met. 'How old is she?' Guessing the answer, knowing Michael was older than Mary, and probably by quite a few years.

Mary shrugged. 'She's forty something: plain, frumpish—he says; she was on the check-out at Safeway's until this week.' She was contemptuous but since she had just walked off her job at a local bakery she had no call to act superior.

'So what did she say to Andrew?'

'Nothing. Gave him the brush-off. But then she let Michael have it.'

'So they fought.'

'No. Michael denied everything, said it was a wrong number, and then he walked out and called me.'

'He's not coming clean with her then. Have you asked yourself why that is?'

Mary gasped. 'Are you suggesting that he doesn't care for me? I know Michael and he worships me; it's not just that he says so, it's obvious by how he behaves, how he looks at me, he'll do anything for me. Why should he have phoned me immediately after Andrew spilled the beans if I wasn't important to him?'

Barbara raised her eyebrows. 'To warn you maybe.'

'Against who?' It was shrill.

'Mary! You've upset—no, you've devastated two people; how do you suppose they think of you at this moment? You figure they're about to give you their blessing?'

'Well, Michael's wife doesn't know about me because he denied it, and she won't so long as he doesn't lose his nerve and tell her, and as for Andrew, I'm not bothered about him. Listen to us: you think the Daynes woman and

Andrew are going to join forces and come after me with a shotgun?' She grinned, enjoying the drama.

'Does either of them have a gun?'

'This is for real, Barbara; it's not the telly. Although'—her eyes were alight—'the sex is better than the telly: sex without violence, that's how it should be, right?'

'Should be.' But Barbara was doubtful.

* * *

Michael sprawled on an old car seat outside Rod Coulter's caravan, a can of Carlsberg Special in his hand, his eyes half-closed against the afterglow. 'You've got it made,' he murmured. 'If I had all this'—his free hand gestured, indicating the caravan, the woods, the first stars glinting—'I'd want nothing else.'

'No woman?' Coulter didn't move from where he sat on the steps of the van, didn't turn his head. Michael studied the man's profile in the fading light but he knew the face would be as expressionless as the voice. He envied the lack of emotion as he envied the other's lifestyle: footloose, unemployed, nonchalant yet always in funds from various suspect activities, but never caught; always with a bottle of Famous Grouse on hand and Carlsberg for chasers.

'Well, there'd be a woman, yes,' Michael admitted, grinning. 'For a while,' he added thoughtfully. 'Mind you, Mary would prefer a proper house.'

'Then you'd be back where you started: just substituting one woman for another.'

'They're not in the same league,' Michael protested. 'Mary's a sweet kid; if you'd heard my wife slagging her off . . .' He crushed the can in his hands, then he giggled. 'She's a vicious bitch,' he added, and there was a note of admiration in the tone.

'Maybe she'll see Mary off—'

'She could but—'

'No, that's the wrong way round. They could fight and Mary could come off best. You should give her the gun, get her to do the job for you.'

'Then Mary would be for the chop. She's got no brains.' Michael stood up and Coulter leaned to the side as he went to the fridge for more lager. He glanced round the interior of the van, thinking it unusual that a fellow could keep a place neat and clean without a woman, but then Coulter had no more possessions than he could pack into his pick-up: a sleeping bag, some clothes and tools, everything else came with the caravan, and that was rented, along with the fittings and the propane cylinders.

There was silence when he'd sat down again and opened a fresh can. After a while Coulter said, 'What did you have in mind?'

'When?'

'Before today: before the balloon went up.'

'We talked about it last time.' Michael was sullen, the alcohol starting to catch up with him after the events of the day, and now his drinking buddy setting out, as he saw it, to rile him. He said crudely, 'The idea was to get rid of her.'

'You were drunk.'

'We both were. You said there are ways of disposing of a body so's it's never found, not in our lifetimes anyway.'

'It was an academic discussion.' Coulter had a command of words, he was no ignorant thug. 'The situation's changed,' he pointed out. 'How do you propose to handle it now?'

'Ride the storm, I guess.'

'More like horses, and you've got two of 'em to ride: your girl and your wife.'

'I've juggled them fine so far; I convinced Sophie it was just a one-off, that I was drunk anyway.'

'You think she believed you? She'll be watching you like a hawk from now on.'

'So what? She has to go to work; she's left Safeway's but she'll be looking for another job on Monday. I'll be free as a bird while she's away all day.'

'But this Mary's pushed you into a corner. You said she's expecting you to leave your wife.'

'Not yet.' Michael shifted uncomfortably. 'I told her: when I'm free. No way can I shack up

41

with Mary while Sophie's—' He stopped and sucked his cheek.

'Alive?'

'No!'

Again they were silent and this time the atmosphere was strained as the denial hung in the air demanding comment.

'That was what you implied last time we discussed it,' Coulter said softly.

'I was fantasizing. I never meant it.'

'You need to get your priorities straight, man. Is the girl expecting you to join her now?' Michael regarded the distant gleam of water beyond the dark trees. The steamer was passing, lit up for a party, only the faintest throb of the engines audible. 'So you have said so,' came the voice from the steps. 'And she's waiting for you. Or to join you in the Boathouse. Your wife might walk out; on the other hand she could get an injunction and turn you out maybe, I'm not a lawyer. She'll definitely make a new will. You said your wills favour each other. That won't be for long once she meets your other woman and finds out how things stand. Besides, you've lied to her. Women don't like that.'

'You don't know what you're talking about. I could win her over, both of them. I know I could.'

'Could,' Coulter repeated. 'But not now. The way you tell it, Mary comes across as a kid who's set on having you, and she's not

42

bothered about other people—like the guy at the hotel, and your wife, maybe you too—'

'She's crazy about me!'

'But not much bothered how she goes about getting you. My point is she's not thinking straight, probably not thinking at all. She's trouble. Now she's left one guy she's expecting you to fill the gap. You said you'd go away with her, and she's just moved the date forward.'

'So what do you suggest?' Feeling himself cornered, he tossed the problem back.

'How much is the Boathouse worth?' Michael's eyes widened. 'Two hundred K?' Coulter answered his own question. 'A quarter of a million perhaps, because there's some land and the lake frontage. I'll take ten thousand to get rid of the body.'

Michael grinned weakly. After a while he said, 'We've been here before except that you didn't name a figure. A hit man would kill for ten thousand, let alone dispose of the body.'

'You'll have to look sharp before she makes a new will.'

Michael licked his lips. 'Where would I find ten thousand?' He gasped as a thought struck him. 'You're mad! If the body's not to be found, I can't inherit, can I? Then where's the money to pay you?'

'You'll have the place to live in. It's as good as yours even if you do have to wait seven years before she's declared dead. You can borrow against the value of the property.

Meanwhile you'd have her plastic.'

'How can I use her credit card once she's gone missing? I'm in deep shit as it is. She's only got one card and I've been milking it this month . . . Now that's a point: if she wasn't here next month she wouldn't see the bank statements. She doesn't know I lifted her card but I've been sweating on how to deal with that statement when it comes . . . on the other hand if she's not here I'd be getting all her mail.' He stopped, thought about it and said sharply, 'Five thousand!'

'Ten, and I'm not haggling.'

'We're joking, right?'

'Right, now let's work out the details.'

Chapter Four

On the Monday Sophie found a temporary job behind the bar at a pub in Ambleside, standing in for a sick employee. The following day, as soon as she left for work, Michael was on the phone to Mary. He couldn't go to her because Sophie had the car so Mary came to the Boathouse. The danger, as much as their enforced separation, was highly stimulating and they made love with abandon in the bedroom where rippled light danced on the ceiling and water slapped against the piles as the steamer passed.

44

It was the sound of voices on the boat that alerted Michael and sent him hurrying out to hide Mary's car behind a stand of Douglas firs halfway up the drive. As he walked back he reflected on what might happen if Sophie were to return unexpectedly. There'd be no car to give the game away but how would she react on finding Mary in her bed?

He climbed the stairs slowly. She was fast asleep. He sighed, not wanting to wake her. She looked as if she belonged here in the lovely light above the sparkling water, in his house which could—should be theirs. To hell with it, he thought, and slipped back into the bed.

It was nine o'clock in the evening when he decided that she really had to leave. She was tired and demanding, turning fractious. She protested that pubs didn't close for hours yet and that Sophie had to drive home all of twenty miles across the pass.

'It's cutting it too fine,' he said reasonably. 'If she was feeling off-colour'—'suspicious' was the word in his mind—'she could be home any time.'

'So what? She knows about me—'

'She doesn't—'

'Then she should do. She has to know sometime. Anyway, would she care?'

'She's possessive about things. Like—it's her bed.'

She was stricken. 'Michael, you don't still

45

sleep with her? You said—'

'No, no. But it's *her* bed. We scr— we've been making love in it. Don't you see? She'd go spare.'

'OK.' It was light and angry. 'Next time we'll screw in the spare room. I take it you have a spare room. Where *you* sleep.'

'Don't be like that, love. Look, next time I'll come to the flat. I'd prefer that; this place is haunted by her. I feel constrained. I think of your flat as home.'

'You've never been there. You could have come any time. I kept asking—'

'Things have changed. What I mean is, where you are is home to me, or will be from now on.' It was over the top but then so was Mary. 'I'll come tomorrow,' he promised, 'but you must leave now. Suppose a neighbour was to come by?'

He was sitting on the side of the bed. She slipped her arms round him and nuzzled his back like a puppy. 'You're sending me away.'

'You know me better than that.' He freed her hands and kissed the palms. 'Look, tomorrow we'll talk about the future, our future. I think she'll be leaving very shortly. There's nothing to keep her here, there hasn't been for a while, and now there's you. She'll understand when I explain about you; she's an old lady, sweetheart, but she's sensible. It's an empty marriage; she knows that.'

'You're saying she'll walk out and leave her

house?' Mary looked round the room as if pricing the furniture.

'We'll come to an arrangement. We're joint owners after all so I can buy her out.' He smiled fondly. 'And then you'll move in.' She looked doubtful. 'Or we'll sell up and buy a place in the sun. How's that?'

'You really think she'll go without trying to make trouble?'

'There's nothing to stay for. She'll be gone within . . .' he hesitated, '. . . days.'

Michael was a compulsive liar; lying came to him as automatically as breathing but in one respect this afternoon he was sincere: he had deep feeling for Mary Spence. Whether it was infatuation, love or lust was immaterial, for the time being she monopolized his thoughts, at least those that were not occupied with problems associated with his wife. So he wasn't lying when he proclaimed his dependence on Mary, and he didn't lie when he said Sophie would soon be gone, although in the latter case his telling the truth was a matter of accident.

He didn't intend to go to Mary's flat the following day but the assurance kept her sweet and was an inducement to get her to leave the Boathouse at that moment. The empty promise came naturally; as the evening wore on he was increasingly aware of the time and he was mortally afraid of Sophie catching him out in a situation from which escape could be difficult.

Michael was no psychopath, he had a dread of consequences. He was a poor judge of character. He thought his wife sensible without realizing that everyone is flawed and that no sensible woman could have lived with him for a week without becoming aware of his fundamental dishonesty.

Sensible Sophie was not, at least in this respect, her flaw being the blind spot of good wives married to rogues. But she had a streak of cunning. Finding lipstick on the pillow when she made the bed the following morning she changed the linen and said nothing. Her hours at the pub were flexible and that day she was to start work after lunch so she was home all morning. Michael worked in the spare room which he had set up as a study and there he received Mary's calls on his mobile. She realized that without transport he couldn't keep his promise so she said she would come to the Boathouse again. She was amused by his protests and ridiculed his suggestion that she should pick him up on the road and they would drive to some secluded spot. That was crazy, she said, when there was a comfortable bed available in an empty house. She told him to expect her at two o'clock and broke the connection. At midday he called her back to say that Sophie had been told not to go into work because the boss's wife was taking over the bar that afternoon and evening. Mary said in that case he could take the car and come to her flat. He said he had to take Sophie shopping. Mary didn't believe a word of it.

She would have liked to talk it over with Barbara but Barbara would only put into words the suspicion that Michael was rejecting her and indeed, thinking back to that airy bedroom lit by golden reflections, hadn't he seemed too much at home in that bed? He's still sleeping in it, she thought; she's his wife, I'm his bit on the side. She agonized over the situation until she felt sick with doubt. She called him and there was no reply. He'd switched off his mobile. He was refusing to speak to her.

She drove to the lake and took the dead-end road that served houses along the south shore. She slowed as she passed his drive but it was long, winding through the woods, and the Boathouse was invisible. OK, she thought viciously, she doesn't know me, I could be any tourist looking for access to the water. She drove back and turned down the drive.

There was no car outside the house. Delight and anticipation replaced anger and then she sobered. He'd lied. Not necessarily, his wife could have gone shopping on her own. She ran to the door, seeing as she did so an empty kitchen behind the window. The door was locked. There was a letter slot. Without thinking she lifted the flap and called his name. There was no sound from the interior.

She walked round the place peering in

49

windows. There was no one at home. Slowly she returned to the car, uncertain again, wondering where he could be. Were they together? She used her mobile but his was still switched off. That could mean they were together and he daren't speak to her. Between misery and anger she switched on the ignition and drove back to the end of the lake, turned left in the village and took the north shore road to the pass and Ambleside.

*   *   *

At breakfast time on the Thursday there came a point when Michael could no longer avoid his wife's eyes. 'Did I cut myself shaving?' he asked.

Sophie had been wondering why she should have to wait for him to speak before she could start but there was no surprise in her response. 'I saw Mary Spence yesterday.'

'Oh yes.' He took a gulp of coffee and prayed not to choke. 'I hope she didn't make a nuisance of herself.'

'She didn't speak. She came in the bar, sat down and stared at me. I assume it was her. A young girl, rather old-fashioned, a lot of eye make-up and a floppy hat with pink roses.'

'Could be anyone.'

'How did she discover where I work?'

'Mm.' The response implied deep thought as he looked away to contemplate the yard beyond the window.

'How many people know?' She was relentless.

'I could have mentioned it to anyone.'

'I'd only been there two days. How many people have you met in two days?'

'I have a mobile. People called me.' He glanced at her. 'Mostly I called them—but not her. She may have tried to get in touch but I had the phone switched off most of yesterday—deliberately.'

'Why was that?'

'She's an incubus.'

'A what?'

He slammed his palm on the table, suddenly enraged. Her eyes widened, shifting an inch to the shotgun behind him on its rack. 'I've had all I can stand!' he shouted. 'What d'you think it's like, eh? Put yourself in my position: there's this tart pestering me all the time, never giving me a moment's peace, *stalking*, that's what it is: a crime, I could get an injunction, and now you twisting the knife as if it's all my fault—OK, it was my fault initially but that was months since. I told you, I admitted it, and you—you made like you accepted it and now, every time you feel like it, you're going to throw it in my face. Haven't you got any sense of—of compassion, any sympathy? We've been together for years, we've shared everything—' He stopped, lost for words, appealing mutely to her forgiving

51

nature.

'We shared our lives,' she murmured.

'Exactly!'

'This house.'

'Yours, but yes, you shared it—'

'Money.'

'I am trying, darling—'

'Shared a bed.'

The silence stretched. His lips parted and she waited for the lie. It didn't come. She said quietly, 'She doesn't shower before she screws. Isn't that rather risky, health-wise? How do I know? She left her lipstick on my pillow.'

His eyes were flat as a lizard's. He said evenly, 'You came home very late on Tuesday and you were too exhausted even to wash your face. That had to be your lipstick.'

She stood up and started to clear the breakfast things. Michael went quietly out of the kitchen and upstairs to his study. Behind him Sophie raised her heavy gaze to the shotgun which she kept for rabbits raiding her vegetables. She was only looking, not consciously considering when it might be used next.

She went to Ambleside and worked through the day, running on automatic pilot, at times feeling close to tears, confiding to the boss's wife that she reckoned it had to be the onset of an early menopause. She didn't need any persuading to leave early and she drove home over the pass, along the lake shore, past the tourists in lay-bys photographing evening reflections, past hikers gleaming with sweat and achievement at the end of a good day on the tops, past a pair of lovers kissing on a bluebell bank. Other people all lost in delight unaware and uncaring that someone passed by in a personal world that was the antithesis of theirs: dark and empty and vaguely menacing.

It was still light when she reached home. The house was unlocked but Michael wasn't inside. Moving through to the sitting room and out to the deck she saw that the boat wasn't at the slip. There were numerous craft on the water but it was impossible to tell if hers was among them.

She was sitting in the kitchen sipping Bell's when the telephone rang. Focused on Michael, schooling herself to be calm, she reached for the instrument, grunting a 'Yes?'

'Michael,' came the breathless voice of a young woman, 'I've been trying to reach you for hours, for days—you were switched off. Listen, sweetie, I can't stand it any longer, being on my own, I have to speak to you. I'm coming down now, I'm on my way—Michael? *Michael!*'

Very gently Sophie replaced the receiver and, turning back to her drink, was aware of Michael himself standing in the doorway.

'Who was that?' It was jerky, as if he had no command over his voice or his curiosity.

A dozen responses passed through her mind

53

but 'Mary Spence,' was all she said.

The gun was on its rack, like a trained dog awaiting action. He followed her eyes and his face changed. It had been smooth, vacant, ready to assume any look that was required, a chameleon face, expression substituted for colour. Now what she identified was unadulterated hatred.

She had the heavy whisky tumbler in her hand and she threw it, not at him but at the cooker. It was a diversion. He winced at the crash, staring at her mother's crystal disintegrating in shards to the floor. There was a slow motion quality about the action and his turning to her must have been relatively slow; he was slower than her anyway because when his eyes came back to her he was looking into the twin barrels of the gun.

'No!' he shouted. 'It's loaded!'

'Loaded?' she snarled at him. 'No one ever keeps a gun loaded.'

'Just joking.' He managed a sickly grin. 'So now she's started pestering you, has she?'

She said coldly, 'Get out of my house.'

'Now look—' But he was going. Not risking passing her to the yard door, he edged backwards, retreating through the sitting room to the deck, walking round the house. She followed his progress from inside, the gun obvious at every window had he looked. He didn't.

The Mini stood in the yard, facing up the

drive. He saw that the keys were in the ignition and he slid inside thinking himself lucky that she'd closed the windows against the dew. At the back door Sophie raised the gun and fired. The Mini jerked forward and went bucketing up the drive.

She stared in disbelief at the place where it had been. She reached inside the door for the outside light, walked forward, laid the gun down and peered at the ground. Unmistakably, when you knew what to look for, when you'd caught the sound of metal striking metal, there on the granite sets were tiny flakes of green paint and a number of shotgun pellets, not to speak of the cartridge case by the back door.

*   *   *

'He was here,' she told Mary Spence when she arrived. 'He left a while ago. I thought he'd gone to join you.'

'I expect he's at the flat. I called from Ambleside so I missed him on the road. I didn't realize I was speaking to you on the phone. Not at first.'

'That was obvious.'

'I'm sorry. I am, truly, but it just happened, you know; you can't help falling in love, and anyway, your marriage was washed up. I mean, you're still young enough to find another chap. I came in the bar yesterday to see what you

55

were like. I thought you looked nice, not at all—well, Michael can be pretty blunt, can't he? But you're attractive.' She sounded surprised, smiling, trying to break the other's attentive gaze. 'You won't be alone for long,' she resumed desperately and then, thinking that sounded cheeky coming from a young person: 'I just want everyone to be happy and you're not really, are you? He said you'd be leaving shortly.'

'Where did he get that idea?'

'Well, you must have suggested it.'

'That I would leave this house.' It was a heavy statement, not a question.

'He would buy you out,' Mary assured her. 'It wouldn't be as if we—he was turning you out; I mean'—she looked round wildly—'it would be worth a bit: your half share.'

Sophie was taking deep breaths. Mary watched her closely. 'It's reasonable, isn't it? He wants to do the right thing by you. We both do.'

'How old are you?' Sophie asked, finding her voice.

Mary was affronted after her attempts at reassurance. 'I'm twenty-two, if it's any business of yours.'

'I would have put you as rather younger.' Sophie considered this. 'And you left a boy of your own age to shack up with this old snake.' She checked. 'That's insulting a snake. You've been lucky—so far. What else has my husband

56

told you? I take it he's going to marry you.'

'He will eventually.' Mary tried to retain some dignity. 'You'll divorce him so obviously we'll marry.'

'How would you live? He's got no money.'

The reasonable tone emboldened Mary to push it. 'I don't know as I want to live here but he says it's worth a bit with the lake and all so we'd sell it and buy a place on the Med. Do you have a problem with that?'

Sophie shook her head. 'No, it's not me who has a problem. This is my house, and all the contents, including the bed you screw on with my husband—the lying bastard—' She had been careful, realizing the immaturity of this child, but it was that very factor coupled with the deceit, the lying . . . She looked at the gun which she'd replaced on its rack, the thing had been loaded, *he'd* loaded it! She shook with rage—and the dam burst.

They moved together, Mary frightened, Sophie hurling herself round the table to put herself between the girl and the gun. 'You shot him!' Mary shouted as Sophie reached for it.

'Guns are always kept unloaded,' Sophie told her. 'He had loaded this one, now why would he do that?'

'You're making it up.'

'He told you I'd be leaving shortly.' Mary nodded, mesmerized by the weapon, the barrels pointed at the floor. 'So,' Sophie said harshly, giving rein to the emotions she'd repressed all day, 'I was leaving and he'd loaded this gun.'

'You shot him.' It was a whimper. 'You shot my Michael.'

Any stricken animal could disarm Sophie, however enraged. 'You silly bitch. I didn't shoot him, he moved too fast—and at that time I didn't know the gun was loaded. He said so but of course I didn't believe him. It was after I fired at the Mini that I found the pellets on the ground.'

'You're lying, you dirty old slag. You shot my man.'

Sophie smiled tiredly. 'If I had, his body would be in the yard.'

Mary said fiercely, 'If he did get away then he's gone to my flat where he'll be safe from you, you thieving murdering cow, you—'

'Oh, grow up. You're not unique. Lots of girls go through this phase. It's a rite of passage, having a crush on an older man, and the old fellows love it. It boosts their ego and it's always the same story: "My marriage is on the rocks, my wife's leaving me; I'll marry you as soon as I'm free." It's a formula, they don't mean a word of it.'

'We're having a baby,' Mary said.

'How can you have any idea who the father is?'

'Because I broke it off with my boyfriend when I met Michael and that was months ago.'

'That's not true. I've talked to Andrew. And

Michael says you're a working girl.' It wasn't true and she regretted it, but too late. Mary came round the table like a panther, arms reaching, long nails flashing. Sophie kicked a chair and brought the gun up as a shield, barrels aimed at the wall. The chair caught Mary below the knees and she stumbled, lurching sideways, hitting a corner of the dresser with an ominous crack. 'Sod it,' Sophie muttered, stepping back before the girl could cannon into her. She made to replace the gun but changed her mind as Mary sat up shakily.

'You tried to kill me too,' she said tonelessly.

'If I had you wouldn't be alive now.'

'I'll have you in court for that.'

'Away you go,' Sophie said blithely, her equilibrium virtually restored even though she hadn't touched the woman. With a pang she saw that her forehead was bleeding. 'Here,' she said, 'let's patch you up before you go.'

'Don't you touch me! If you lay a finger on me I'll—'

Sophie held up her hands in surrender, remembered the gun and put it on the table.

Moving a little unsteadily Mary walked along the passage and out of the house.

Chapter Five

Before dawn Michael came home to an empty house. He went to bed and fell asleep immediately. He woke late and as he surfaced he knew a strong sense of foreboding. What did the new day hold for him?

He pulled on his Levis and lurched downstairs, switching off lights, fumbling with the kettle. His mobile, left on the table last night, started to chirp. He tried to orientate himself, reaching slowly for the instrument, speculating on the identity of the caller.

'Hello?' he said carefully.

'You owe me ten.' It was Coulter.

'What?' He was utterly confused.

'Ten K. Don't come here. Keep away. And get the money quick. I'll call you.'

'What—' But Coulter was gone.

Michael cast round wildly as if the fellow's number was scrawled on the walls. Rod didn't have a mobile. No, Rod *said* he didn't have a mobile. Or he'd just bought one. But he couldn't be reached because Michael didn't know the bloody number. How did you get a mobile's number? Was there a directory service? Should he try . . . This was ridiculous, bizarre. Paying no heed to the warning he rushed outside and jumped in the car.

Coulter heard the Mini coming up the drive

and waited, stiff with hostility. Sensing this as he flung open the door Michael felt himself at an advantage. He'd had time to think. He wasn't surprised that, on his arrival, Coulter should wait for him to take the initiative.

'What d'you mean, I owe you?' he snapped.

'That was the arrangement.' It was dismissive. 'I told you not to come here.' The anger was obvious now. 'You're mad. I'm not bothered about you incriminating yourself but if we're seen together you put me in the frame.'

'You are in the frame. How did you do it?'

'Do what?' Coulter's tone was too casual.

'You killed her.'

'I haven't killed anyone.'

So that was how he was going to play it. They were two animals, standing off, eyeing each other, looking for weaknesses. Michael licked his lips. 'What's the ten thousand for then?'

'We agreed that you'd kill her and I'd remove the body—but the rules got changed because you disposed of the body yourself.'

Michael retreated until he was leaning against the side of the Mini. Coulter advanced a few steps. Michael's mind was racing and his mouth was dry. 'Where's the body?' he asked.

'Where you put it.'

There was a pause. 'We're friends, right?' Michael tried to find level ground. Coulter said nothing. Michael looked bewildered. 'I asked what the ten thousand was for.'

'If you don't pay up then you did the job yourself and I mean all of it.'

Michael's brain slipped into gear. 'You killed my wife—and put the body somewhere—and you're making me the fall guy.'

'You got it.'

'You botched it, man. You'd never go to the cops, you have to steer clear of them. Anyway, it would make them suspicious, wondering how you come to know I killed my wife, first thing they'd think of would be collusion.' He glanced at Coulter's pick-up. 'Besides, there'll be traces. She had to be transported.'

'Oh yes, there'll be traces,' Coulter said heavily, staring at the Mini. He stepped to its rear and looked through the back window. 'In the boot,' he said: 'traces on the floor.' He looked down, focused, and stooped. Michael's jaw dropped but he closed his mouth with a snap. Coulter saw none of it. He had extended a hand but he withdrew it without touching the metalwork. He straightened and stared at Michael who knew without any doubt that their positions had changed. Coulter had the advantage.

'You shot her.' It wasn't a question. 'You carried the body in this car—' Coulter stopped for comment but Michael only frowned. 'You'd best get rid of the car,' he went on. 'What I suggest is you leave it in a back street in

Kelleth with the keys in the ignition. It'll disappear soon enough.'

Michael said, 'If I killed her *and* disposed of the body what are you asking the ten K for?'

'To keep quiet about it,' Coulter said.

*   *   *

Ollie Ashton, thirteen years old, bored, playing truant, opened the bathroom window and stared sullenly at the derelict factory on the other side of the stretch of weeds and dust they called the Waste. It was late morning and his house was empty, his mum at work, dad somewhere between the Social and the Legion and not home till teatime with a skinful. So what was he to do with himself? No windows left to break in the factory, not right time of day to go round backs of houses looking for unlatched windows. He scowled at the factory, at the loading bay bristling with razor wire—a lot of good that was, every local knew where to enter the place and the interior was stripped of anything useful. So what was left—hold on, someone was about. A Mini came creeping across the Waste, stopped, circled and reversed into the loading bay.

'You'll be lucky,' Ollie muttered. The guy had to be a stranger, hadn't realized the wire barred access completely at this point.

He studied the hooded figure that emerged from the driver's side. Only one of 'em:

biggish, not a boy. He went to the rear of the car and Ollie expected to see him against the wire, looking for a gap, but he didn't show. Ollie frowned, the guy had to be *down*, below the back of the car. What was he doing?

He came in sight again, moving to the front, carrying something, laying it on the ground, stooping . . . Ollie grinned, number plates were being changed on a stolen car. Immediately he started to calculate how he might use the situation. If he had the old number he might inform the owner—for a price—if he could find the owner, and if he could see the old number, but one plate lay on the ground, the other was hidden by the thief—and Ollie had no binoculars.

The fellow straightened, holding a plate, picked up the first and walked away. Ollie was gobsmacked. The chap hadn't been interrupted, no one else was about, he hadn't glanced towards the backs of the houses, seen someone watching; he'd acted as if he didn't care, as if it had all gone to plan—and he'd left the driver's door wide open. Ollie, alight with possibilities, raced downstairs.

*   *   *

It was a quiet night. The owls were silent and only occasionally a coot gave a sleepy squawk in the reed beds. The water made no sound, there was nothing to make ripples. There was no moon, but the fells were dark against a myriad stars. There was no light along the south shore but high above the level of the lake a faint glow showed, pinkish and alien in that setting. It bloomed and sank and rose brighter. Amazingly no one saw it, but then at three in the morning only an insomniac making tea might be looking out of a window, and that night there were no insomniacs on the north shore. The odd motorist, late-night party-goer or emergency worker, had his eyes on the road.

It wasn't until eight o'clock that Marjorie Neville, judging all foxes had gone to their beds, went to let out her hens and ducks, and smelled smoke. Alert immediately, as any countryman would be, she called her neighbours but even those who lived on the north shore could see no sign of fire. They were hampered by the mist which would burn off shortly but for the moment it hung in the trees and could have been smoke itself. However, after only a short time her nearest neighbour, old Colonel Fairburn, called back to say that now he could smell it, and he was incensed. Hikers, he blurted, they were camping in the woods and had lit fires: 'I'll give them the "right to roam",' he shouted. 'I'm going up there to turn out these louts and give them a piece of my mind: teach them some manners.'

'You do that,' Marjorie said grimly, thinking

she should lend support; he was an old man and some hikers could be very aggressive. 'I'll join you; they could be on my land.'

'The dogs'll find them.'

She met him at her boundary, on a level with her house but some distance from it. He had come up the hill from his own place, his two Labradors and a retired foxhound leaping ahead to greet her enthusiastically. 'We'll let them follow their noses,' he said. 'They can do the work, pin the vandals down.' He grinned, he was a spare old chap, as attractive in his tanned leathery way as he must have been as a young subaltern. Marjorie was fond of him and his equally active wife.

As they went they chatted casually while the dogs ranged ahead leading them upwards on a diagonal line.

'Can't think what hikers are doing up here,' he said, grumpy because, without a path, they were crushing bluebells. 'It's not as if they were going anywhere. There's no footpath, public or private. Why come on our land?'

'Quite. Divers would stay on the shore.'

'What made you think of divers?'

'Sophie says people have been diving off the point east of the Boathouse. She's seen them in the woods.'

'Is that so. How is Sophie? We must have them up for a drink. Haven't seen her for a while.'

'She's well. I saw her last week—listen!'

'What?' His hearing wasn't as acute as hers.

'The hound's speaking.'

'So he is. Ah, at last: Coulter's track; we can take this for a spell, the dogs seem to be above us.'

He was right. As they quickened the pace the Labs came bounding down the dusty trail, obviously excited, then turned and rushed away, to race round a bend. The smell of smoke was quite strong now and they were puzzled.

'That's not wood smoke,' Marjorie exclaimed. 'The buggers are burning plastic!'

He glanced at her, opened his mouth and thought better of it. They rounded the bend and saw the dogs ahead, silent now, fidgeting on one spot, focused on something the people couldn't see. As they approached the animals slunk down the track and took up positions at the colonel's heels.

'What's the fellow done?' Marjorie breathed. 'Set his place on fire?'

The colonel was hoping the man wasn't inside, that vandals had found the caravan when Coulter was away, but as they came to the open glade and were shocked even though they'd steeled themselves to see a charred shell, they saw—with mounting horror—a pick-up standing to one side.

The vehicle was untouched and the fire had scorched only the sides of the nearest trees. Smoke still rose, stinking of burned plastic, but not enough to be visible at a distance. All the siding of the caravan had gone and only mangled bits of the frame remained.

They moved closer. The dogs hung back. The colonel put out a restraining hand and Marjorie said, 'Don't be silly, Gerald; my guts are as strong as yours. That appears to be him.'

'It's a man anyway.' He tried to be resolute. He swallowed and looked away. 'That is,' he said to the trees, 'it's human. Presumably it's Coulter.'

The object lay on its back and would have been difficult to distinguish among the debris but for the fact that the arms were obvious: seemingly locked and bent at the elbow with clenched fists. The figure looked like a boxer squaring up to an opponent.

'He was fighting,' the colonel said.

'No.' Marjorie was brusque, mastering her horror. 'That is natural—normal, I mean—in the circumstances. It's to do with tightening of the ligaments or something from intense heat.' She turned and stumbled over a long log. 'What's a pit prop doing here?' she demanded angrily, kicking it away.

They'd seen enough and they didn't stay. As they started down the track she said, 'I'll leave you to report it, you'll be more used to that kind of thing.'

'Indeed I'm not!'

'I meant, reports, dealing with authority and

68

so on.'

'Of course I'll do it.' She was just as accustomed as he to dealing with the authorities but he was sympathetic; she might maintain she had a strong stomach but she'd had her fill of horror for the day and it was only courtesy that he should take on this onerous chore. The police would need someone to conduct them to the scene, at least he could spare her that.

'Someone has to do it,' he told his wife over coffee in the kitchen where Davina was taking the mid-morning break with Josie, the girl from the village who cleaned for them.

'Could it have been a gas leak?' Davina asked while Josie stared, awe-struck at the news.

He blinked. 'Could be. I was thinking more of vandals; the man drunk perhaps and them coming along and setting fire to the place, not knowing—surely not knowing that there was someone asleep inside?'

'Never!' Josie exclaimed. She was a little thick, in both senses; overweight and not highly intelligent. The colonel glanced at her uncertainly but addressed his wife. 'Marjorie says there have been people in the woods.'

'Trespassing?'

'What else?'

'Poaching.'

She'd startled him. 'Now that's another thing we didn't think of. Vandals yes; hikers possibly: looking for shelter to get their heads down—although not with a man already in possession. But poachers? Now that's a thought.' He frowned then shook his head violently. 'They'd never set the place on fire; last thing poachers would want to do: attract attention to themselves.'

'It was just that you said there were people in the woods. Marjorie saw them? Did she approach them?'

'She said it was Sophie who'd seen them.'

'We'll ask Sophie then. Let's have them up here this evening—Marjorie too. We're not doing anything, are we? I'll give them a ring.'

Michael took a few moments to answer the phone and when he did he sounded out of breath. Davina announced herself and asked to speak to Sophie. Michael said she wasn't there. 'I called to suggest you come up for a drink tonight,' she explained. 'You've heard about the fire?'

'Fire?' His voice climbed. 'Where?'

'Coulter's caravan burned in the night. I'm afraid the poor fellow was inside.'

'Coulter?' Michael was puzzled. 'You mean that guy up in the woods? Got an old pick-up . . . That's right, he's living on Braithwaite's land . . . in a caravan. I remember now.'

'That's the man. Gerald and Marjorie smelled smoke this morning and went up there. Burned to a cinder—oh, bad taste. I mean the caravan is a wreck.'

'Then how do they know—'

'You'd better talk to Gerald.' Her husband came out to the hall, mumbling crossly, taking the phone from her. 'Fairburn,' he grunted.

'Nasty business,' Michael said. 'You were up there?'

'She told you so. Nothing more to say until they've investigated.'

'Who? Oh, the fire brigade. Is the fire out now?'

'They'll bring experts in to search for "the seat of the fire", I believe it's called. And the propellant.' He savoured the word. 'I'm tending towards vandals rather than poachers, but she thought of a gas leak. Of course he didn't have gas.'

'Propane,' Michael said.

'Oh, he had Propane, did he?'

'I'm asking: did he have Propane gas?'

'No doubt. Must have done, eh? Had to have something to cook with. Come up this evening, the two of you, and we'll talk then. I have to report the bloody business now.'

*   *   *

A patrol car came first, the occupants noting that the informant appeared to have taken his time between finding a burned-out caravan with a corpse inside and reporting it. The combination of a huge region, much of it upland, an overstretched police force and a

71

spate of hoax calls in the holiday season inclined the police to view the report with suspicion. It wasn't until they were out on the shore road that the men in the patrol car realized that their destination, Oakshaw, was more likely to be a substantial house than a camp ground. Campers' children were often the source of hoax reports.

Gerald met them on the forecourt of his glorified cottage. There was no offer of hospitality; opening a rear door almost before the car came to a halt he climbed in and settled himself. 'It's not far,' he said comfortably.

The man beside the driver turned, fumbling for notebook and pen. 'If we could have your full name, sir—'

'That'll do later,' Gerald said, knowing that later more senior men would arrive; these were only checking to make sure he wasn't barmy. 'You need to see the body; that's the priority.'

Constables don't argue with colonels, however long retired. The driver put the car in gear and they moved off, Gerald taking note of the interior of the strange car, sniffing as he caught a trace of cigarette smoke, disapproving the length of the driver's hair. They turned left at the end of his drive and shortly left again off the paved road to take a rough track that climbed through the woods.

'Who owns this land?' asked the one who

wasn't driving.

'A man called Braithwaite. Absentee landlord.' Gerald was censorious. 'I'll give you his number when we come back to the house.'

'And you say there's a body in the caravan.' There was an undertone of disbelief in the statement.

'In the remains, yes, in the debris.'

'Did you touch it?'

Gerald stifled a gasp. 'No, we didn't touch it.'

' "We", sir?'

'I came across here with a neighbour.'

'We'll need to talk to him too.'

'It was a lady: a Miss Neville.'

The silence that followed was full of conjecture, amusing Gerald momentarily but he sobered as they rounded the last bend and the track straightened to end in the glade.

The car stopped and for a moment the police sat mutely, staring, then in slow motion, glancing at Gerald who regarded them blandly and made no move to follow, they got out and advanced to the wreckage.

*　　*　　*

The investigation started; senior uniforms, the police doctor, SOCO (because it could be the scene of a crime), the pathologist, fire experts. Josie cycled home to the village for her dinner and within the hour the rumour was abroad

73

that the recluse who lived in old Braithwaite's woods had been murdered by a drugs gang and his body set alight. 'Stunk like a barbecue,' were Josie's words, 'you could smell it all along the lake, it were what sent them up there in first place: himself and Miss Neville. It were dogs led 'em to it.'

Marjorie, feeding two detectives coffee and shortbread on her sunny terrace, said she was thinking in terms of a cigarette end possibly combined with heavy drinking. There was a bin bag beside the pick-up full of empty lager cans and at least one whisky bottle.

'You handled it, ma'am?'

'Just the edge of the bag. You're suggesting he had visitors?'

They regarded her thoughtfully, two men in plain clothes, dressed casually in deference to the warm day, shirts but no ties, laundered jeans, shoes not trainers. The senior man was wiry, in his thirties, a touch of class about him, maybe a graduate, the other was heavy, balding, flushed. Should be wearing a hat, Marjorie thought: self-conscious but not unintelligent, piggy eyes, but pigs aren't stupid.

'Apparently there have been strangers hanging around,' said the senior man, recalling her to the subject in hand. He was a detective sergeant: Mackreth. The border country was full of Scots. Canny Scots, she must watch her back. Joke, she thought.

'I've heard something,' she said.

74

'You've seen them, ma'am?'

'No, it was my god-daughter who thought there were trespassers, but that was down nearer the water. At the time there were people diving off the point, so they could have gone into the woods to relieve themselves.'

'Could we have a word with her?'

'She doesn't live here. She—and her husband, they have the Boathouse on the shore west of here.'

'How well did you know Coulter?'

'I didn't know him at all. I never met the man. I'd seen him occasionally, driving his truck, but I've never spoken to him.'

'Despite him living so close, and he's been there for what—a year?'

'I don't go on my neighbour's property if I don't know the owner well and unless I have good reason, like a lost animal.' She paused, then added, 'Particularly if there's someone living on that land. But the caravan was over a mile away and on a higher level. No, there was no contact.' She returned his gaze blandly, armed against further questions on the subject.

*   *   *

'So we have a mystery man,' DC Rumney said as they left. 'You reckon we're going to find that he's got—had form?'

Mackreth nodded, breathing deeply as the scent of bluebells filled the car. 'He had a reason to be living alone up here, hidden away. On the run from someone?'

'Like us, for instance?'

'Someone. Maybe this Sophie, who saw strangers in the woods, she can fill us in on his background, or her husband more likely. The Boathouse: sounds more downmarket than most of the places round here.'

This seemed to be borne out when they found the Boathouse. No car was visible, only an old bicycle propped against the wall beside an open door. As they approached, a man came towards them backlit in a passage that ran through to a room that was full of light.

They produced their warrant cards. Michael looked at them curiously, then at the men. 'Detectives?' he observed. 'Is this something to do with the fire?'

'Could we have a word, sir, if you can spare the time?'

The diffidence delighted him. 'Come in!' he gushed. 'Anything to distract me from work. I was just about to have a lager. How does that sound? Come along and I'll bring it out to the deck.'

Bemused and amenable they went through to a homely sitting room and out of wide french windows to a slatted wooden platform with a table and chairs in ironwork with cushioned seats. Below them the lake stretched to left and right, sail boats like bright butterflies flitting across the water. On the far shore the trees clustered in shades of hazy emerald and above it all the fells were gauzy against a heat-soaked sky.

'I could live here,' Rumney said, passing his tongue over dry lips, thinking a cold lager would be the finishing touch.

Mackreth was thinking: why didn't Coulter make a move to get out of a burning caravan? Could we have a murder investigation here?

Chapter Six

The lager was Carlsberg Special. Rumney drank deep, sighing with appreciation. Mackreth tasted and nodded gravely. Michael took the third chair and smiled amiably. 'How can I help you?'

The police had agreed to keep it informal. The man might know nothing but he could provide background information. Keep the locals sweet. 'You're Mr Daynes?' Mackreth asked pleasantly.

'That's me. Call me Michael. And you?'

'DC Rumney and DS Mackreth.'

Michael nodded and waited. A worldly man would have asked why it was necessary for detectives to visit local people after a fire. Michael had to think for a few moments then his expression changed, his interest quickened. 'Why CID?' he asked. 'Was Coulter into something?'

'Why would you think that?' Mackreth looked across the water and his tone was casual, even lazy; the question could have been one on a list that he was obliged to utilize when working door to door.

'I'm a journalist,' the other told him. An embarrassed smile. 'Working for myself at the moment. I never did crime as such but naturally I picked up something of police procedure. There's been gossip about Coulter; of course there would be about anyone living alone in the woods. He wasn't a tramp, he owned a truck, you saw him in it but no one knew what he did for a living.' He paused. Mackreth said nothing, Rumney's eyes were half-closed against the sunshine and most of his drink had gone. 'We'd got used to him,' Michael went on reflectively, 'but this—' gesturing to the woods behind the house, 'it's revived interest. There's a rumour that he was involved with drugs.'

'We only knew about the fire this morning,' Mackreth said.

Michael laughed. 'You have to be a townie. Josie Warburton helps out at the Fairburns' and she goes home to the village at noon. Within the hour not only did everyone on the lake know about the fire but there'd be a dozen theories as to the cause.'

'Which one would you favour?'

'Me? I haven't considered it. Chap dies in a

fire: the obvious cause is drink and smoking, isn't it? Could be a chip pan fire,' he added after a moment.

'How did you hear about the fire?'

'People called me. For information actually. You see, some of 'em would think with us being only a mile away, we'd have seen something, but it happened in the middle of the night—so they say—and our bedroom faces this way.' He gestured upwards to what Mackreth assumed was the relevant window.

'Perhaps your wife saw something, if she was awake.'

'She's on holiday.'

'That's a pity; we wanted to ask her about these strangers she saw in the woods.'

'Good heavens! More gossip?'

'It's been mentioned. It could be important.'

Michael's jaw dropped. 'You suspect foul play! You reckon someone was here scouting . . . looking for Coulter . . . Now I come to think of it, Sophie did mention . . . but she didn't put it like that: "strangers in the woods". She did say she thought there was someone . . .' He was worried. 'I'm afraid I ridiculed it, said it was imagination, said she should be writing the book.' Mackreth raised his eyebrows, Rumney didn't react, he was staring morosely at his empty glass. 'I'm working on a book,' Michael explained. 'That's why I don't have much time for the neighbours. Like today: phone calls were a distraction.'

Mackreth came to a conclusion. 'I need to speak to your wife—' he began.

'Why?' It was belligerent.

'About these strangers she saw. You have the number of where she's staying?'

'She's touring.' Michael spread his hands. 'She's in Ireland actually, at least she should be. She called me from Stranraer just before she went on board the ferry. So far as I know she's not booked anywhere, that's how she likes to travel: stop wherever she can find a bed.'

Suddenly they were surprised by a faint and tinny tune vaguely reminiscent of 'Scots Wha Hae'. Mackreth reached for his mobile and stood up, moving to the end of the deck.

Rumney came to life. 'Good lager,' he observed genially. 'Just the ticket for a warm afternoon.'

'Yes.' Michael did a double-take. 'Yes, let me get you another.' He hurried indoors.

Rumney beamed. Mackreth came back, pocketing his mobile. He looked a question. 'Gone for more booze,' Rumney told him.

Mackreth nodded and sat down as Michael returned with three cans of lager although two glasses were only half-empty. They settled again with an air of satisfaction.

'We have to find your wife,' Mackreth intoned as if for the first time, and Rumney froze in the act of pouring from his can.

'What's happened?' Michael asked.

'The caravan was torched.'

'Arson,' Rumney mumbled for the layman's benefit.

'So what was your wife driving?'

'She took the Mini.' Michael was unhappy. 'I still don't see how she can help you—and how d'you know it was arson?'

'It would appear that some—substance was introduced.' Rumney stared blandly at his superior who continued, 'It's essential we find your wife because she saw strangers hanging around and as far as we know at this moment she's the only person who did. Coulter's a mystery man but someone fired his caravan. Which is it likely to be: a local or someone from his background—a background no one knows about because the dead man didn't know any locals? Now do you see why we have to speak to her?'

Michael didn't appear convinced. 'I'm just trying to protect her. She's on holiday, for God's sake! But like I said, she's touring; your guess is as good as mine where—'

'Ireland's not all that big; we'll find her.' Mackreth glanced at Rumney, now deep in his second Special. 'Give me the particulars of the car and we'll start things moving over there.'

'I hope the Garda will be circumspect. If she comes on a road block and police approach—armed? Are they armed in Ireland?—she'll think the worst. Like a terrorist situation—or something's happened to me. Nasty shock that: police asking you to come to the station or wherever.'

'They're used to delicate situations. Innocent members of the public are treated different to villains; you should know that, being in the media.'

*   *   *

'That was snide,' Rumney said as he completed his three-point turn and started up the drive. 'The media treats everyone according to how much can be got out of 'em.'

'He talks too much. What did you make of him?'

Obviously Rumney was unaffected by the drink. He never was but he could put on an act, lulling interviewees into thinking they had only one individual to reckon with, unaware that a second pair of eyes was watching, another brain processing information.

Rumney was on his own tack. 'Bit of a coincidence,' he said: 'the only person who might be able to give us something on the arsonists has gone missing.'

'She's not missing; she's touring Ireland.'

'He says she's touring, and don't you think that's a coincidence?'

'That's exactly what it is. What you're implying is that two events are related: the fire and the absent wife. You've built a whole scenario round just two facts.'

82

'One fact actually.' Rumney was unmoved, all his attention apparently on the road. 'The *fact* is that we've got a corpse in a fire that was set. But the other—the missing or absent wife—isn't fact, it's hearsay. It's a fact that he *says* she's away. Why'd she go on holiday alone?'

'She's Miss Neville's god-daughter.'

'So?'

'The old girl has to know something about this Irish trip. Maybe she's in touch. Let's go and find out.'

* * *

A strong spicy smell met them at the open front door of the house called Losca. Mackreth apologized for interrupting preparations for the evening meal. Marjorie said coolly that it could wait for a few minutes and showed them into a room full of light and air and cushions covered with cat hairs. A rangy black animal with a white-tipped tail followed them and made straight for Rumney who had no time for cats. He crossed his legs deliberately but he didn't stand a chance. Sharkey leapt on the back of his chair and nuzzled his ear. 'Allow me,' Marjorie said, removing the cat and disappearing with him draped over her shoulder. Behind her a tortoiseshell queen entered, sat down and regarded them with basilisk eyes.

'Now!' Marjorie announced briskly on her return. 'What can I offer you? Whisky, beer?'

Mackreth declined politely, explaining that they'd been consuming Michael Daynes' lager which would keep them going for a while, directing a meaning glance at Rumney. There was a faint sound elsewhere in the house. 'I've shut him in,' Marjorie assured them, 'he'll create hell until he's let out.'

'Michael Daynes,' Mackreth began, 'says his wife is away on holiday, touring Ireland.'

'Oh yes?' She was startled. 'Sophie said nothing to me. I thought she was at the Boathouse; that's why I sent you there.'

'She said nothing about going away, sometime in the future perhaps? What I'm trying to say is did she bring the date forward?'

'No-o.' It was hesitant. 'Although on that score my memory isn't what it was; it could be that she mentioned taking a break and I've forgotten.'

'Does she normally keep in touch with you when she goes away?'

'Not if it's for a short period. How long did she go for, did Michael say?'

'He didn't, and he doesn't know her whereabouts. Apparently she's not booked anywhere.' He paused but she made no comment. He asked carefully, 'Would she have gone with a friend perhaps?'

'Possibly.' Marjorie was thinking hard.

'Mr Daynes is unhappy about us trying to

trace her but I think we managed to convince him that the Irish police will handle the matter discreetly.'

'You're going to look for her? Why?'

'Because,' he said patiently, 'we need to talk to her about those people she saw in the woods. There may be no connection but I'd like to eliminate them if possible. The caravan fire was arson.'

She drew in her breath but she didn't appear to be all that surprised. 'We mentioned it, the colonel and I: wondering about vandals. It was deliberate then? But they, whoever did it, couldn't have known that there was a man inside.'

He wouldn't rise to that. He repeated stubbornly, 'It's why we need to find your god-daughter, ma'am.'

'But she had nothing to do with—'

'No, no! Of course not, but she may be able to point us in the right direction of the— people responsible.'

'I doubt it. All she saw was a shadowy figure—or two, and they were right down by the water. Why don't you find the divers? That shouldn't be difficult; they're probably still about, and they would have been in that area, around the point, longer than Sophie ever was. She just passes through the woods on her way up here; she prefers to walk rather than take the car.' No one spoke, it could be that the men were envisaging a woman walking alone

85

in woods where killers were abroad. Marjorie broke the silence: 'How do you propose to start looking for her?'

'We'll start with the car. Mr Daynes gave us its make and registration number.'

'Oh, she took the car?'

'A Mini, right?' She nodded. 'We'll circulate the Garda with its particulars. They'll find her soon enough unless there are more old green Minis in Ireland than in this country. She crossed from Stranraer to Belfast last evening so we have a fixed point to work from. But if she does contact you before we find her you will let us know, won't you? I'll leave you my number.'

*   *   *

By the following morning Michael was castigating himself for his mistakes while knowing that the only way to deal with them was to turn them to his advantage. This was possible because he was in possession of most of the facts, at least those that mattered, whereas the police were groping in the dark—fishing, they called it. If it had been a mistake to lie about Sophie's movements, it didn't have to be a lie, it was what he assumed had happened. If it was a mistake to dispose of the Mini, that was done out of embarrassment because . . . because, a sly inner voice pointed out, the marks of shot on the metalwork

86

indicated a quarrel—a shooting, for God's sake! A shot-up car coupled with the absence of his wife did more than suggest foul play, it signalled it.

They wouldn't find her of course, they couldn't find her; she didn't exist. But she does exist, insisted that other, logical self, there is a body. He breathed deeply, longing for a whisky, knowing he must keep a clear head (last evening, when the police left, he had poured his unfinished drink down the sink); whatever happened he must act naturally. He was a grass widower, his wife on holiday in Ireland, in touch occasionally—but what about Marjorie? Sophie should be in touch with her too! Well, she could have left on the spur of the moment, after a row—no, no row—hell, he'd think of something. He'd called Davina Fairburn last night and apologized because he hadn't joined them for a drink; the police kept him, he said, making no mention of Sophie. He must find some plausible reason for her absence before he dare meet any of their friends.

Meanwhile he would cycle to town for provisions. It was Sunday but the supermarket would be open. On his return he would call at the pub, show his face and incidentally get a line on the gossip. It was a warm day for cycling; he would have liked to buy a car but this was out of the question. Frustrating when he thought there was something like seven thousand in her personal account but he wouldn't be able to touch that for years. For the time being he was stuck with the bike unless he could raise some cash himself, by writing for example. And there was Sam Lewthwaite in Lancaster, his father dealt in old cars. Mary had a car but for a while, a long while, Mary was forbidden fruit. He was dreadfully unhappy about that but the likeliest motivation for getting rid of a wife—after money, and he had that motive too—was in order to be free to enjoy a mistress. The only marginal comfort he had in a delicate situation was that Mary had at last accepted his pleas not to phone him, above all not to come to the Boathouse. He had been so concerned that she might turn up at a crucial moment, when the police were with him for instance, that he had even contemplated telling her why it was essential they remain clear of each other. If nothing else would convince her he'd imply that the police could look on her as an accomplice. She'd be frightened but she'd know he wasn't rejecting her, which could be what she was thinking at this moment, since she was staying away and not telephoning. He was miserable to think she was going through a bad time, that he was responsible, but he'd make it up to her. As he cycled to town he considered how they might meet in safety, but she wasn't answering her mobile and he daren't go to the flat where he'd run the risk of being spotted by Barbara Howard.

Once in Kelleth and intensely aware of her proximity caution left him and he convinced himself that he need not be recognized, he'd been quite confident when he'd dumped the Mini. He bought a cheap drab anorak at the supermarket and, with the hood up, he drifted down the cobbled yard, glancing sideways at her flat as he passed. No one was in evidence; windows in the upper flat were open but not those on the ground floor, and he knew she had the lower flat. Everywhere there were flowers: camellias, tulips, early lilies, all in riotous bloom. He focused on Mary's window box and could see, in the brief moments it took to pass, not daring to brake, that not only were her blooms thriving but there was water below the window ledge. So she was home. He gave a helpless whimper but he continued through the yard and out of town.

In the village he stopped at the pub and walked in, steeling himself for questions, relieved to find a number of visitors in the bar and only a few locals. Ralph Fisher, the tenant, plumply amiable, drew him a pint of draught lager without asking. 'They let you go then,' he observed weightily.

Michael, accustomed to the man's facetiousness, said they could find nothing to hold him on. People regrouped, Michael now the focal point. No one showed surprise at the exchange.

He looked round. 'Where are the press? I thought the place would be swarming.'

'They were here yesterday,' Fisher told him. 'We were packed out. Oh yes, indeed, we had our nine minutes of fame. Didn't you see us on the News?'

Michael shook his head. 'I was working.' He'd been occupied with the police last evening but he wasn't going to be the first to mention them.

'Some reporters were here this morning,' Fisher said. 'Latecomers, nothing left for them. They took the body away yesterday. Didn't you see—or hear—anything? You're his nearest neighbour. Were, I should say.'

Michael allowed them to wait while he considered the colour of his lager. 'We heard the sirens of course. But that was the first we knew that anything had happened. Our bedroom looks out on the lake. Anyway his caravan's deep in the trees.' He stopped and drank deeply. It was another sweltering day, everyone was sweating profusely.

'Is it right the CID came to you?' Fisher asked, politely now that he was serious.

'Naturally.' Michael was quite relaxed. 'Like everyone else they thought that since I lived nearest, I must know the chap.'

'Did you?'

'No more than anyone else. I've no idea what he did or where he came from, whether he was on benefit . . .' He shrugged.

'He wasn't on benefit,' Fisher said. 'He came from Manchester and he didn't have form. Clever bugger.'

'How d'you find that out?'

'Me family connections.' Fisher's brother-in-law was a special constable.

'Coulter hadn't got form?' Michael was amused.

'All that means'—Fisher was patronizing, in the position of mentor—'is that he'd never been caught. No sign of how he made enough to live on. He wouldn't need much but he had to buy petrol, food, pay rent for the caravan. He didn't steal, not around here he didn't: too wily. He must have had a store of cash. The police are working on the theory that's why he was killed: robbery.'

'You don't have to kill to rob,' Michael said. 'They could have just clobbered him, like a heavy mugging.'

'It went wrong.' Fisher was mulish. 'They hit too hard, then they had to torch the caravan to cover up: fingerprints and so on.'

Michael nodded. 'So that's why they're so keen to find my wife. Because she was saying last week that there were trespassers in the woods between us and Marjorie Neville. They'll be thinking in terms of criminals from Manchester who knew he had a load of cash squirrelled away.'

'Why do they need to find your wife?' Clem Dover asked. He owned a guest house and his wife knew Sophie from the Women's Institute. 'What happened to her?'

'Nothing's happened. She's away, touring Ireland, and I don't have a contact number.'

'The cops think she can give them a description of these trespassers?'

'That's the idea,' Michael said slowly, frowning.

'Now what?' Fisher was sharp.

Michael fingered his lips. 'I was just thinking . . .' He trailed off.

'Thinking the police had better find her first,' Dover announced generally, and stopped in consternation as he realized the tenor of what he'd said.

'She'll be all right,' Fisher intoned, concerned at Michael's obvious dismay. 'The villains won't know that they were seen, nor who saw them. They can't identify her.'

'I have to get back.' Michael looked sick. 'She could call me any time, maybe has; I've been shopping, I left after breakfast.' Leaving his drink he hurried out and a moment later they saw him pedalling past the windows.

'He's not thinking straight,' Dover said. 'He should have his mobile with him.'

*   *   *

Michael pushed steadily along the shore road, heedless of rucksack straps cutting into his shoulders, considering the new scenario:

that Coulter could have been killed for a hoard of cash. He liked it; he wished he'd thought of it himself, he could have done with a windfall, and if it had been illegally acquired, the proceeds of a bank robbery perhaps, then there could be no follow-up. No robber goes to the police to complain that he's been robbed.

He hadn't locked the Boathouse. He owned nothing valuable, no computer, only a typewriter. He parked the bike, eased the rucksack off in the kitchen, rolling his shoulders with relief, went to the sitting room and poured himself a whisky. Sunday afternoon: even the police wouldn't come calling on Sunday afternoon. He unpacked the food, ate a sandwich and went upstairs to his study.

He liked this dim quiet room, it was conducive to work; had his outlook been the lake and the fells he would have been continually distracted by skimming sails, by laughter, by people having fun. He stood in the doorway and looked at his typewriter: uncovered, a sheet of paper inserted. He never left the machine like that.

He moved forward. The carriage had been turned so that the one word in the centre of the sheet was conspicuous. It was capitalized and said:

MURDERER

Chapter Seven

The bell chimed and Barbara Howard opened her door to a big fellow with a ravaged tanned face, a stranger and well past the first flush of youth.

'Good evening.' She was expressionless, wary.

'Good evening.' He was grave and polite. 'I'm looking for my sister.'

'Your—' She stared. 'Your sister?'

'Mary Spence. I've been knocking. No one seems to be home.'

'Ah.' Light dawned; she knew a little of the family background—but he'd come all the way from Essex? The stepbrother actually, but if he preferred to drop the 'step' that was his affair. 'She's away. I'm Barbara. I don't think she told me your name.'

'Keith Weston.' He smiled and the rocky face broke into attractive lines. Nice eyes too. 'We're really steps: different parents.'

She nodded non-committally, she wasn't going to ask him in; he'd have questions which she wasn't prepared to answer, if indeed she could. Compromising, she moved out on the landing and looked over the railing at Mary's front window. 'I don't know when she'll be back,' she said vaguely. 'She didn't say.'

'I know about the boyfriend.'

She stiffened and just stopped herself from asking which one. 'Both of them,' he said, watching her. 'Perhaps she took off with the new one. What do you think?'

'She said something about him.' She wouldn't meet his eye.

'Do you know where they were planning to go?' She stared at him like a defiant teenager. 'Because she could be there now.' She hesitated. 'I *am* her brother.' It was insinuating.

'I don't *know*! She doesn't tell me all her private life, it's not my business, I'm only a neighbour. We're not close.'

He regarded her thoughtfully and seemed to reach a decision. 'She's young for her age,' he said gently, 'and this is a married man who, I understand, is living with his wife. Mary and I have a good relationship and I'm concerned about her. Andrew was all right: her own age, unattached, but this one's different. She won't say anything about him except he's married and supposed to be leaving his wife. When I asked what he does for a living she told me to get out of her hair, and now she's not answering her phone, and I find she's left her flat without telling you or me where she's gone. She knows I'd disapprove of this chap. How do you feel about him?'

'It's nothing to do with me,' she insisted wildly. 'She's over twenty-one.' Weston said nothing. Despite the fact that he appeared to

95

offer no threat to her, he made her uneasy, and she wanted him to go away. 'Why don't you talk to the fellow?' she said weakly. 'His name's Michael Daynes and he lives along the south shore of the lake, a place called the Boathouse.'

But he knew that already; what he wanted was to locate his stepsister and he saw that at least for now Barbara couldn't or wouldn't help him.

*   *   *

'Mary who?' Michael looked past the visitor to his nondescript Land Rover then stepped back involuntarily as Weston pushed into the passage and turned left into the kitchen.

'We'll sit down, shall we?' He pulled out a chair. He nodded to Michael, directing him to the opposite chair. Weston had positioned himself below the gun on its rack.

Michael remained standing. He said stiltedly, 'There's some misunderstanding here. You seem to have a problem. Do you mind explaining how you think I come to be involved in it?'

'If you didn't know what the problem was you'd be ringing the police by now. Where's my sister?'

Michael said cautiously, 'You say you're Mary's brother. I knew a Mary but she didn't have a brother. I mean, the Mary I know

96

doesn't have a brother.'

Weston didn't respond to that. He was listening: listening for movements elsewhere in the house. 'Wife in bed?' he asked genially.

'She's—not home—yet.' The pauses were infinitesimal.

'Let's go and see, shall we?' Weston stood up and took down the gun.

'This is crazy,' Michael breathed, mesmerized by the weapon.

'I'm not crazy,' Weston told him, suspecting it was unloaded. Michael would know where the ammo was but he didn't have the gun.

They went over the house slowly, Michael careful not to make a sudden move, Weston raking every room with his eyes: the big bedroom with the unmade bed, an indentation in one pillow, a second on a chair; a room in use as a study with a single bed, papers and a map spread on the quilt, bookshelves, a table with more papers, an electric typewriter. In the bathroom there was one toothbrush only, one face flannel; nowhere were there any women's things on view.

They returned to the kitchen and Weston broke the gun, saw it was unloaded, sat down and placed it on the table in front of himself. After a moment Michael took the opposite chair.

'Where's your wife?' Weston asked.

'She left. For Ireland. She's got friends there.'

'Left because you brought Mary here?'

'Look,' Michael had been thinking and was suddenly expansive, 'I did meet Mary—Mary Spence—some months ago. I gave her a lift home; I'd had a skinful, we . . .' He spread his hands. 'I promise you, it wasn't anything—I wasn't serious, just an aberration on my part. My wife was away.'

'That's not what Mary says. She says you plan to leave your wife and marry her.'

'I'm not responsible for what she says. The kid took a shine to me.'

'She's no kid, but she is immature. You have no intention of leaving your wife, have you?'

'No. I haven't.' They regarded each other: Michael penitent, Weston only mildly reproving. 'You had a fight with your wife,' he said slowly, as if feeling his way, 'and she walked out.'

'No, no, we didn't—my wife's broad-minded. I don't mean she *approved*, of course not, but she wouldn't make an issue of a thing like that. It was already history anyway; as I see it your sister got tired of her boyfriend, in fact that was Sophie's reading of it—Sophie's my wife—that Mary had a new friend but wanted to keep it quiet, a married guy probably, some big fish in the area—you know: big fish in a small pond? So Mary had a showdown with Andrew—that's a chap she was having a fling with across the lake there— and she blurted out how she was going off with

98

a married chap, and she substituted my name. That's how I come to be involved.'

'You talk a lot.'

'Just trying to get to the bottom of it.' His eyes jumped as a car appeared beyond the open window and came to a halt beside the Land Rover. 'Visitors,' he said brightly. 'Do put the gun up, there's a good chap.'

Weston stood and replaced it on its rack. Mackreth and Rumney emerged from their car and approached the back door, standing aside as the big man stepped out. All three said good afternoon, the words automatic as they eyed each other. Weston, seeing that they carried themselves with an air of authority, guessed them to be police. The detectives, overtly curious, tried to place him: creased jeans and shirt, old Land Rover but not a local registration. He looked like a farmer but not from around here, and not to be eliminated from their inquiries. Mentally Mackreth filed him for reference.

Michael was bland, speeding one party, welcoming the next, any emotion controlled and concealed. The detectives allowed him to usher them into his sitting room but they remained standing.

Rumney asked bluntly, 'Have you heard from your wife?'

If Michael noticed the absence of a 'sir' he didn't react. 'Not today,' he said and waited expectantly for the next question.

'She's not in Ireland, is she?'

'Oh, you've found her?'

'We have her car.'

He was bewildered. 'You've found the car but not her? I don't get it. Where's the car?'

'With our forensic people.'

Michael swallowed and looked to Mackreth for enlightenment. 'Had she been in it? There's been an accident?'

'Someone fired at the car,' Rumney told him.

Michael's eyes came back to him slowly. 'What? I'm concerned about my wife and you tell me—Where was the car found?'

'Who shot at her?'

'She's been *shot*? Is she—*Where is she?*'

Mackreth said quietly, 'Someone shot *at* her. Presumably as she was driving.' He glanced at Rumney who went out. Michael's eyes followed him but his attention remained with Mackreth. He said, 'How can you tell she was shot at? Is there blood?'

'How do you explain pellet marks on the boot?'

'Oh that!' Michael gestured impatiently. 'She fired at a rat in the yard. We're overrun with rats and rabbits, that's why she keeps—it.' He stumbled as Rumney returned with the shotgun.

Some signal passed between the police. 'Is your wife proficient with firearms?' Rumney asked stiffly.

100

'It's her gun. She uses it.'

'So she is used to guns.' Mackreth answered the question.

'I said so.' Michael was showing strain.

'It's been fired recently,' Rumney said.

Michael nodded slowly, controlling himself with an effort. 'She—shot a rat. And hit the Mini.'

'Show us where,' Mackreth said. It was an order, not a request, and when they went out he kept Michael between them. At the back door he stood close, too close, while Rumney stooped awkwardly in the yard squinting at the sets.

'What happened to the rat?' Mackreth asked.

'She missed it.'

Rumney picked at the ground a few times and straightened. He came over, tiny balls in his big sweaty palm. 'She didn't clean the gun,' he told Mackreth and turned to Michael. 'She's used to firearms and she replaced the gun without cleaning it?'

Michael shrugged. 'She probably meant to and forgot.'

'How good are you at shooting?' Mackreth asked.

'I've no idea how I'd be. I've never fired a gun. You haven't told me where you found the car. Was it at the ferry terminal?'

'Ah yes.' Mackreth led them back to the sitting room where the light was good, revealing small changes of expression. This time he sat down. Michael offered drinks but he declined for both of them. He regarded Michael with mild curiosity. 'You told us she was in Ireland.'

'That's what she said. And Stranraer: that's the port for Belfast, isn't it? Or for Larne.'

'The car was found in Carlisle.'

Michael stared. 'Well then, she came back. Or she wasn't in Stranraer when she called me.' He thought about this while they waited. 'What condition was the car in when it was found? Why are you searching it? And exactly where was it found?'

'On a housing estate,' Mackreth said. 'A former police officer wondered why under-age kids should be doing wheel-brake turns in a Mini that had lost its registration plates. They said a hooded man brought the car to some waste ground and removed the plates and the keys and walked away. They hot-wired it. People are very clever nowadays.'

'How do you know it's ours?'

'We traced its Vehicle Identification Number. Easy enough to remove registration plates but not the VIN.'

'So it was stolen, but what's the point in Forensics going over it for prints? The kids' will have covered the thief's.'

'They'll be going over it with a fine-tooth comb, and there again, there could be traces of your wife inside.'

'It was her car! Of course there'll be traces.'

'But if she was conveyed in it, sir—like, helpless, tied up or worse?'

That 'sir' was the more unnerving introduced at that moment and only then. Michael was clearly agitated but any man would react fearfully when it was implied that his wife could be a murder victim.

*   *   *

'He's edgy,' Rumney said. 'But then you'd expect it even if he was innocent. Wife missing, car found, foul play suspected, his—her gun confiscated . . .' It was in the car's boot. 'He knows he's a prime suspect.'

'And all this time she could well be having it off in Ireland or Scotland with a boyfriend. One thing: he can't sue us—yet. We were only tracing ownership of a shot-up stolen car.'

'We have the gun. He has to know we're thinking it's a murder weapon.'

'So it'll be interesting to see if he threatens us with legal action, won't it? If he doesn't we'll be wondering why, right?'

'Right.'

'Go back to Marjorie.'

'What? Again?' Rumney pulled into a gateway and stopped, the engine running.

'Motive,' Mackreth said. He felt very tired. 'And I don't believe that story about the rat. It's too neat. I don't like the smooth way he adjusts his story to account for new facts. The wife didn't phone from Stranraer, she just said she was there when she phoned, and on her way to Ireland—but did she call at all, eh? Is the phone call itself a fabrication? If we find his prints on the gun how much d'you bet he'll remember handling it at one time?'

Rumney watched a tractor go by, spilling slurry. 'Be interesting to see the sequence of prints on it. If he shot her his prints should be superimposed on hers.'

'He may not have used the gun, plenty of weapons to hand in a country house.' Mackreth stared into the trees. 'Not a posh place of course, but worth a bit with the lake frontage. That's why I was thinking about motive, and who owns the Boathouse, and did Sophie make a will.'

*   *   *

Her god-daughter owned the Boathouse, Marjorie told them stiffly, it had been the family home, and no, she hadn't any idea of the contents of Sophie's will, even if she had made one.

Mackreth evinced surprise: 'You're by way of being family, ma'am,' managing to convey scepticism without being rude. Familiar, yes, crass, and she could have castigated him for that but she didn't. She had been eating when they arrived and she was not in the best of moods, still chewing as she appeared, slamming the kitchen door on the cats, evidently doubly embarrassed that they should catch her eating in the kitchen instead of the elegant dining room glimpsed through an open door. She took them to the sitting room and offered drinks in a tone so coldly polite that to have accepted would have been gross.

Marjorie said, 'Family or not, sergeant, it's a curious time of day to come calling to inquire into a family's most private concerns.'

He was irritated. 'It would be, but your god-daughter's car has been found, riddled with shot.'

Her expression didn't change and he had to conceal his own astonishment. Beside him Rumney shifted in his chair. Marjorie remained silent as if waiting—and not, he thought, for a blow. He could detect no sign of fear but then she was old and old people have less to lose than the young or middle-aged. And they have more experience at hiding their emotions.

'You don't seem surprised, ma'am,' he said gently, trying to needle her with exaggerated deference.

'I'm waiting to hear the rest.' Which was reasonable.

'It would appear that someone attacked Mrs Daynes.'

'What makes you suggest that?'

'The shot?' His heart sank as he spoke. Was

105

there a rat after all?

She gave a tight smile. 'It was a mistake. She didn't know the gun was loaded. One never keeps a loaded gun in the house. She was furiously angry and pulled the trigger without thinking.'

Rumney gaped. 'Who—'

Mackreth said loudly, 'Did she hit him?' and Rumney subsided, abashed.

'I doubt it.' And now her smile was grim. 'Since he was inside the car and you've been interviewing him, he can have fielded no more than the odd pellet. But you thought Sophie was in Ireland with the car. Where did you find it?'

Mackreth ignored that. 'When was it they had the—altercation?'

She gave the ghost of a shrug. 'Sometime last week.'

'Can you be more specific?'

'Not with my memory. Why is it important?'

'Because we know the gun has been fired, and there are pellet marks on the Mini. Because we have a story that Mrs Daynes fired at a rat, and now we've taken the gun to test for fingerprints.'

'Red herring,' Marjorie barked. 'She fired, he drove off—' She stopped.

'Yes, ma'am?'

'Then she left.' It was lame, and said lamely.

'On foot?' Mackreth was sceptical.

'How would I know?'

106

'Because you're in touch with her.'

'Indeed I'm not.'

'Then how do you know about the row when she shot at her husband?'

'That was another time.' There was strain now and as she became more stressed Mackreth started to push.

'It makes you wonder,' he said chattily, 'who loaded the gun that Sophie thought was unloaded.'

'*She* didn't!' Marjorie was fierce. 'No way would she keep a gun loaded. She took it down and he warned—' Her jaw dropped.

'Michael warned her that it was loaded,' Mackreth put in, suppressing a sense of triumph.

She stared at him. 'She phoned me,' she said weakly and then, recovering her belligerence: 'Where was the car found?'

'In Carlisle.' Mackreth, suddenly exhausted, motioned to Rumney, who told her about the car thief, the youngsters hot-wiring the Mini, the missing registration plates, how they traced the ownership to Sophie Daynes.

She listened attentively. 'What does Michael say?' she asked at the end.

Mackreth said, 'Either it was stolen from Stranraer ferry terminal or Sophie lied, that she never left—that it was stolen here, in Cumbria. Your stories don't tally, ma'am.'

'I wouldn't say that.' She was too casual. 'There are discrepancies certainly, gaps, and it's those that are the problem. No one knows what happened between the salient points.'

'And what are those?'

'Well, my god-daughter has disappeared and isn't in touch with anyone—'

'That's a fact?'

'—so far as we know. She quarrelled with Michael, her car was stolen. How do you tie those together?' Her equilibrium was back and she'd placed the ball in his court.

'You said she could be with a friend.'

'Did I? It's possible of course.'

'A male friend.' It was a statement.

'I didn't say that.'

'But is that possible?'

She thought about it. 'Anything's possible.'

'What did they quarrel about?'

'I have no idea.'

'It must have been pretty serious for her to fire at him.'

'She didn't know it was loaded.'

'Did she know Coulter?'

'Coulter? The man in the fire?' She shook her head angrily. 'She never met the fellow. These questions are random, sergeant; you're scraping the bottom of the barrel—and keeping me from my supper.' She stood up. 'I suggest you have an early night. You look shattered.'

*   *   *

108

Heading back to the station Rumney said, 'Do you really think there's a link with Coulter?'

'Coulter?' Mackreth had been on the verge of dozing. 'Time that guy was identified. For my money he was a small-time crook, lying low.'

'But if he wasn't Coulter—'

'What? Who wasn't Coulter? And what's a name mean anyway? A rose by any other name . . .'

'You're half-asleep. What I'm saying is that the body burned in the caravan may not be the chap who lived there. Like substitution?'

There was no response. Mackreth was asleep.

Chapter Eight

'You can charge him with keeping a shotgun unsecured,' the superintendent said, 'but how would you tie that to a charge of murder?'

Myles Mettam was portly and astute, a desk man with the overview.

'The point is, he loaded it.' Mackreth, bright-eyed and sharp after a good night's sleep, had wakened to the conviction that this was the simplest of sex crimes: the murder of a wife by the husband.

'Where's the motive?' Mettam asked. 'Who benefits?'

'Money. The house is hers, she inherited it. The car's in her name. She's working so the chances are she's the one with the bank account, but the house is the main thing.'

'He's enjoying all that while he's married to her,' Mettam pointed out. 'What was there to fight over, let alone kill her for?'

'There could have been friction over him being unemployed. The godmother's holding something back there. Sophie was the breadwinner, she could be resentful. He's got expensive tastes, drinks Carlsberg Special. Has Glenfiddich on the sideboard.'

Mettam was shocked. 'If she's working as a barmaid I don't wonder she fired at him. I'm only surprised she didn't hit him. But I agree, if she's a sportsman, she didn't keep a loaded gun in the kitchen. Naughty, all the same, keeping any gun unsecured these days.'

Mackreth refused to be sidetracked. 'I want to search the house.'

'We're overstretched,' Mettam grumbled. 'Here's Forensics employed on this guy in the caravan fire, and the stolen Mini, and now you and Rumney chasing a fellow who loaded a shotgun but who was the victim—almost. And there's the divers. All adds to the cost; forensic charges alone are prohibitive.'

But the divers hadn't involved Forensics, they didn't even have to be traced; they were around most weekends, including this last, and had been interviewed. They maintained with some indignation that there was no call for them to go in the woods, except just the margin for a piss; they weren't interested in woods, nor had they noticed anyone among the trees, neither substance nor shadow.

'If trespassers were there,' Mettam ruminated, 'and they were looking for Coulter . . .' He glanced expectantly at Mackreth but the DS was dismissive.

'Coulter's caravan was over a mile from the lake and hundreds of feet above it.'

'But if they were searching, knowing there was a caravan somewhere in the woods? They could have encountered this missing woman—Daynes—'

'No, she only ever saw shadows.'

'Suppose they were on the prowl at the same time she disappeared, suppose she saw something? The fire was arson, we suspect there was foul play where Coulter was concerned. Did the fire occur the same night she disappeared?'

Mackreth produced his notebook. 'The caravan was torched early Saturday morning. Sophie called—no, Daynes said she called him the previous evening. Originally he said she was in Stranraer but since the Mini was found he says she could have been lying to him. But lies come natural to him.'

'Find out when the woman Daynes was last seen, who saw her, what was her state of mind. Go to the pub where she worked.'

'She wasn't well,' the licensee's wife told them, wondering if there was trouble in the wind. Business-wise she thought they were in the clear but she wondered about her husband; they were both middle-aged and she was feeling it, particularly in the season, but everyone knew that the forties was a dangerous age for men.

'What was wrong with her?' Mackreth asked.

'Menopause.'

He gulped. 'She told you that?'

She stared at him. So old-fashioned. 'Said she thought so. You reckon it was something else?'

'She's disappeared.'

'Never!' She was fascinated. 'Her husband said she was getting over it, that she'd be back this week. Disappeared? When?'

'That's what we have to find out. So far we've not found anyone who saw her Friday. You must be the last people to have seen her—Thursday? What time did she leave?'

'She left early.' Her eyes gleamed, she was putting two and two together. 'I let her go; she was obviously sick—'

'She was vomiting?'

'No, no. I mean she looked s— not well, depressed, like she'd burst into tears any

112

minute.'

'Shocked?'

'Now you come to mention it, yes. She was acting like someone had died, you know?'

*   *   *

'She'd had a shock,' Mackreth mused. 'And was acting as if someone had died.'

'Coulter died,' Rumney said in the same tone. 'But not until Saturday.'

'But Sophie—' Mackreth's tone hardened, 'she was acting strange just before he died.'

'Not just before: two days before.'

Mackreth savoured his beer. They were still at the pub, drinking Theakstone's. 'She left here Thursday,' he said. 'Coulter died Saturday. What was she doing Friday?'

'Michael says she drove to Ireland, which could be partly true if the Mini was stolen from the terminal at Stranraer. They could have quarrelled Thursday night or Friday, she fired at the Mini—wait a minute! It was Michael drove off in the Mini, according to Marjorie Neville.'

'He's got some questions to answer.' Rumney was grimly amused and at that moment Mackreth's mobile started its alien rendering of 'Scots Wha Hae'. He checked the display and went outside. Rumney, receiving no signal to follow, drank his beer quickly.

After a few minutes Mackreth appeared in

the doorway and jerked his chin, ignoring his own drink. Rumney joined him outside.

'They've had a text message.' Mackreth didn't need to identify the source. 'Anonymous: "Daynes is a murderer. Ask him about Mary Spence." We're going back.'

'Does the name ring any bells?' he asked as they left town.

'Mary Spence? No.'

'Interesting. As you said, he has a lot of questions to answer. Wonder who sent the text.'

* * *

Nothing seemed to have changed at the Boathouse. The back door was open, the bike leaning against the wall; there was no sound of human activity except, blended with birdsong, distant voices of people out on the water. When Michael appeared he looked as if he hadn't slept.

'Any news?' he asked, coming along the passage.

'We should have news?' Mackreth asked, feigning surprise.

'Of my wife.' Michael led the way to the sitting room and stood, half-turned and dejected, looking across the lake.

'We haven't come about your wife,' Mackreth said. 'Tell us about Mary Spence.'

Michael nodded once and sighed. 'I tried to

114

convince the chap but I got nowhere.' He turned to them, spreading his hands in a gesture of helplessness. 'I scarcely knew the girl; it was only a casual thing but she had to go and take it seriously. My wife knew—I told her immediately—and she wasn't bothered.' He grinned weakly. 'Well, not after the initial tantrum: throwing the odd plate and that—'

'Firing at you.'

'OK, but that was recently.' He checked. 'Ah, she's been talking to you—no, to Marjorie—I told you it was Sophie who fired the gun, I lied about the target. I substituted the rat. Which was appropriate, I have to admit.'

'Why did you load the gun in the first place?'

'Protection. She'd seen these prowlers. I was worried, this place is too remote; people can come at us from any direction, including the water. We were—we are vulnerable. What good is a gun unloaded? You'd never have time to get to the ammunition—'

'Where is the ammunition?'

'In the kitchen drawer.'

'But you didn't tell your wife you'd loaded it.'

'I did—'

'Not until she was pointing it at you.' Michael bit his lip. 'You drove away,' Mackreth went on. 'You came back and she'd gone. You said she was in Ireland in the car.

But you had the car. How did you get back from Carlisle?'

'I don't know what you're—When was I in Carlisle?'

'Where does Mary live?' The questions came like automatic fire.

'I don't *know*.' Michael sounded exhausted. 'I said, I told her brother: it was just—it wasn't serious, not even a one-night stand, I was drunk. But she's young, immature, and now she's bored with the boyfriend and left him and she's picked my name out of a hat, told him she was going away with me, told her brother too. Which of them got in touch with you, Lambourne or Weston? He's not her brother, you know, only a stepbrother. But very close, I understand.'

Mackreth ignored the innuendo. 'Your wife came home early from the pub and caught you in a compromising situation with Mary.'

'No!'

'And threatened you and fired at you, and you drove away, and then you came back.'

'So that's it.' Despite his drawn features Michael sounded relieved—like they all do, Rumney thought; they're glad it's over, no more running, no more subterfuge. 'Someone's got it in for me,' he was saying, 'and doesn't this dovetail with the theory that when the wife disappears the prime suspect is always the husband?'

'When she's murdered,' Mackreth

116

amended.

Michael shook his head, seeming at the end of his tether. 'There's no sign of that. She's away somewhere, she doesn't know what's happened.'

'Is that why you called her employer, said she'd be back this week?'

'You know everything.' He was resigned. 'That's right, I didn't want her to lose her job. For all I knew she'd called them herself but I thought I'd be on the safe side.'

For him it was an unfortunate turn of phrase. Mackreth said: 'She hasn't been in touch with you. She's not touring Ireland in her Mini, that call was a fabrication on your part. You had the car, you dumped it, removed the registration plates and left it where kids would cover any incriminating traces and likely torch it. Why?'

Michael sighed, beaten. 'There were the pellet marks. She'd vanished. It looked bad. I had to get rid of the car.'

'Not if she'd just walked out!' Mackreth was incredulous. 'It was she who fired the gun. What did you have to be afraid of? What was that?' Michael had mumbled something.

'I thought she'd drowned herself. She threatened to swim out in the lake, not come back. I wasn't thinking straight.' He collapsed in a chair and fixed his gaze on Mackreth. 'It was like this: when she fired at me I was terrified. There are two barrels, see. Before she could fire the other one, I was up this drive in the Mini like a bat out of hell. I spent the night in the car and in the morning I left it some way off in the woods and came down here on foot, praying that she wasn't still in a vile mood. I came in very quietly and crept all over the place and she wasn't here. I got to wondering: where had she gone? That's when I thought she could be in the lake—and there was the car with the pellet marks. It had to be got rid of. I took it to Carlisle, came back on the train.'

'It didn't occur to you to go out on the lake and look for your wife's body? You have a boat. Or to alert the rescue services?'

'All I was thinking about was my own skin.'

They thought that for once he was speaking the truth.

'Let's get this straight,' Mackreth said firmly, sitting down, glancing at Rumney who took out his notebook.

'Are you arresting me?' Michael asked.

'No.' But the tone wasn't reassuring. 'We need times,' Mackreth explained mendaciously. Times might help but what he was after was more *time*, more rope for the man to hang himself. Michael was devious and aggression could have the effect of making him clam up. On the other hand and in view of what had already been exchanged, he would suspect any hint of sympathy, of fellow feeling, seeing these as a ploy to lull him into a false

118

sense of security. Could he be distracted? 'No,' Mackreth repeated thoughtfully, 'the reason we need to keep a record'—glancing at Rumney poised to take a note—'is because there could be a link between your wife's disappearing and the caravan fire.'

Michael had been slumped in his chair, now he straightened with a jerk. 'You're joking!'

'It came close.'

'What came close? No one knew the fellow! We didn't: Sophie and me. No way can you be thinking—'

'Listen!' Mackreth held up a hand. 'You were worried yourself about prowlers in the woods—'

'Not him surely. You're not saying it was that Coulter guy?'

'What I'm saying, what we're considering, is that these strangers were looking for Coulter, who could be a crook from Manchester or some other city.'

Michael was silent.

'So we need some times,' Rumney reminded him gently.

'Yes. Yes, of course.' But he was still thinking about prowlers.

'Where did your wife go on Friday?' Mackreth asked, sounding bored.

'Last Friday?' Michael blinked rapidly. 'I haven't the remotest—no, wait. She wasn't here! She left Thursday evening so Friday she'd be driving to—no—' He collapsed in dejection. 'I don't know where she was.'

'With Coulter.' It wasn't a question, merely a diversion.

'She didn't *know* Coulter. He died in the fire anyway. There were people looking for him? So the guy was a criminal. There were rumours.'

'People looking for him could have known he was living in a caravan in the woods but not specifically where. Your wife could have encountered them, seen something she shouldn't.'

'She never said anything, not that she'd actually run into anyone.'

'It's possible that when she did, she didn't come back.'

'Oh, my God! You mean they—No, I don't believe it.'

No more do I, Mackreth thought. Aloud he said, 'Let's think about the timing. You left here after she fired at you. When would that be?'

Michael's eyebrows climbed in amazement. 'Man! I wasn't looking at my watch!'

'Was it daylight?'

'No-o, it was dark.'

'Before or after midnight?'

Michael shook his head and shrugged.

'What time did she get home from the pub?' Rumney asked. They knew she had left at eight o'clock.

'It was still light, must have been before

nine.'

Mackreth let that go. 'How did she seem to you?' This was the moment he'd suggested that Sophie found him in bed with Mary Spence, but now he was into the business of distraction.

'She wasn't herself.' It was grudging.

'What was wrong?'

'Mary Spence had come in the bar and stared at her: just stared. Didn't say anything. Sophie found that disturbing.'

'Stalker behaviour.'

'Exactly,' Michael agreed eagerly. 'That's what I told her. Unfortunately I'd also told her Mary was unbalanced. Not nice that: a crazy woman knowing where you work. Naturally Sophie'd be on edge driving home: that difficult pass, big drops below the road. She was worried every time she passed a stationary car, thinking it might shoot across and push her over the edge. By the time she reached home she was a wreck.'

'So she took down the gun and told you to get out of the house.'

Michael gave a sharp snort, not amused. 'Right. That's just what she did do—and I'd completely forgotten that I'd loaded it! She didn't believe me, pulled the trigger after she'd driven me outside, and I heard those pellets: like a rain of hail it was.'

'Where did you spend the night?'

'Up on the hause'—he gestured—'away

towards the head of the lake. I pulled off the road there and got my head down.'

'Can anyone verify that?'

'Not a soul.' Suddenly cocky.

'You came back—when?'

'Before sunrise. It was bloody cold in the night, and did you ever try to sleep on the back seat of a Mini? Hell, by first light I'd have faced the second barrel rather than spend another hour on top of the hause.'

'And when you came in where was the gun?'

'On its rack.' Less voluble now.

'Where was her handbag?'

'She'd taken it.'

'Sponge bag? Brush and comb?'

'Those too.' He was alert, watching Rumney's pen.

'What clothes had she taken?'

'Only a few, and her raincoat.'

'And you thought she had committed suicide.'

'Yes, *then*. It was later, on the Friday, after I dumped the car, that I started to think rationally again. I knew it could be wishful thinking but when I got off the train and reached home I looked for her things: the handbag and the rest, and they weren't here so I knew she was alive.'

'Let's go back a bit,' Mackreth said, and castigated himself because it sounded as if they were in an interview room, which they were in a sense, but he didn't want Michael thinking

122

that way. 'When your wife got home Thursday evening what did you do, the two of you, between then and when you left?'

Left so abruptly, Rumney said to himself.

'We talked.'

'About what?'

'This girl. She was on our minds.' An understatement surely.

'This conversation went on for how long? An hour? Two?'

'Not two hours but it rumbled on a while. Rows do that. Finally it got too much for her.'

'This was all about Mary Spence coming in a bar and staring at your wife.'

'It sounds trivial, the way you put it, but that was the basic cause of the squabble, yes.'

'The two women never met—not to speak.'

Michael hesitated. 'They talked,' he said cautiously, 'on the phone.'

'Go on.' This was blood from a stone.

Michael swallowed. 'I was out. Mary called and Sophie answered.'

'This is that same evening, when you had the fight?'

'It wasn't a fight, it was a—tiff, just. Yes, it was that night.'

'What did they talk about?'

'I don't know.'

'Oh, come on! If that phone call was fuel on the flames your wife would have flayed you with every detail.'

'It was a load of bull. The woman was

obsessed, saying how it was her—Mary—who I fancied, not my wife, and Sophie should do the right thing and let me go. Sophie wasn't making any allowances for the girl being crazy, in need of treatment, she took it all at face value. She was in a spitting rage when I came in but more because Mary was making such a bloody nuisance of herself than because I'd made one stupid mistake months since. I don't blame Sophie for anything, and she never meant to hurt me, she was the wronged wife. Happens all the time.'

Mackreth rose, stretched his legs and moved to the open french windows. He stood on the deck and his gaze wandered over the water and the coloured sails and came back to rest on the little dock below, the dinghy rocking in the last ripples of the steamer's wake. He looked from the boat to the vast expanse of the lake then he returned to the room and regarded Michael thoughtfully. 'These prowlers,' he said. 'There was a shot and you drove away fast. I'm thinking that someone in the woods that night could have heard that shot and a racing engine and come down to see what was happening. Did they come here?' He glanced towards the passage. 'Encountered your wife?' It was repetition but would Michael rise to the bait?

He did, but warily. 'I'm beginning to think you may be right on that score.'

'They came in the kitchen?' Mackreth

mused. 'Left prints?'

'Not if they were wearing gloves.'

'I don't think so. If they were only looking for Coulter—remember he wasn't killed till the following night—they wouldn't be troubling to wear gloves.'

Rumney's face was wooden as his brain raced, trying to figure out what his partner was aiming at.

'We'll get your wife's prints for elimination purposes,' Mackreth said. 'They'll be all over her pots and pans. And other visitors who were here, we'll be seeing them; Miss Neville, I presume, and ourselves of course. You don't mind, do you, no objection to giving your prints for elimination?'

'No.' It was surprised and shaky. 'Not at all.' Michael looked round helplessly. 'You do it here?'

'We'll run you down to the station—and bring you home.' Mackreth grinned, it was a joke; he wasn't about to allow a cooperative member of the public to find his own way home. 'And I'd like your permission to print this place. We don't need your say-so, we could always get a warrant but then we don't need that either, do we?'

Chapter Nine

'Can you be convicted of murder if there's no body?'

Gerald Fairburn straightened from his dwarf beans. 'Mice are at it again,' he barked. 'I'm going to ask Marjorie for a cat. What are you doing in your slippers?'

Davina, exotic in silver mules, said, 'They haven't found her body but they've taken him in. I didn't think it was that bad a marriage, did you? Although you always said he was a sponger.'

'You're wearing your new slippers in the garden!'

'So I am. I was speaking to Elaine Dover from Glendene. The police have arrested Michael. I thought you'd be interested.'

'Village gossip. I'm coming up for me tea. Marjorie will be down shortly with the eggs. We need a good mouser here, the buggers have taken half the early crop.' They couldn't use traps because of the dogs.

They had tea on the terrace. A cuckoo called from the trees at the back. Here the low wall that bounded the terrace was cushioned with aubretia, purple and magenta, and clumped with yellow stonecrop. A red admiral caught Gerald's attention as it checked at the alpines and then passed on. 'Michael will be

126

helping them trace Sophie's movements,' he stated. So he had been listening.

'They're searching the Boathouse.'

'Rubbish. Need a warrant for that. No grounds for one.'

A latch clicked and Marjorie came through the side gate carrying a basket, Sharkey mincing after her, arching tall as the younger Labrador advanced with circumspection, keeping well out of striking distance of claws.

'Just talking about you—or rather—' Gerald gasped as Davina nudged him, then the message penetrated. 'That cat will do,' he said loudly. 'We need him for the mice. They've taken half our beans.'

'You can have him if he'll stay,' Marjorie said, but she'd seen the nudge. She glowered at Davina who asked politely, trying to be casual, 'Have you heard about Michael?'

'What's he done?'

Only murdered your god-daughter, Gerald thought, and guessed his wife was on the same lines, but what she said was, 'The police have taken him in—for questioning.' She could be indiscreet with Gerald but now was not the moment to suggest that Michael was a murder suspect.

'Is that all?'

Davina gasped. 'Isn't that enough?'

'What I meant was: do you know more? Why question him at the police station—I assume that's where he's been taken—instead of at home? What sort of questions?' She didn't press for the source of the information; in small villages there are jungle drums, omnipresent, not always accurate; in this village the drumbeat started with the special constable, Fisher's brother-in-law.

'His story doesn't jell,' Davina said. 'Apparently he keeps adjusting it. Now he's saying—' She stopped.

'Something about Sophie?' Marjorie's eyes were intent. ('I felt I was *skewered*,' Davina told Gerald afterwards.)

'You've got to know sometime,' she mumbled. 'He's saying Sophie threatened suicide—in the lake: to drown herself.'

'She did?' Amazingly, Marjorie smiled, resembling one of those huge lizards that eat people.

'Personally I don't believe it.' Davina was reproving. A joke it may have been, but sick, no cause for amusement.

'What else does he say?'

'That she—this has to be fantasy too, Marjorie, but it's what people are saying, and it must have originated with him—that Sophie could have been—could have run into the men who killed Coulter. You see, he swings back and forth like a gibbon.'

'Coulter?' Marjorie dropped into a chair. 'The body in the fire, that man?' She glared at Gerald.

'Sophie's intruders.' He was angry now, he

128

didn't like this. 'There seems to be a theory that people were after Coulter, that the fire was the work of a gang, but if so, none of it has anything to do with Sophie. Michael's trying to confuse the issue.'

'Ah, there you're wrong.' Davina was intrigued by the intricacies of the scenario, then she remembered that it was this woman's god-daughter they were discussing; checking in mid-stride, she was pinned down by Marjorie's eagle eyes.

'Go on,' she ordered. 'You're suggesting Sophie had got herself involved with a gang?' That reptilian grin again.

'She could have run into them that night, the night she—walked out.'

'That's absurd!' Gerald was concerned about Marjorie's state of mind. She was old, she was acting as if she were close to the edge, amusement bordering on hysteria. 'It's a load of tittle-tattle. For my money, Sophie had an almighty shindig with Michael—there's a woman in it, isn't there? Some barmaid on the other side of the pass. *Cherchez la femme.* Michael's kicked over the traces, Sophie read the riot act and cleared out. Gone north. You've got people in Scotland, haven't you?'

'You think there's a woman in it?' Marjorie asked curiously.

'He doesn't know.' Davina was contemptuous. 'Certainly there seems to be a woman, that's what the quarrel was about, when Sophie shot at him. D'you know, he's actually admitted that he loaded Sophie's shotgun without telling her. You don't look surprised but there, you know him better than we do; after all, he's by way of being a relation, sort of . . .'

'You're rambling, Davina,' Gerald grunted. 'And that gun should have been locked up; asking for trouble, keeping a firearm in plain view.'

'A woman?' Marjorie repeated, ignoring minor considerations.

'Yes, but not on the other side of the pass; Gerald's confused with the pub where Sophie worked for a day or two.'

'Where does this woman live, the one who Michael is supposed to be—"seeing" is the current expression, I believe?'

'I don't know.' Davina's disappointment showed. 'But the police will find her. It seems that Michael's shifting the blame to her.'

'Blame for what?'

'Now why did I say that?' She was nonplussed. 'I do get the impression that the focus is shifting to this mystery woman. Did Sophie ever hint that Michael—oh sorry, none of my business.'

'Can't remember.' The old lady was suddenly curt. 'Where are these mice? Let's take the cat and if he won't stay at least he can leave his smell: act as a deterrent.'

After Michael's fingerprints were taken he elected to stay in town rather than be driven home, a move that surprised Mackreth since it pointed to the man's total lack of interest in anything that the search might find in the Boathouse; that search, ostensibly for prints but actually designed to uncover any indication of foul play. With the odd exception there was nothing to be found: no incriminating letters (but who wrote letters nowadays?) nor any clothes or make-up that didn't appear to belong to one woman, and that was surely Sophie. The exception could be fingerprints on the headboard of the bed, on a bedside table and on a wardrobe door. These had been made by a smaller hand than Sophie's, hers assumed to be those found on the kitchen equipment. Nothing could be matched on site of course and if those in the bedroom belonged to Mary Spence, it was a moot point whether they did anything more than confirm the existence of a current affair rather than a one-night stand.

Mackreth, looking in on the search, wondered whether they were wasting their time, whether the answer to Sophie's disappearance lay elsewhere—if, that is, she had disappeared and was not at this moment recovering her equilibrium on the far side of the Scottish border. Wandering about the

131

house, he stopped at the laundry basket in the bathroom, rummaged through it and paused at a cotton pillow case smudged with lipstick. Dropping it with an expression of distaste he went downstairs and returned to the station considering how he might obtain Mary Spence's prints.

*   *   *

Rumney was to find her flat without trouble. Although the address given in the telephone directory was no more than Gideon's Yard the only person visible when he came down the cobbles from the street turned out to be watering Mary's plants. Barbara Howard said she didn't know when her neighbour would return, she was away on holiday. In view of Rumney's occupation her attitude was rather careless, turning her back, nipping off a dead leaf. A more normal reaction would have involved some measure of curiosity. When he asked if she had a key to the flat she turned and eyed him belligerently.

'I have. Why?'

'If we need to go in—'

'Not without a warrant!'

'Why would you be thinking in those terms?' She was silent; no doubt she knew the system in theory from watching cop shows on the telly but she was unable to cope with the reality. 'We know about the boyfriend,' he said

132

comfortably.

'So?' She had no idea of the moves, but since she wouldn't play he was left dangling. 'Are they together?' he asked desperately, anything to get her talking.

'I shouldn't think so, not in the season. He won't have time off until the autumn.'

He blinked. She smiled. 'A sweet boy,' she assured him. 'They make a lovely couple.'

'Are we talking about the same man?'

'Andrew.' She was more sure of herself now. 'Andrew Lambourne.'

'This is the married chap?'

'Bless you no! Andrew's not married—yet.' Her gaze sharpened. 'They're only engaged. You thought they were together?'

'Andrew Lambourne.' He was thoughtful. 'Where can I find him? He must know her whereabouts.'

'Of course he does. He's at Marten House, down the lake—' Her eyes widened and he turned to see a big man had stopped at the foot of what he took to be Barbara's steps. It was his size as much as anything that identified him; he was the fellow who'd been at the Boathouse yesterday when they arrived.

'I got company.' Barbara pushed past the detective and came up short against the stranger who blocked her escape route. Behind her Rumney smiled amiably. The fellow ignored him and addressed the woman.

'Have you heard from her?'

133

She licked her lips and glanced at Rumney who said brightly, 'We met yesterday at Daynes' place. You're a friend of Mary's?'

'I'm her stepbrother. And who are you?'

He had his card out. 'DC Rumney, Kelleth CID.'

The man's accent puzzled the DC, not that he couldn't place it more or less, thinking it was London or thereabouts, but what was the chap doing here?

'I'm Keith Weston and I come from Essex.' He was telepathic? 'And I'm looking for my stepsister.'

'Why?' He dared not interrupt the flow by suggesting they find a more suitable place to talk than a public thoroughfare. 'What made you come all this way?'

It was Weston who solved the problem of privacy. He turned to Barbara who seemed fascinated by this brief exchange: 'You have the key, perhaps we could go inside her flat and talk.'

'I can't do that.' She was suddenly defiant. 'I don't know you, you could be anybody; she'd have said if I was to let anyone into her home—and as for him'—nodding fiercely at Rumney—'he has to get a warrant.'

'You're within your rights,' Weston told her. 'Mr Rumney and I will find somewhere else.'

'No.' She was quick. 'I can ask you in.' But she meant into her place. Rumney guessed that she was eager to know what the men had

134

to say to each other; no way was she going to let them go off without her. He wondered why she was taking her neighbour's business so much to heart. Was it curiosity or loyalty, or did she know something that the stepbrother didn't, let alone himself? That rough southern accent made him suspicious. They'd considered a gangland murder but that was Coulter, and little more than a ploy at that.

They were taken up the steps to find themselves in a living room that was quite opulent for a Kelleth yard. Chairs and sofa were in crimson leather, there were exotic drinks on a trolley and brilliant posters from Turkey, Poland, Bulgaria. Barbara brought coffee immediately, evidently keeping warm on a hotplate.

Weston took the initiative before Rumney had a chance to settle: 'Why are you looking for Mary?'

Most officers would point out that it was usual for them to ask the questions but Rumney decided that with this chap you trod softly. 'We're investigating certain activities, and her name came up.' He paused and Weston waited for more. There was no sound from Barbara who was sitting with them, ignoring her coffee. 'We're trying to trace a woman,' Rumney elaborated. 'Mrs Sophie Daynes.'

Silence. Weston drank. Barbara's attention was fixed on Rumney. 'Mean anything to you?'

135

he asked politely of the man, then his eyes came round to Barbara, including her. She clenched her jaw as if to bear down on speech.

'Sophie Daynes is the wife of the man Mary's having an affair with,' Weston said calmly. 'Which is why we were all at the Boathouse yesterday.'

Rumney looked a query at Barbara who said shakily, 'Mary? An affair?'

No one responded, perhaps taking her loyalty for granted. Weston said, 'Has Mary committed a crime?'

'Not to my knowledge,' Rumney said.

'Then why do you need to find her?'

'Good question.' He hadn't seen that one coming because he hadn't anticipated Weston's appearance on the scene: a simple man asking awkward questions—well, he looked simple in the sense of ordinary, rough. 'Daynes is helping us with our inquiries,' he said blandly, 'and your sister's in the frame because of the close relationship.'

Weston was very still. 'How can I help?' he asked.

Rumney's mobile started to ring. He excused himself and went out to the landing at the top of the steps. Behind him Weston said earnestly, as if continuing a conversation: 'I feel responsible, you see. He's not going to leave his wife.'

'No?' Barbara's voice climbed, her eyes on Rumney's back. He had left the front door open.

'You're close to her,' Weston said. Barbara was silent, red-faced. 'Where would she go?' His very bulk made him intimidating, particularly to a woman unaccustomed to deceit.

She shook her head. 'She didn't tell me. If she wouldn't—didn't tell you, and you're family, why would she tell a neighbour?'

'Because you're a woman and she's in love.'

'There's that,' she conceded unhappily, 'but she went so sudden, she always told me before, because I watered her plants when she was away—'

'Where did she go?'

'She never said! Why does it matter so much?'

'She could be there now.'

'No.' It was definite. He was surprised. 'She went there with *him*,' she muttered, glancing at the landing. 'But if he's at home now, she wouldn't go there on her own.'

'Where?'

'Some little place in the Borders but honest, I don't know exactly, she didn't say—'

Rumney was back. He said, 'There are fingerprints in the Daynes' house that have to be identified, and we need Mary's for comparison.' He glanced at Weston. 'We're going to want yours too because you were there.'

'You can have mine,' Weston said evenly,

and might have said more but checked himself.

Rumney addressed Barbara: 'We can get a warrant, ma'am.' His tone was as intimidating as Weston's size. Now they were both looking at her. She shrugged defeatedly and went to a wooden key rack on the wall behind the front door.

Rumney took a key from her. 'Where does she keep her car?' he asked.

'Usually in the street at the bottom of the yard'—she gestured—'but she's been putting it in my garage for a while. There's some lock-ups—'

'Why was that?'

'Andrew keeps hassling her. Andrew Lambourne, the boyfriend.' She was uncomfortable, knowing that the image conjured up one of promiscuity. 'She hides her car so Andrew won't know she's home.'

'Where's her car now?'

She gaped. What a stupid question—or was it a trap? 'She took it of course—when she left.' She was frowning, wanting to be rid of them but feeling responsible. She said tensely, 'I'm coming in the flat with you. After all, I have charge of the key.'

But Rumney wasn't having that and, citing contamination which, he noticed, Weston appeared to understand but not the woman, he insisted that they remain on the patio at least until he had retrieved the items he needed for prints.

It was a tiny flat: two rooms, a galley kitchen and a minuscule bathroom. Barbara said the place was let furnished and the only sign that the living room was occupied by a young woman was a stack of *Hello!* magazines and *Easy Living*. The kitchen told a different story, the refrigerator holding an assortment of food: butter, cheese, bread, yoghurt, eggs, and a stack of TV dinners in the freezer compartment. On the draining board there was a cafetière, disassembled, a mug and cereal bowl, all washed and set to drain.

The contents of the bathroom were even more striking. On a shelf above the cistern was all the paraphernalia that Rumney associated with women, including a hairdryer. On a glass shelf above the basin was a spool of dental floss, toothpaste and a plastic mug containing a toothbrush. A face flannel was draped over the side of the basin, bone-dry.

In the second room the bed was made. There were more jars on a dressing table, lipsticks, eye make-up, a brush and comb. He collected anything that might be expected to produce prints and, as an afterthought, those that might harbour DNA.

Chapter Ten

'She's done a runner,' Mackreth growled on hearing the news.

'That's not all,' Rumney told him. 'I had Barbara show me her garage and at that point she decided to come clean about something else. When she went to see if Mary had taken her car she found the doors closed but not locked, just a bolt shot on the outside, and the padlock that should have secured the bolt, that was missing. She reckons Mary threw it in her car when she left. Incidentally, she drives a Mini too, same as Daynes.'

'So? Popular old car. Everyone had a Mini at one time. But if Mary hung on to the padlock she was intending to come back. But she didn't; she went to the Boathouse and Sophie came home early and caught them together. Daynes is toughing it out, Mary panicked. If the prints match they will put her in the Boathouse at the same time that Sophie disappeared.'

'By all accounts Mary's immature. She's the one who'll break when we find her.'

Mackreth was surprised. 'You're thinking collusion. But we've got no proof, nothing to say when those prints were put on the headboard.' His eyes glazed. 'Wait a minute! There's lipstick on a pillow case in the laundry basket. I took it for Sophie's, but do middle-aged women leave make-up on bed linen? They don't wash before going to bed? Maybe we can match the DNA. For all that, sleeping with Daynes don't make Mary a murderer, nor even an accessory.'

'When we find her we'll get a confession.'

'You hope. Actually I don't think Michael's got that much backbone; we'll have him back once we've matched those prints. Meanwhile I want a word with this stepbrother.'

Weston had come to the station to supply his prints and had been asked to wait. Now, meeting Mackreth, he seemed quite happy to talk: about himself, about his garden centre in Essex, his home life—he was a bachelor. On request he listed names and numbers of his colleagues. He agreed it was a bad time of year to leave such a business. He called them each evening and they had his mobile number for emergencies.

Mackreth said diffidently that he failed to understand why a chap should find it necessary to desert a garden centre at the busiest time of the year merely because his stepsister was having an affair with a married man.

'It's only for a couple of days.' Weston was on the defensive. 'I'm much older: step-siblings, you see. I feel responsible.'

'She's not under-age.'

Weston said nothing. Mackreth, trawling for enlightenment, stared into the shadowed eyes, the features so intent and resolute and, sensing the determination of the man, with a flash of insight guessed at his motivation. Of course, they were 'steps': close but not incestuous; if he wasn't in love with the girl the bond could be as good as, if not stronger than, a blood tie.

'You're concerned about her,' Weston said, and Mackreth realized that he'd been silent for too long. He played for time.

'We've talked to Daynes.'

'I did that too.'

'Yes, you were with him when we arrived yesterday. I assume you talked about Mary. What did he tell you?'

'He swore that there was no affair, that he met her only the once, that they were intimate that one time but it was months ago.'

'Do you believe him?'

'It's not how she tells it. We keep in touch. Our parents aren't that interested so it's like there's no one for her to turn to.' Smothers her, Mackreth thought: possessive sort of chap. Weston was saying: 'At first I thought Daynes was just another boyfriend, like Andrew. Andrew Lambourne: he works at one of the local hotels. She didn't tell me Daynes had a wife until she mentioned marrying him. I took her up on that and then she had to admit he must get a divorce first. Things cooled between us after that—and then young Lambourne called me last Saturday week to tell me she'd gone off with Daynes. I kept trying to contact her but couldn't get through so in the end I had to come north and try to find out what was going on.'

'And found she isn't with Daynes after all.'

'That's right.' They regarded each other levelly.

'Where do you think she is?' Mackreth asked.

'She could be away with someone else.' It would appear that he'd given the matter some thought. 'Daynes strung her along while it suited him but when his wife put her foot down he chickened out. Mary had already finished with Lambourne, burned her boats there, Daynes turned out to be a wimp, so off she goes with some other chap.' He sounded bitter.

'You don't reckon she was serious about Daynes.'

'No.' Weston stretched his legs, giving the appearance of casualness, even boredom. Was it genuine or assumed and, if the latter, why? 'She's young. While she's with them it's the real thing: she's never been in love before, they're golden boys—until the gilt wears off, and then it's on to the next one.'

'So you'll be heading back south now.'

'That's right.' He stood up easily. 'Seeing as how I can't help you here . . .' He trailed off and Mackreth saw that, for the first time, he seemed at a loss.

'Why did you think we wanted to talk to

143

you, sir?'

'You know, I didn't think.' He beamed. Acting dumb?

There was a knock at the door and a uniformed man entered, handed a sheet of paper to Mackreth and left. The detective regarded the few words of the message and looked up. 'We wanted some background on Mary because of the close relationship with Daynes,' he said. 'The man's wife is missing.'

'I see.' Weston sat down slowly. He didn't look at the paper which Mackreth had placed face down on the desk.

'The relationship was serious until recently.'

'That's what I understood from her.' Now Weston did look at the paper. 'How recently?'

'Her fingerprints are in his bedroom at the Boathouse.'

Weston said nothing for a long moment then: 'Can you be certain when they were left there?'

'We might work it out but what we can be certain of is that the relationship wasn't confined to just one meeting months ago.'

'I knew that.' Weston was contemptuous. 'Daynes is a liar. I believed Mary—while it lasted, but she was goading Lambourne when she said she was going off with Daynes—had to be, he's still there.' His tone changed. 'What are you saying? You found she was in the Boathouse recently—' He stopped.

'Yes.' Mackreth's tone was heavy. 'And

Daynes' wife is missing. Disappeared around the same time as your sister.'

'Mary's not missing.' He didn't trouble to correct the mistake in the relationship. 'She'll be back.'

'You didn't enter her flat, did you?'

'No, Rumney insisted—*what! Mary's there?*' He came to his feet in one movement, his chair tossed over like a child's toy.

'No!' Mackreth remained seated although it took some strength of will given the man's bulk. Weston glared down at him, his mouth working. 'No,' Mackreth repeated quietly, 'she's not in the flat.' The other picked up the chair and sat down, blood darkening his face. 'What *is* there,' the detective went on, 'are all her toilet things, her brush and comb, toothbrush and so on.' He didn't add that some items were on their way to the laboratory.

Weston was thinking. 'She changed her mind,' he said at last. 'Met someone like I said, went off for a few days. Young girls, they're all the same: irresponsible. I can't spend more of my time up here, I'm needed back at the business. I'll let you know when I hear from her, shall I?'

'No way is he going home,' Mackreth told Rumney when the big man had gone. 'He was devastated when I told him how she'd left her flat. He's going to look for her, find out if she's an accessory, and then he'll do all he can to

145

protect her. Now where's Daynes?'

*   *   *

Rumney, not troubling to search the town, would have gone straight to the Boathouse but then he had the idea to look in at the Lurcher, Michael's local pub. He was there and drinking whisky which boded well for the police. He might be indiscreet. He made a fuss when asked to return to the station but that might be no more than resentment at having to abandon a lunchtime drinking session. He did demand the reason but he dried up when Rumney said vaguely that there had been a development. Back at the station he had the bewildered but eager air of an innocent party anxious to answer inquiries and get back to his mates in the Lurcher as soon as possible. He did ask again and in a jocular fashion if he were being arrested and was reassured on that score. In the interview room Mackreth seated himself comfortably, genial and a trifle bored. He was a man forced by circumstances to go through with a daft rigmarole, raising wry eyebrows as Rumney inserted the tapes and conducted the preliminaries. Michael had given his permission to be recorded and he watched the routine with absorption. This behaviour seemed a trifle over-played. Rumney blessed the whisky.

'So,' Mackreth announced when the

146

formalities were over. 'You own the Boathouse?'

'No, my wife inherited it from her mother.'

'Ah. And what happens to the property if your wife should die?'

'I don't know.' Michael looked surprised. 'To my knowledge Sophie hasn't made a will.'

'I see. If that were the case you would inherit everything, right?'

Michael blinked, serious and disconcerted. 'Presumably. You'll have to ask her. I—she doesn't have much.'

'The house alone must be worth a quarter of a million.'

Michael gaped. 'Wh—' He frowned, calculating. 'You could be right, lake frontage and all. Yes, that's possible, I suppose.'

'If she died by accident or suicide you'd be a relatively rich widower.'

He shook his head firmly as if he'd only just picked up on Mackreth's drift. 'She's alive; she took her things.'

'Her things were taken,' Mackreth amended, 'but not her car.'

'She couldn't; I had it. She must have been picked up by someone: a taxi or a friend.'

'But you disposed of the car. And said she was in Ireland. And that she'd phoned you.' Without a change in tone: 'And you never handled the gun.' Michael said nothing. Mackreth continued: 'How does it come to have your prints on it?'

147

'Of course I handled it. I loaded it because I was worried about the intruders.'

'You told us originally that you knew nothing about firearms.'

'I don't, but I'd seen her load and fire—at rabbits in the garden. I knew how to do it. Certainly I lied about the car and I've explained why I had to do that: to dispose of it. For God's sake, it was only a domestic spat. Why should I tell you all our private business?' His brain was leap-frogging.

'Why did she fire at you?'

'I told you! She was livid because that girl—Mary Spence—she was making waves: she was stalking Sophie. It was the final straw: coming in the bar where she worked. And the phone call with a load of lies—all fantasy. Sophie was scared and very, very angry. She flipped.'

'Because she discovered that you were still seeing Mary.'

'No.' The man's eyes were steady.

'She came to you at the Boathouse.'

'No.'

'Had sex with you in the bed you shared with your wife.'

'No.' It was quiet, unemphatic.

'And left her mark. Mary didn't trouble to remove her make-up just for a quickie in the evening.' When it became obvious that Michael wasn't going to respond, Mackreth resumed: 'You quarrelled violently and your wife shot at you. You didn't sleep on the

148

hause; you came back, found her still in the house, killed her and disposed of the body—and the items that she would have taken with her supposing she'd left voluntarily. What did you do with the body?'

Michael raised his head. 'I didn't kill her.' He sounded tired. 'She's alive and she'll be back as soon as she hears I've been arrested'—he smiled—'for her murder.'

'We'll drag the lake and we'll impound the boat. There have to be traces.'

He shrugged. 'You won't find her because she's not there.'

'She'd be there if she'd committed suicide,' Rumney put in.

'Then how would you account for her taking her things?' Michael asked.

* * *

'He's forgotten one item; well, two,' Mackreth said viciously when they broke for tea and the detectives retreated. 'It was him who suggested suicide in the first place. And then, if she was alive she'd be using her credit cards. If they're not used, she's dead.' He paused, then added wryly, 'Except that Mary could be using them, of course.'

'We can't go forward,' Rumney said gloomily. 'So far we've got nothing to hold him on, not even circumstantial evidence. The car's clean—at least as far as murder's concerned.

149

Sophie's prints are there naturally, likewise they'll be all over the boat: it's her boat, like everything else. The guy can't be charged, let alone convicted just because he was having it off with another woman. His story could be true, basically: that Sophie called a cab and drove away.'

'We need to circulate local taxis.'

'Or she could have phoned a friend to pick her up, like he said.'

'That's more difficult.' Mackreth frowned. 'I'd trust Marjorie Neville just as far as I can throw her. She'd lie in her teeth . . . and that makes two of 'em, her and Michael, but each lying for different reasons. He's out to save his skin, but she wouldn't give a damn for herself, only those bloody cats and, of course, her god-daughter.' He wasn't maundering, just chasing open-ended notions.

'You don't reckon anything to the Coulter angle then?' Mackreth stared at his partner, lost. 'Someone after Coulter.' Rumney was patient with him. 'A gangland killing. Sophie Daynes ran into them unexpected like.'

'Oh no. That was just a ploy to distract Michael, to confuse him. No, Coulter has nothing to do with us. Wonder how they're getting on down there.' The Coulter case was in the hands of an inspector who was working with Manchester CID trying to establish the man's affiliations before he arrived in the Lakes.

Chapter Eleven

Mrs Foley receipted the bill, acknowledged the departing guests' thanks for their visit with her social smile, then switched it off as the big man in open-neck shirt and jeans approached the desk. 'My name's Weston,' he said. 'I'm looking for Andrew.'

Mrs Foley's expression hardened. 'He told me about you.' She picked up a phone. 'Andrew, Mr Weston is in Reception. Will you come down?' She listened and her lips thinned. 'Don't make it too long,' she said acidly. She replaced the receiver. Her eyes lingered on Weston's trainers.

'I'll be outside,' he told her equably.

He waited on the forecourt automatically assessing the condition of the herbaceous borders but his thoughts were on Mary and this lad whom he'd not yet met, only spoken to on the phone. Nevertheless their common interest showed in their intensity of expression and when Andrew emerged they identified each other immediately. The lad sketched a nod; he was carrying a soft suitcase and a bulging sports bag. He crossed to an old Fiesta and unlocked it. Weston strolled over. 'I'm Keith. What's going on?'

Andrew needed a shave and his features appeared to have crumpled. He moved like an old man. 'I'm leaving. She won't give me time off so I've handed in my notice.'

'Where are you going?'

'I don't know. She's not at her flat. I was there the same night but no one was home.'

'The same night as what?'

'Didn't I say on the phone? She came to see me in my lunch hour, told me she was leaving with *him*, that she was pregnant.' Weston flinched. 'I went to her flat that evening. No lights anywhere. I've seen Barbara since; all she'll say is that Mary's away.'

Weston thought the lad was close to collapse. 'I was talking to Barbara yesterday,' he said. 'The police were there. Have they been to you yet?'

'No. Why police?' But it hadn't really registered. 'What did Barbara tell you?'

'Nothing useful. The police will come to you because they suspect Daynes of doing away with his wife; for all I know they'll have charged him by now, they were close to it yesterday. They suspect Mary could have been an accessory.'

'Balls.' No anger, not even contempt, merely dismissal.

'She was in the Boathouse around the time that Sophie Daynes went missing. Her prints are in the bedroom. The police reckon the wife caught them together and they turned on her.'

Andrew opened the back of his car and

152

stowed the bags among more luggage on the seat. He closed the door and turned to Weston. 'Get in,' he ordered, indicating the passenger side. Weston was startled as much by the tone as the order itself. 'We have to talk,' Andrew said. 'Not here, somewhere more private.'

'You lead the way. I'll follow.' Weston's old Land Rover was close by, incongruous between a Jaguar and a Shogun.

Andrew led him down to the lake and a lay-by above the shore where he parked facing the water. Weston joined him, pushing back the passenger seat in the little car, leaving the door wide. They were shaded by leafy alders but the morning was gearing up for another hot day.

Andrew looked across the water. 'That's his place,' he said tonelessly but Weston could see only trees on the far side. 'Where that sailing dinghy is now.' Andrew pointed. 'Beyond its bow you can see glass shining. That'll be his windows. The walls don't show up through the haze.'

'Right.' Weston wondered where this was taking them.

'You can see it from the upper rooms at the hotel. I've watched through binoculars.'

'Did you see anything—significant?'

'I never saw Mary. Saw lights sometimes but I was too far away to see what was happening in a room. And he'd hardly kill his wife without drawing the curtains first. Unless it happened in the kitchen. What's that got to do with Mary anyhow? I'm not bothered about Daynes' wife; that's his problem.'

'Except that we're involved now.' Weston was tart. 'What I'm concerned about is my sister's safety.' He dropped the 'step' for emphasis as much as simplicity.

'No way is she an accessory to anything.'

'It could have been an accident—a blow during a fight, for instance—and then he took the body away in one car while Mary drove the other, and she brought him home again. Then she panicked and scarpered.'

'So she'd be innocent of murder—unless it was her blow—'

'That would be manslaughter.' It *could* be, but Weston didn't correct it. This guy was on a short fuse.

'We have to find her,' Andrew persisted. 'The longer she stays away the worse it is for her. Barbara must know where she is.'

'Why? Mary never intended to go, she left all her toilet things in the flat. Barbara swears she doesn't know where she is. My mobile's on all the time and she's never contacted me—' Weston stopped, apparently absorbed in a family of tufted ducks floating past.

'She's scared of you—'

'No! I'd be the first person she'd come to for help. That's what worries—'

'Not if it wasn't an accident.'

154

'What?'

'Maybe they did—' Andrew stopped and shook his head. 'It doesn't bear thinking about. It terrifies me. I had him pegged for a killer—I accused him, went in the Boathouse, it wasn't locked, left a message on his typewriter. I pointed the cops his way, I sent them a text'—Weston was staring, amazed—'but it never occurred to me, never in a million years—if I'd suspected I'd never have fingered him. Oh, my God, what have I done?' He clapped his hands to his mouth in a curiously feminine gesture.

Weston saw that the youngster had leapt from total denial to a dawning awareness that his love could be a killer; now he was wallowing in guilt because he thought he'd steered the police in her direction. The lad needed to be controlled before he could do more harm. 'What did you want to talk about?' he asked bluntly, trying to establish some sense of order. 'You said you needed somewhere private to talk.'

'Did I? Oh yes, I lost my job and I need to find Mary. That's all, that's the situation. I don't know where to start. If the people closest to her have no idea where she is, what can we do?' Now he'd reverted to a childlike state. Weston was the father figure, the leader.

'Leave it to the police,' the big man said, with a confidence he didn't feel, but the lad was a loose cannon. 'I'm staying at a pub in town. Book a room there and I'll try to find out what the police are up to. I have a handle, you see, being family. For my money they'll broadcast a description, a request for her to come forward. What we have to do is try to reach her before they do, make sure she doesn't say anything to incriminate herself. She'll need a solicitor. I can handle that part.'

'Daynes would know where she's holed up. I phoned him, you know, right at the start, asking where she was. He denied everything. That's why I went there, to see if she was in that house. He *has* to know where she is.'

'He's in custody—or was. But if he's charged with murder he can't be bailed and there's no way we can get at him.' But Weston was thinking that if Michael were released from the station and could be reached, he might be prevailed upon to talk.

*   *   *

'They let him go! He was hauled out of the Lurcher by the scruff, taken in for more questioning and then released. What d'you make of that?'

Davina winced as Marjorie severed the rabbit's cervical vertebrae with a hatchet. The young Labrador whimpered and squirmed, trying to pluck up courage to snatch the skin from the chopping block.

'They've got nothing to hold him on,' Marjorie said as she made for the house

156

carrying the bloody knife and the carcass. Behind her the Red Baron leapt on the block and crouched, snarling at the Lab. 'Bugger,' Marjorie said. 'Meant to bury that skin.'

'Well, of course they haven't got a—c-crime.' Davina stuttered, took a breath and went on weakly, 'They're dragging the lake,' which was equally crass considering the identity of the body the police were looking for. She followed the older woman to the kitchen and the double sink under the window. Marjorie glanced at the lake as if checking the condition of the water for diving. Davina, unable to think of anything to say that was innocuous, waited nervously.

'What's Michael's story?' Marjorie asked.

'He hasn't confessed. We don't know all the details but we know that.' They took it for granted that between the members of the Fairburns' social circle and the publican's brother-in-law they should be able to monitor most of the police activity. Only more recent events escaped them and that merely by virtue of the time element. If Michael confessed to murder this morning they should know by noon.

'I wasn't thinking so much of confession,' Marjorie said, rinsing the skinning knife, 'but his version of what happened that night.'

'To my knowledge it's never changed—basically. He came home and Sophie had gone.' Regarding the solid figure at the sink, now deftly dismembering the rabbit, cleaning joints, piling them in a colander, Davina was exasperated. 'Gerald and I think she's just gone away for a time, to find some space.' She felt she should be offering reassurance but she was confused. Marjorie gave no indication that she was listening, even that she'd heard. Too late Davina thought that if the old girl was in shock she'd only exacerbated matters by implying that poor Sophie's body was lying on the bed of the lake. 'Is there anything I can do?' she blurted, and then, strident: 'How do you *feel*?'

'Feel?' Marjorie repeated. 'How should a person feel when a man keeps a loaded shotgun within reach in her god-daughter's own house?'

Davina blinked, then grasped at one interpretation. 'You're thinking he shot her?'

'What do you think?'

Marjorie pushed a pan on the Aga's hob and reached for the oil. Ripping paper from a roll she started to dry the rabbit joints. 'Looks Spanish,' Davina said inanely, avoiding the question, moving to watch. Mustard seeds were scattered on the hot oil and started to pop.

'Lunch party?'

'No.'

Davina sighed. 'I'll go then; I think you'd rather be left on your own.'

'You'll have to forgive me.' Marjorie turned

158

but refused to make eye contact. 'If I keep working it stops me thinking of anything else, you see.'

Davina nodded, biting her lip. 'You know we're at the end of the telephone. Or come down, any time.'

She left by the back door, collecting the reluctant dog, dragging him away, his eyes still fixed on the Red Baron who was crouched in the shade with the rabbit skin.

The young Lab's companions were down on the shore with Gerald, the trio observing the preparations for dragging the lake. Lakeside dwellers were accustomed to the sight of divers going about their mysterious business but this was something else. Nevertheless around eleven o'clock Gerald lost interest; nothing seemed to be happening of any consequence and he abandoned the vigil to tramp home for morning coffee with Davina.

*   *   *

There was nothing in the lake. The parcel had rested on the bottom a few yards in from where the bed shelved steeply into deep water. It was weighted with an old fly-wheel but iron and parcel were too heavy for the length of sisal connecting them. The constant passage of the steamer set up enough agitation that eventually the worn strands parted and the parcel floated clear. It didn't rise to the surface

159

immediately but drifted with the current towards the outlet.

At the foot of the lake was an old humped bridge which caused much confusion in summer because it was single-track and traffic often met head-on at the blind top. At such times pedestrians clustered like flies in the embrasures above the piers. Downstream of the bridge the river bank was manicured: spruce and colourful where the village gardens came down to the water, the first of these belonging to the Lurcher: a beer garden given over to a lawn and picnic tables where obese ducks accosted customers and demanded food.

The parcel had reached the outlet this morning and, the river being shallow, it showed intermittently above the surface. A photographer stationed on the bridge thought it was an otter but when it didn't raise its head or dive he dismissed it as farm litter and concentrated on the view. A glimpse of bright orange as it passed below him confirmed that it was nothing alive, no living animal anyway.

The parcel emerged from the bridge shadow and, as if attracted by the spectacle of small children feeding the ducks, it grounded gently on mud at the edge of the Lurcher's beer garden.

The ducks saw it of course, opportunists as they were, and rejected it as inedible. The children were first to show more than a passing interest, not because it was litter, not even by virtue of its size—they were accustomed to bulging bin bags; they were puzzled by the way in which the gaudy baler twine had been trussed so methodically about the contents of this mysterious parcel. They didn't like to touch it, nor did their fathers. Ralph Fisher, summoned from his bar, stared dumbfounded, his mind a confusion of guilt (were all his accounts in order against the arrival of Authority?), of disbelief and fascination. Reason evaporated in the face of this object which had appeared so dramatically on his property. A woman had been missing, there had been speculation concerning murder, and here was—well, it was over five feet long, and it was the right shape . . .

'You'll have to call the police,' someone said.

'My brother-in-law is a—' Fisher checked himself. 'I'm about to do just that,' he said loudly. 'Perhaps you, sir,'—his confusion was unprecedented, he never called a customer 'sir'—'perhaps you'd remain here and keep folks at bay until such time as—as . . .'

'No problem. You reckon it was the woman that was murdered?'

Fisher blundered indoors to call the police. After a while Mackreth and Rumney arrived to find the village humming. The garden had been sealed off as far as possible and a makeshift screen erected, but because of the height of the bridge spectators could see the

161

heads of people inside the screen, if not what lay at their feet. The bridge was so crowded that uniforms had been placed at either end to direct traffic.

The news travelled like a grass fire before the wind. The pub was full to overflowing, customers spilling out to a road now lined with cars. Fisher, quickly recovered, was harassing his suppliers, demanding more of everything. In contrast the beer garden was quiet.

Mackreth and Rumney sat at a picnic table waiting for a camera man to finish inside the screen. There was no question of preserving the surroundings for traces; the garden was no crime scene. The parcel hadn't arrived in the village until this morning. The photographer had come forward, the one who had seen it approaching the bridge from open water: 'I thought it was an otter at first but it didn't move so I knew that, whatever it was, it wasn't alive.'

The occupants of a patrol car had been the first police to arrive and they had agreed with him, had gone further, noting that the proportions of the object were suggestive, even that at one end there were small but familiar shapes under the plastic. A constable reached out gingerly and felt toes.

'Would it be like tides?' Rumney asked, regarding a fat mallard with disgust. 'These birds are gross.'

'Make good eating,' Mackreth pointed out.

'Tides?'

'The lake has to have a current: water comes in and goes out. Could someone calculate how fast the body would move, so we can work out where it was put in?'

'Not without we know when it was dumped.'

The camera man emerged from behind the screen. 'All yours for the moment,' he said, joining them as they waited for the arrival of Forensics.

'Anything special about the knots?' Mackreth asked.

'No. Just ordinary overhand stuff like anyone'd tie up a package for the post. Carefully done though, and something weighting it down; there's a length of old rope broke off. It was fastened round the neck. He didn't intend it to come up.'

Forensics arrived, followed by the pathologist. With each new arrival the hum and jostle on the bridge was momentarily stilled as if the audience held its breath.

The orange baler twine was cut and the heavy but flaccid bulk eased up enough to allow the string to be drawn clear. The photographer took more pictures.

Three bin bags had been used, the middle one slit at the base so that it formed a tube to overlap the other two thus completely concealing the contents until the top one, the one they now knew was at the top, was cut sufficiently to be peeled back. Initially the face, with its dead eyes and rictus of agony, was near sexless but the plucked brows and long hair marked her as a woman.

Mackreth and Rumney were stupefied. Anyone, everyone would stare at a corpse in horror or compassion although, in people accustomed to violent death, emotions are suppressed. Mackreth couldn't have said what he was feeling, he didn't know. For days he had been preoccupied with the possible movements, the probable fate of Sophie Daynes. This very day they had started to drag the lake, and here was a body, a woman's body, but they had photographs and they knew Sophie was in her forties and this, if you could ignore the terrible expression, appeared to be a girl.

The remaining bags were cut and they found her shoes and, more importantly, her handbag. The bag contained a sodden cheque book and a wallet (with thirty-five pounds in notes) and credit cards in the name of Mary Spence.

Chapter Twelve

Identification was imperative; credit cards were not enough, personal confirmation was needed. Mackreth had a momentary qualm; he respected Weston and dreaded the big man's

164

reaction. Rumney, floundering as he tried to recover balance, appreciated his partner's scruples but reminded Mackreth of murder cases where ostensibly grief-stricken relations turned out to be psychopathic killers.

'The man's not devious,' Mackreth said. That was basically true although Weston had attempted to sidetrack them concerning his plans. A phone call to the hotel where he'd been staying elicited the information that he hadn't given up his room but that he was out at the moment.

As they considered their next move the inevitable happened. They had been engaged in a search for a woman who might be missing, no more than that, although the decision to drag the lake suggested that the situation was being taken more seriously by the authorities. They had anticipated that shortly they would be joined by a senior officer but they would still be in charge at the lake—dogsbodies—until and unless the divers found something that might indicate foul play. But now, suddenly and undeniably, they had a murder on their hands, and although as yet the cause of death was unknown—a bruise forward of the temple was obvious but hardly fatal—the meticulous packaging of the body suggested a calculating killer.

Everyone knew that this was the big one. Mackreth and Rumney weren't demoted, they knew the background and were a mine of information, but the DCI who had been in Manchester, winkling out Coulter's contacts, was brought back to take charge of the case involving the body in the Lurcher's beer garden. Appropriately the DCI was a woman, Annabelle Warwick: close to retirement, heavy and plain but smart in both senses of the word, an Oxford graduate who wore tweeds and a Burberry raincoat. Her assistant, on the other hand, DS Lorton, was lissom with the wide green eyes and small mouth of a cat, a woman who was street-smart, ex-grammar school, who favoured clever copies of designer labels. People who didn't know the pair were inclined to dismiss the DCI as past her sell-by date and the DS as a bimbo who had bartered sex for promotion. The attitudes of their colleagues varied between awe and wary suspicion but always imbued with respect.

A briefing was called and Mackreth summarized the work he and Rumney had been engaged in, his own bewilderment evident as he tried to relate the search for a missing wife to the appearance of the dead mistress—although he was careful to remind his listeners that the body was as yet unidentified. The expressions on the faces of the hastily assembled team showed that they were even more baffled than he, a state borne out by their questions. Were they to continue looking for the missing woman? Did he still suspect she'd been murdered? Did they have a serial killer here?

DCI Warwick intervened at this point to say that Mackreth had been stating the facts leading up to the discovery of the dead woman. The direction of the investigation would be determined only after she was formally identified. But, assuming that this was Mary Spence, and she was definitely *not* Sophie Daynes because the age was wrong, the situation had to be re-evaluated.

A telephone was ringing. The constable who answered signalled a development. Weston had arrived.

*   *   *

Mackreth received him. He seemed to have grown bigger and darker but that, thought the DS, was subjective. Quite frankly, the detective was diffident, but anyone would be when about to share confined space with a powerful and unpredictable animal. Although he would be accompanied by Rumney, as further back-up he chose DC Heslop who played rugby and was built like a barn.

The autopsy hadn't started, which was as well, Weston was spared a prolonged wait. He said nothing on the way to the mortuary, nothing as he stood before the slight and sheeted form. Watching closely Mackreth saw him wince as her face was revealed, then his features softened and there was such a depth of yearning in the eyes that even the pathologist looked away. No one spoke; they waited for him to ask to be left alone with her, but then it became obvious, as they stood there like attendant statues, that he *was* alone. After a while he turned and walked out, striking the door jamb with his shoulder. Lurching, he came up against Heslop's bulk. He recoiled and walked down a passage. Turning blindly through a doorway into an unoccupied office, he sat down on the first chair. Mackreth stood, the DCs behind him but remaining out of sight in the passage.

Mackreth said gently, 'Identification, Mr Weston?'

He looked up and now it was the detective who winced. 'That's my stepsister, Mary Spence,' he said.

Mackreth realized tardily that no one had thought of providing a cup of tea, let alone something stronger. 'When you're ready,' he said kindly, 'we'll go back to the station, get us—'

'Of course,' Weston interrupted coldly, 'you don't know who's responsible. Not that it matters. The bruise doesn't look much, does it?'

'Not really.'

'Not a fracture.'

'No.'

'It would be preferable if it was. Otherwise she could have been alive when he put her in

168

the water. Like an animal drowned in a sack.'

Mackreth could think of nothing to say. Weston looked up at him again and something vital flickered in the eyes. 'Like a kitten,' he said, 'fastened in a plastic bag and thrown in the lake, right? *Right?*'

Rumney and Heslop loomed behind Mackreth who said firmly, 'We'll get him, Keith. Give us time.'

He bared his teeth. 'Take as long as you want. It's nothing to do with you.'

'What the hell did he mean by that?' Heslop asked of Rumney later.

'He'll get over it. It was the shock.'

'Even so he meant something; why, it's everything to do with us.'

'Not in his book. He's the brother, stepbrother, whatever. He's thinking in terms of family business.'

'Oh, like the Mafia.'

'I hope not.' Rumney shivered and wondered why this case should seem so fraught.

*   *   *

'We turned him loose.' Despite himself Mackreth felt defensive as Warwick betrayed neither surprise nor disapproval. 'What else could we do?'

'The closest relative?' she murmured.

'I know, and they could have been lovers,

and she was going with at least two other men—but his employees state categorically that he was working at his garden centre until the Saturday morning. Mary went missing on the Thursday.'

'That doesn't have to mean she was killed Thursday. She could have holed up somewhere and still have been alive on the Saturday when Weston reached the Lakes. Ah!' Eyes sharpened behind Armani spectacles. 'You have a preliminary report on the autopsy.'

'Not for a while yet, but even when we have the stomach contents, the hard part will be finding where she ate her last meal.'

'Young girls.' Warwick sighed. 'A sandwich from a bar? In summertime she'd be lost in the crowd. Who saw her last—to our knowledge? Someone on the Thursday obviously.'

'Not to see,' Mackreth said slowly. 'Barbara Howard, her neighbour, heard her about that morning and since she didn't see or hear her from mid-morning on, reckons she left sometime after breakfast. No one has been found who actually saw her Thursday.'

'So you're saying the last known sighting was Wednesday?'

He nodded. 'Of course she must have been seen by dozens of people but the only one we know about is Sophie Daynes. That lunchtime Mary entered the pub where she was working and sat down and, according to Michael

Daynes, "stared at her".'

'She didn't speak at all?'

'No. He says she was stalking his wife.'

'Oh my.' Up went Warwick's eyebrows. She looked past Mackreth who turned to see Lorton leaning against the door jamb. She was wearing a striped top and a scarlet cap and carrying paper bags with the logo of the Indian take-away. 'The girlfriend was stalking the wife,' the DCI said, 'and the girlfriend's found dead. Wife's disappeared. It's too obvious except it's the wrong way round; how often does the prey kill the stalker? Alternatively some dull spark suggested a serial killer. That would be the husband. Obvious again.'

'He has a strong motive for killing his wife—if he inherits,' Mackreth contributed. 'The house must be worth around a quarter million.'

'But it isn't the wife who's been killed,' Warwick reminded him, adding coolly, 'as far as we know. And as for his killing both women, where's his motive for the girlfriend?'

'They were still intimate until shortly before her death.' Mackreth was thoughtful.

'If that's a euphemism for fucking, men have been known to fake it. Passion, I mean.' Lorton's listeners were disapproving but alert. 'Women are better at it,' she added, unabashed. 'Not that it seems to apply here; as I understand it the dead girl was mad about Michael. When are we going to see this

171

lecher?'

'We're looking for him.' Mackreth resented their concerted attention. 'He's not at his home; incidentally, we've taken away bin bags and baler twine, even sisal rope from the stables. The Boathouse is being kept under surveillance and his description's circulated. Since he has no transport and no money— again as far as we know—either he's hitching lifts or he's still in the area.'

'Suicide.' Lorton was lugubrious. 'You may never find him.'

He shook his head. 'Michael isn't the man to take that way out. Mind you, he's just the kind of fellow who would think of faking it. Clever bastard.'

Warwick beamed at him. 'You'll find him,' she assured him, but thinking that, as Lorton had observed, Michael was, like many next of kin in domestic murders, the obvious suspect, and 'obvious' had led many a good man astray. Women too, on occasions.

*   *   *

Michael was in a Bed and Breakfast over the border in Annan when he heard the news. He had sold some jewellery that had belonged to Sophie's mother and with the proceeds had managed to get this far. Tomorrow he would have to steal, or devise some scam, or hitch south and beg help from his pal in Lancaster.

172

But tomorrow was another day; he was tired, in need of sleep, he'd come up to his room after a fish supper and switched on the television. He caught Channel 5 News to see a woman at a desk who was saying: '. . . the search for the woman who was missing from her home on the shores of Kettlemere in the Lake District ended today with the discovery of a body, said to be that of a woman, but not yet identified. And now Sport . . .'

He stared at the screen where footballers converged on a goal. He saw nothing but recalled words out of sequence: 'body', 'Kettlemere', 'missing', 'Lake District'. He breathed fast and shallow, felt heat then cold as sweat ran down his back. She's beaten me, he thought, the bitch, she got me after all. She's surfaced and I'm the next of kin, the prime suspect. So why aren't they looking for me?

They were, they just hadn't caught up with him yet. Weston was searching too, but he had the greater incentive and his mind was working with the intuitive skill of a predator. Putting himself in his quarry's place, knowing the fellow was without transport, he considered where a man would go to pick up a lift if he didn't want to be seen thumbing vehicles on the roadside. The answer was the big truck stop in Kelleth where long-distance drivers pulled in for a meal or to spend the night.

While Weston was at the truck stop Andrew

returned to Kelleth unaware of the latest development. He had been driving through the Borders searching for Mary's car. He came back to the hotel to be accosted by a striking girl in a red baseball cap who produced a warrant card and asked him to go with her to the police station. No explanation, only a feline smile and candid eyes. He went without protest. It was something to do.

After the introductions Warwick surveyed him benignly. 'You've been away all day,' she observed.

Andrew was so tired that his brain felt scrambled. He shook his head mutely. Should he have stayed at the hotel? Not left Marten House? Had he broken some archaic term of employment? Who cared?

Tea appeared and then this motherly soul produced a half-bottle of Martell from a huge leather bag. Andrew realized that he must be looking like death. Brandy would be good. She poured lavishly, adding a few drops to the other mugs. The young detective sat down.

'You were looking for Mary,' Warwick said.

He nodded, then brightened. 'Have you found her?'

'Yes.' A flicker towards Lorton. In his eagerness Andrew missed it. 'It's bad news, I'm afraid. Mary died some days ago.'

He didn't react. 'No,' was the immediate response, then, 'You don't know her,' meaning they couldn't identify some unknown as a

174

woman they'd never met.

'Keith Weston identified her this afternoon,' Warwick said. 'Drink your tea, Andrew.'

Obediently he sipped, registering its strength, forgetting it wasn't only tea. He said in a curious hollow tone, 'Tell me the rest.'

'Perhaps—' the girl began.

'How did she die?' he demanded, and now there was an unnatural resonance to the voice. Lorton stiffened in her chair.

Warwick was thinking that he'd find out as soon as he left the station. If there were no media outside, they'd trap him at the hotel. Besides, said the detective's brain, he is a suspect. She sought to tread the line between suspicion and compassion and failed.

'It appears that she was murdered,' she said, 'and her body put in the lake.'

No—but the denial was only a thought. His eyes rolled up and they were only just in time to stop his head hitting the floor. Callous old cow, Lorton thought. Aloud she said accusingly, 'He wasn't ready for that!'

'Never would be,' Warwick rejoined, 'but it's a moot point.'

As they eased him back on the chair, steadying him as he recovered, she was thinking that, given a shot of brandy on top of a high state of exhaustion—and a quick brain—it might be possible to induce a faint.

Chapter Thirteen

Michael went to ground. He checked out of the B and B next morning, running a risk but it would have attracted attention had he left the previous evening. He carried a rucksack and resembled any other hitch-hiker, too old for a student certainly but he could pass for a man down on his luck and looking for work. He headed west making for the Galloway hills with the idea of stealing from cars at trail heads in order to survive. Occasionally he caught glimpses of the Lakeland fells across the Solway Firth: too close, and now he saw his mistake in taking this route. He was more conspicuous in rural areas than he would be on major roads and in cities. He should be making for Glasgow. He thought of turning round—then he saw the Primera.

It was stationary in a lay-by: an estate with a grille but no dog, a laptop on the rear seat, and the driver in front checking a map. Michael coveted the car but prudence said it was far too distinctive a vehicle even if he could separate the owner from it. The laptop was another matter. Moreover the guy, who was probably a sales rep, might have an expensive mobile.

The window was already rolled down and the driver looked up. 'Lovely morning,'

Michael said, grinning engagingly, hesitating. 'Lost?'

'No, no.' Lacklustre eyes surveyed him from behind aviator shades. 'Not really.' The tone was dull. 'Going far?'

'Galloway, Newton Stewart. I'm making for the hills.'

'So am I. Newton Stewart anyway. Put your gear in the back.'

Surprised, Michael obeyed, gingerly pushing the laptop along to make room for his pack, nipping round to the passenger side.

The chap tossed the map behind him. 'How far have you come today?' It was the usual gambit and Michael answered truthfully, then turned the question back.

'Not far,' the driver said, adding, 'You're going in by way of Glen Trool rather than Clatteringshaws?' He seemed to be making conversation as if he had something more pressing on his mind. Maybe he was ill and on drugs.

'It's one way of doing it.' Michael was hedging, the names meant nothing to him.

'The Gairland Burn is recommended for the Merrick,' the chap said. 'Can you get to the Dungeons from there? Where's the Silver Flowe?'

'Somewhere in there.' Michael's eyes were active although his head didn't move. Would the mobile be in the glove box or a door slot, or in the guy's jacket? Where was his jacket?

Not visible, must be in back of the grille; what else was back there? It was a classy new car—he ached to drive it—but he'd never get far, chap would report it as soon as he made off—unless, of course . . . No, that would be madness. Theft yes: of anything he could lay his hands on, but violence was out, it was impracticable. No, the obvious and safest course was his original plan of breaking into walkers' cars when he could be miles away before the theft was discovered.

'There's been more than one death.'

'*What?*' Belatedly Michael was aware that the chap had been droning on about lanes and forestry and water and now—death? 'I nodded off,' he gasped. 'Not much sleep last night. You were saying?'

'I was saying that some people do the Dungeons from the north but whichever way you go in watch out for the lanes. They look harmless but a number of people have been drowned. The Silver Flowe is notorious.'

'Right.' Michael was cheery, not following. 'I'll be keeping to the lanes.'

'Don't leave the paths.' It was emphatic, this chap was becoming a bore. 'The ground is pretty rough.'

'I'm used to it.' He felt the other's eyes on him. 'I walk on the Pennines,' he explained. 'You can't get much rougher than the northern Pennines. In winter too.'

'I see. You're camping?'

'That's right.' His pack wasn't large enough to contain a tent and sleeping bag and all the other stuff he'd need in rough country but this chap, in his naff glasses and Pringle shirt, wasn't to know that.

'I thought of stopping for coffee,' the guy said.

'Good idea.' It was early but a halt might offer the opportunity to get his hands on the laptop. A pity about the car; he still hankered after it but it was too much of a risk.

They stopped at an hotel set back from the road with tables and umbrellas on a terrace. 'You'll be wanting to push ahead,' the driver said. 'If you're still on the road when I'm finished here, I'll pick you up.'

Michael breathed deeply and reached for the door handle. Should he snatch the laptop at the same time that he pulled out his rucksack? Could he get away? As he closed the door he glanced behind him at the surroundings. It was bare fields. No concealing woods.

The driver reached back for the computer and set it on the passenger seat. As Michael retrieved his pack and closed the rear door there was the gentlest of clicks as all doors locked. He stared, his resentment showing. The driver nodded pleasantly. The window opened a crack. 'You'll soon get a lift.'

Michael shouldered the pack and trudged away.

'We've got him!' Mackreth announced as DS Lorton, luscious this morning in caramel shirt and chocolate cut-offs, glanced in as she passed his office. 'They've picked him up in Galloway.'

'Michael?'

'The same. He hitched a lift with a chap working for the Ordnance Survey who'd lost his dog.'

'The man was looking for his dog?'

'No, it died. He was miserable or he wouldn't have picked anyone up but he wanted distraction. Seems to have got it because the way Michael aroused his suspicions was by pretending to be a bona fide walker when he knew nothing about the dangers in the area. "He wasn't genuine," he told the local cops: didn't know the lanes, they say. Lanes are deep water creeks in Galloway. And then the OS man had heard this morning's broadcast appeal for Michael: a middle-aged chap from Cumbria, possibly hitch-hiking. So he reported it on the off chance and the Dumfries chaps picked him up on the road to Castle Douglas. They're bringing him to Carlisle now.'

*   *   *

Genuine hikers were abroad in Lakeland and

one of them, Thirza Barber, turned eighty and old enough to know she should take more care, was trying to get into a position to inspect a nest on the wall of a quarry not far from Kettlemere. It was an old slate quarry, deep and in the shape of a half-moon, the curving arc some two hundred feet high, dropping sheer to a pool of black water. On the straight side the wall was lower, perhaps only fifty feet, and here there was a smooth broad terrace with no parapet, not even a fence. Some way back from the edge was an unpaved road giving access to a pair of old quarry cottages now done up and let to holiday people.

Peregrines had built their nest on the smoothest and tallest section of the big wall and Thirza was angling along the lip from tree to tree trying to make out if there were chicks. She decided the site had to be abandoned when she could see no heads in the nest and no adults were calling, let alone attacking her. She turned back and at that moment a twig caught her favourite ball cap and it went spinning into the void.

'Shit!' she hissed, craning to see if by some miracle it might miss the water, although there was no beach. Water lay rather than lapped against vertical rock all around. And there it was: upside down, floating, mocking her. And there too, just below the surface, was the roof of a little green car.

The first police on the scene reported that the dimensions were those of a Mini, which made sense to Mackreth who had been wondering about Mary's car. However, nothing could be done until it was recovered, and that was going to take time. Meanwhile, and as they waited for Michael's arrival, the preliminary report of the autopsy came through. There were no details such as analyses of blood and tissue, but rough answers to specific questions posed by the police. There was no water in the lungs and air passages, nothing in the stomach, and Mary wasn't pregnant. Which meant that she died some time after she'd last eaten and that she was already dead when she was put in the water. The cause of death was not yet specified.

Michael arrived under escort but before he was interviewed the escorting officers spoke to Mackreth. The man had been morose on the journey south but he had spoken once or twice and the police listened without parting with any information. Their report was astounding. Michael was under the impression that the dead woman was his wife, and so far no one had enlightened him.

He was isolated and given tea while Warwick and Lorton, Mackreth and Rumney convened in Warwick's office and tried to make sense of the events of the last twenty-four hours.

'You've been in on this one since the start,' Warwick conceded, addressing Mackreth and including Rumney. 'So what's your opinion? Is the situation clarified now or more complicated?'

Mackreth transferred his gaze to the window. Rumney stared at his knees. The women waited attentively.

Mackreth drew a deep breath and turned back to the room. 'Both,' he said, and qualified it instantly. 'On the surface Mary's death is simplified.'

'We never knew she was dead,' Rumney protested, 'so it couldn't be complicated.'

'She'd disappeared,' Mackreth said firmly. 'So her disappearance is simplified, is what I meant. She was murdered, stuffed in bin bags from his—no, from the Boathouse, dumped in the lake. He—the boat was used. Her car was put in the quarry.' He stopped, uneasy. After a moment he muttered, 'And Michael thinks the body is Sophie's.'

Lorton, not yet inured to horror, said, 'At least we know she was dead. She didn't drown trussed inside those ghastly bags.'

Mackreth blinked at her. 'Weston thought of that; he said it was preferable for her to have died before she was put in the water. He was overwhelmed when he saw her body.'

'Remorse can be mistaken for grief,' Warwick pointed out. 'But if we were to

183

exclude Weston and if, for the sake of argument, Michael is in the clear, who is the most likely suspect?'

'Sophie Daynes is missing.'

'Ah yes, the classic triangle—and where you were working on the theory of the husband killing the wife, now we consider that the wife could have killed the mistress?'

Mackreth looked doubtful. 'Or Michael killed Mary because she threatened his prospects. He stood to inherit a quarter million. Sophie would change her will, or make a will if she hadn't already, leaving the Boathouse to Marjorie, once she knew he was having a protracted affair with a girl half her age.'

Warwick said thoughtfully, 'According to all reports his attitude until now is that he despised Mary and loved his wife.'

'They all say that,' Lorton put in darkly.

'And now,' Rumney uttered with a kind of smug anticipation, 'he thinks his wife's dead, and has no idea that it's his lover. She was, you know; they were f— sleeping together the day she disappeared.'

'Not the same day but near enough,' Mackreth murmured, adding, surprised, 'or maybe they were. We did consider that Sophie could have come home early and caught them together.'

'It will be interesting to see how this interview goes,' Warwick said, adding wryly, 'but two strange women may constrain him and we don't have the facilities for observation. So we'll leave him to you.'

They conferred further, discussing how to proceed but reaching the conclusion that they could make no plan because it depended on Michael, and they didn't know whether he was in the dark or conducting a careful and clever game. They would play it off the cuff.

*   *   *

Michael was gaunt, an ageing charmer. He shambled into the interview room and sat heavily, not troubling to watch Rumney fiddling with the cassettes. He stared at Mackreth with dislike. 'How many times does this make it?' he asked.

Mackreth didn't respond but opened the file in front of him. Rumney went through the preliminaries and Michael said, unprompted, that he didn't want a solicitor to be present.

'You're not charged with anything,' Mackreth pointed out.

'And before we go any further,' Michael was venomous, 'I want to know how she died. I have a right to that. The men who brought me here wouldn't say a word.'

'The autopsy isn't finished,' Mackreth said. 'We do know she didn't drown. She was wrapped in bin bags that were fastened with baler twine and the body was weighted, and secured with sisal rope. The plastic bags, the twine and sisal are all similar to those taken from outbuildings at the Boathouse.'

Michael nodded. 'I've been set up.'

'By whom?'

He shook his head. 'I've no idea. That's your job: to find the killer.'

'Why should anyone set you up?'

'Because I'm a sitting duck: the obvious suspect.'

'Because she was an obstruction, because—'

'What the hell does that mean? I loved my wife; we had a good marriage. If you think, just because I went off the rails with some little slag who—who—' Michael choked to a halt. The police regarded him in simulated surprise. 'I loved Sophie,' he declared. 'I never laid a finger on her.'

'Of course you didn't. It was Mary Spence who was put in the lake.'

Michael blinked, then shifted his eyes to Rumney. His face smoothed out but his nostrils flared. 'This is a trick,' he said harshly.

Mackreth glanced at his partner who got up to stand to one side, not too close to intimidate but near enough to reach Michael should he make a lunge. Delicately, as if it were fragile, Mackreth placed a photograph in front of him.

Michael looked down at Mary's face, the eyes open, obviously lifeless. He sat back and returned Mackreth's stare. His mouth worked.

After long moments Mackreth asked, not unkindly, 'What do you have to say?' He didn't know whether the man was in shock, grief or despair.

'I didn't kill her,' he said hoarsely. 'Who do you suspect, other than me? No, you can't say.' He thought about it and they watched his eyes widen, his jaw drop then close, his lips turning in like those of a toothless old man.

'Who did you think of?' Mackreth asked. 'Andrew?'

Michael showed a trace of bewilderment.

'Weston?' This produced calculation.

'Sophie?' The features hardened but gave nothing away.

'You acted in collusion,' Mackreth surmised. 'Sophie struck the blow and you disposed of the body and the car.'

'The car?' He looked surprised then reverted to truculence. 'I told you how it was: I slept out on the hause and came home to an empty house. Sophie had gone. I—' He stopped.

'And Mary? Where was she?'

'I'm not saying any more till I've seen a solicitor.'

*   *   *

'No fireworks then.' Warwick was disappointed.

Rumney said, addressing his partner, 'Did

187

you notice, when you said how she was found, tied up in plastic bags, he didn't turn a hair? A normal man would have exploded.'

'Not if he did it. He knew already, there was no surprise.'

'But if he was acting . . . He did say he'd been set up; what he should have come out with was "The bastard!" or some such. He's not showing much feeling against this guy who's supposed to have killed his lover and set him up for the fall guy.'

'He's been knocked off balance. If he didn't do it he knows who did. He could be thinking it's Sophie. His orientation's turned around; one moment he's thinking his wife's been murdered, the next she could have murdered his lover. He doesn't know where he is.'

'He'll change his story again,' Lorton said. 'He has to; there's proof that Mary was in his bed at the Boathouse so he can't keep denying it—and now there's a new scenario: Sophie caught them so Sophie killed the girl and attacked him but he got away.'

She could be right but before they could question him further, to find out what story he would tell now, they must wait until he had consulted a solicitor. But he surprised them: he decided he didn't need one. After an hour he asked to see Mackreth again.

He entered the interview room carrying himself better. He'd washed and although he was still drawn the despair of an hour ago was gone. Mackreth regarded him blandly, thinking the fellow was strung tight as a bow, himself emptying his mind of speculation, ready to receive new lies and some truths or, most likely, a deliberate confusion of both which the schooled brain must sift and analyse for facts.

'I don't need a solicitor,' Michael was telling Rumney. 'I'm innocent and no way can you prove me guilty. Of murder, that is.' He paused. They were going to play games.

Mackreth asked, as he was expected to ask: 'What are you guilty of?'

'I've lied to you. About Mary.' There was pain in his face, a quick spasm. 'We were lovers. We were having an affair. She used to come to the Boathouse.'

Mackreth nodded encouragement. Rumney didn't react; as Lorton said, he had to admit that much: lipstick on the pillow, the fingerprints . . .

'Mary phoned that evening,' Michael said. 'That was the time my wife answered.'

'You told us,' Mackreth murmured.

'Did I? I'd forgotten.' He relaxed; his face softened, he was suddenly boyish, presenting an air of helplessness. It didn't deceive them but it gave them a glimpse of the charm he might exert over women. 'I've been . . .' He shook his head and sighed heavily. 'I adored her, I can't bear to think of . . . You said she was tied up! In plastic bags?'

189

'I'm afraid so.' Mackreth was so gentle that Rumney had to resist the impulse to glance at him. The fellow was a suspect, for God's sake.

There was a long pause to be broken by Mackreth. 'Mary talked to your wife that evening . . .' It was the most delicate of probes.

'And earlier.' Now he was listless. 'She called several times: wanting to come to the Boathouse. I tried to put her off, I was terrified of their meeting; both highly emotional, you see, there'd be hell to pay, and Mary's only—was only a little thing.' He put his head in his hands.

'She did come however.'

'No.' He looked up, surprised, even bewildered, then a new thought registered. 'Of course she came,' he whispered. 'That's when it happened. My—our bin bags, our baler twine—' He stopped, staring from Mackreth to Rumney and back again, his eyes intent, seeing images in his mind while they sat like stones awaiting the next revelation. He resumed, with an effort to be firm: 'She didn't come while I was there. That's what I'm saying: she had to come after I'd gone, after Sophie fired at me and I left. Maybe she heard the shot, she knew there was trouble, came to see if I was all right. I was away all night, remember—for hours, maybe six hours. Plenty of time. That's when it happened,' he repeated bitterly.

'And Sophie?' Mackreth asked. 'Where is she?'

Michael grinned horribly. 'Well, she's not the sort to kill herself; that was just my ploy to protect her, suggesting she'd topped herself. She'll be on the Continent, or Scotland maybe. Marjorie Neville's got relations up there.'

'Why did you need to protect her?'

He shrugged as if it were of no consequence. 'We'd had a hell of a row. She'd tried to kill me—or at least wound me, and then she'd walked out. What guy is going to admit his wife's treated him like that? Besides, I had to pretend there was nothing in the Mary angle, that there wasn't any affair.'

'Why was it necessary to pretend that?'

'Well, you see, Mary was missing and I put two and two together and Sophie was missing as well and I thought that Mary—who really had been stalking Sophie, you know—I thought Mary could have killed Sophie, probably pushed her in the lake, like they'd been standing down there on the slip and things turned violent . . .'

'Why that way round? Why not Sophie pushing Mary?'

Michael appeared confused. 'But the atmosphere was all the other way, wasn't it? You were so sure that I'd killed my wife—hell, that was why I scarpered: because it looked so black against me! Everything was focused on Sophie. I believed it myself, not that I'd killed her of course; I knew I was innocent, I hadn't even been drinking that night, if that was when

191

it happened. But I did believe—like I was brainwashed, you know—that Sophie had been murdered. Surely everyone thought, when—' He choked, took several deep breaths and resumed on a high note: 'That when the b-body was washed up, it was Sophie?'

'And now?' Mackreth asked. 'What happened after you left the Boathouse and went to sleep on the hause? What do you think happened after you'd gone?'

Michael looked exhausted. 'They fought. Sophie's a powerful woman. She didn't mean to do it, I'm sure. Two women scrapping, that's all. Manslaughter.'

'And the bin bags?'

'They're mine—ours, sure.'

*   *   *

'Not what I meant,' Mackreth said afterwards. 'I meant how did Sophie have the guts to truss Mary's body in plastic and dump her in the lake?'

'Yes, he'd forgotten that bit,' Rumney said.

'Had he forgotten?'

Chapter Fourteen

The woods were full of birdsong, and butterflies flitted in and out of sunbeams chased by Sharkey leaping through a sea of bluebells. A blackbird fled shrieking. Wild garlic replaced the delicate scents and then, as they emerged in the glade, even that was overwhelmed by the lingering stench of burned plastic and, unmistakably, a whiff of petrol.

Marjorie looked around. She hadn't been here since she discovered the fire with Gerald Fairburn. The pick-up had been removed and if there had been tape marking the crime scene someone had been meticulous in clearing up the last scrap. Apparently the place held no further interest for the police, or the interest was focused on Manchester. She walked round the mangled shell of the caravan; any gas cylinders were gone too. She came to the front and studied the gap where the door would have been, a couple of steps above ground level. There had been a metal contraption here comprising two steps, made of diamond-shaped grating. It had been thrown to one side.

The bin bag which had contained beer cans was missing but some clutter remained: old tyres, rusty metal objects, spars and planks and bricks—Coulter, or some previous occupant of the caravan, could have used the bricks as extra security when working under a vehicle. New grass showed about a log, amazing how quickly grass grew but then this was the best time of the year for growth . . . The birds were very quiet, why weren't they scolding the cat? Where was he? Gone home? Unlikely, they were some distance from the house and it was a long walk for a youngster. She called him but he didn't come. After a rabbit no doubt.

She turned back to the log which, she remembered, had been here before: a pit prop, she'd surmised, although she couldn't imagine any modern mine shoring up its levels with timber. But then, she recalled, short lengths of soft wood were also used in smelters, aluminium being stirred with wooden pokers which disintegrated without harming the compound. I've lost my marbles, she thought, what an idea: stirring aluminium with spruce pokers. So why should timber be cut into such short lengths as this: five feet? She stooped and peered. One sawn end was marked with paint, white paint.

She glanced up and back at the charred shell and saw a pale flash in the woods. 'One of these days you'll get stuck down a hole,' she shouted. 'Come on, we're going home.' But that was just something to say to him; she didn't start home but picked up the log and carried it to the discarded steps. She tried to wedge one end into the grating but the mesh diamonds were too small.

She carried the prop to the shell and planted the end in the soil below the gap where the door would have been. She did this gently, taking care not to mark the ground. Tilting the wood at an angle she held it there, considered, and tossed it aside. She studied the ground. There where she had been careful not to superimpose a fresh mark was a deep indentation.

She smiled grimly. They'd known all along that the fire had been set, and it was possible that the investigators had deduced that the piece of wood had been used to wedge the door, ensuring that the occupant was trapped if he managed to recover from his injuries sufficiently to crawl to the exit. Had Coulter been injured? He must have been; an able-bodied man would have got out through the window. The wedged wood was a backstop and unimportant in itself. What was important was its origin, and what she was to do about it. And where was that bloody cat?

'I'm going,' she shouted. 'And I'm not coming back for you. Sharkey! Treats!'

He came bounding out of the trees like a ballet dancer. 'Good lad,' she told him, reaching for a chewie, running her eye over him for signs he'd been down a hole, forever thankful that the woods were private, and poachers would dare use only ferrets. Every local man knew that if Miss Neville were to lose a cat in a snare, she'd shoot the man who set it and serve a life sentence in penance for the cat, not the shooting. The odd thing was that this day, swishing through the bluebells, she sensed that there was someone else in the woods. This was borne out by Sharkey's attitude; he kept stopping and looking back. There was something of interest behind her, and she remembered that pale flash which she had thought was the white tip to his tail yet now, recalling the moment, she knew that it had been several feet above the ground. And light, not white; no cat up a tree then but— metal? A gun? An *armed* poacher?

They came to a deer trail and followed it as far as a stand of silver fir offering cover. Scooping up the cat she walked round the trees and stopped. She didn't attempt to peer through the foliage but waited: a small round figure in drab clothing, the cat draped over one shoulder like a boa.

After a moment Sharkey stiffened and his head lifted, ears pointed, his eyes following something on the far side of the firs. He wasn't frightened or hostile but interested. Now, on the path, proceeding purposefully in the direction of Marjorie's house, a large woman appeared. She was wearing chinos, a beige shirt and a safari hat, and carrying a trekking pole. She moved well for a big woman but not all that flexibly. She had to be middle-aged and the watcher's hackles rose; the older trespassers came, the more resistant, particularly women. And one's peers were always the most difficult to deal with. She stepped out from the trees and followed.

The stranger had good hearing. Hardly was Marjorie on the path before the other stopped and turned, spectacles glinting—there was the flash of light. She'd been spied on. Marjorie went on the offensive.

'This is private ground,' she grated, an opening that was spoiled by Sharkey's leaping down and rushing to twine himself about the stranger's ankles. Worn, expensive boots, Marjorie noted absently.

'I know. I'm Annabelle Warwick. You must be Miss Neville.' A hand was extended. Baffled, unable to do anything else, Marjorie shook it.

'You were watching me,' she said, then, aware that this sounded petulant, tried to temporize: 'What interest do you have in that place?'

'Coulter was my pigeon. I'm by way of being official.' She produced her warrant card. 'What's the significance of that piece of timber?'

Marjorie's mouth opened and closed. She played for time. 'I think it was used to trap Coulter: wedged against the door.'

Warwick nodded, indicating that this was no surprise to her.

'Is this your first visit to the scene?'

Marjorie asked politely, falling back on etiquette.

'Yes. The case was fragmented. Other people worked here, although once the fire investigators had done their part, the focus shifted to Manchester. I was down there, trying to discover his background and contacts.'

'We never heard the result of the autopsy. We were disappointed, it was a gap in our knowledge.' Marjorie grinned her lizard grin and Warwick knew a trade-off was being suggested.

'There was a crack fracture to the skull,' she said, 'a blunt instrument, not due to the heat of the fire. And quite a lot of whisky and beer in the stomach. He died from smoke inhalation—soot in the air passages—but he was—one hopes he was unconscious by that time.'

'There was a rumour that he'd got on the wrong side of a gang, and that someone was sent here to settle the score.'

Warwick said easily, 'That was one theory. You have another?'

'Oh no, no.' Marjorie was cheating. 'Why should you think that?'

'Local folk must have discussed it.' A pause. 'The piece of timber played a part.'

'It did? Well, of course! The door was wedged.'

Warwick said nothing but stroked the cat.

Sharkey butted her affectionately and Marjorie realized that all the time she was engaged with that log her cat was wooing a stranger. Sleeping with the enemy?

'The log had been sawn,' Warwick said slyly. 'Timber operations.'

'I didn't see any in this wood. Someone must have brought it with them.'

Marjorie threw a panicked glance at her watch. 'Teatime! I have to get back and feed the animals. My house isn't far.'

'That will be lovely, thanks.'

The bloody woman thought she'd been invited to tea! Marjorie opened her mouth to enlighten her and checked. That could be taken as hostility, at the least as reluctance to have a detective in her home. The woman might even wonder if there was something to hide.

They started along the narrow path in single file, Marjorie in the lead, walking fast. There was no chance for conversation but some opportunity for thought, on both sides.

When they reached the house it was no surprise to Warwick that food put down for the cats was ignored. It wasn't their feeding time. Rather, Patchouli and the Red Baron vied for her attention, ousting Sharkey. Marjorie served tea on the terrace using her Minton service and producing a Victoria sandwich. She was aiming for a note of high formality and determined to keep it there. She saw that

Warwick was quite at her ease, not unaccustomed to afternoon tea in gracious surroundings. She showed no surprise, made no facetious remarks, indeed no remarks, but the eyes behind the stylish spectacles were absorbing everything: the alpines in cracks of the sandstone flags, the lawn sloping to the crowns of mature trees, the lake and the fells.

Marjorie cut the cake and passed it, oozing cream. Her eyes were on Sharkey, who was a thief.

'Do you look after your garden yourself?' Warwick asked. There was a trace of Cumbrian below the Oxford English.

'What?' Distracted, glaring at the cat, Marjorie replaced the cake slice without serving herself. 'I do the borders and the vegetables. A neighbour cuts the grass in return for eggs, and I get a youngster in for the heavy work: trenching and so on.' She bit her lip. She was saying too much.

'Good neighbours are a treasure: always someone on hand when there's a problem.'

Marjorie took a deep breath. No doubt that the woman was probing. She had no problem that a stranger should be aware of, or was one suspected? She said coldly, 'Is this your afternoon off, or are you working?'

'A necessary trip.' Warwick sipped her tea. 'I needed to see where Coulter was living.'

Marjorie frowned. 'We'd forgotten Coulter. After the body was found this morning . . .'

200

Her voice faded; here she'd meant to stay on the high ground and she'd not only come out with a palpable lie about Coulter (when she'd been poking about the ruins of his caravan) but she'd introduced the subject of murder. 'Everything else faded into the background,' she said, adding with an attempt at reproof: 'We're trying to block it out.'

'What? Coulter or Mary Spence?'

'Either. Both.' She was floundering.

'And your god-daughter?' came that gentle voice, dripping with something: compassion? Innuendo?

'No.' Marjorie rallied. 'I think about Sophie all the time.'

'It must have been a relief when the body was identified as someone else.'

'Oh, a tremendous relief.'

'She can come home now.'

The ensuing pause wasn't silent. Two thrushes were shouting for dominance, and then Sharkey leapt on the table, landed on Warwick's plate, sent a fork skittering and bounded away dribbling sponge cake and cream.

'Bastard!' Marjorie shouted, retrieving the fork and plate. 'Sorry about that.' She disappeared indoors, returning with a clean plate and fork. She served Warwick fresh cake with a steady hand and sat down. 'Where were we?' she asked brightly.

'Sophie *could* have killed Mary,' Warwick

201

said, as if they'd been speculating on the possibility for a while.

Marjorie was expressionless. After a moment she nodded and said calmly, 'Could have done but she couldn't have put her in the lake.'

'Why not?'

'Because she has compassion.'

' "Has"?' Marjorie was silent. 'She's alive,' Warwick went on. 'She should come back now and face the music. You have to see that yourself.'

'She didn't kill Mary.'

'She didn't *murder* her. But Mary was there that night, at the Boathouse. Michael's admitted it. He suggests your god-daughter was responsible for Mary's death.'

'Michael's putting the blame on Sophie?' The old eyes were blazing.

'Someone trussed her like a fowl.' The tone was designed to inflame.

'That was him! Women like Sophie gravitate to freeloaders. And then they have to protect them. Like old damaged cats, she said, you can't turn them away when they come crying . . . I should have known something was seriously wrong when she said that, it was around the time that he was supposed to have sold a story for a hundred pounds. I smelled a rat there, always distrusted the fellow—you know he was sacked from his last job? Something about claiming expenses for work he didn't do. I'll bet he got hold of Sophie's credit card and invented selling a story to account for that hundred pounds. She'll know when she gets her next statement. Perhaps she's guessed already; she has this blind spot—' She stopped, stricken.

'I've only just arrived on the scene,' Warwick said mildly. 'But Mackreth knew you were protecting Sophie; he guessed she was here in this house when he was here himself. Admittedly it doesn't seem to have occurred to him that she was protecting her husband.'

Marjorie glowered but she was thinking hard. 'Whatever happened,' Warwick went on earnestly, 'it's surpassed by what he's accusing her of. There's no one so evil as a man who turns against a woman who's prepared to give him everything. If we still had capital punishment he'd allow her to go to the gallows to save his own skin. Give me animals any time.'

*   *   *

'I haven't met Sophie,' Mackreth said, 'but the way I look at it at this moment is that she's as likely a suspect as her husband.'

'The clock's ticking,' Warwick reminded him. 'He'll have to be charged tomorrow.'

'It's all circumstantial,' he protested. 'Like the fellow says, the outbuildings were never locked; there's no disputing the sisal came from there, and the baler twine: the dust matches. But anyone could have walked in and taken the stuff. Same applies to the boat, the oars weren't secured.'

'Who else had motive?' Lorton wondered.

They were in Warwick's office again: exhausted, bloated with coffee and fast food, craving showers and their beds. There was a feeling that everything was on hold in anticipation of Sophie's return, and yet they couldn't resist speculation after Warwick's report on her encounter with Marjorie.

'The motivation doesn't have to be crucial,' she said in response to Lorton's question. 'If we can bring it home to one of them, we can worry about motive afterwards.'

'One of who?' Lorton queried ungrammatically. 'Weston was in Essex, and Lambourne—he would have been on duty part of the evening but we don't know when she was killed.' She looked at Mackreth who ignored the question of timing in favour of character.

'Lambourne's too young, he could have hit her in a jealous rage but he could never have brought himself to package her. Emotional sort of chap, it was him who sent us that text accusing Daynes of murder.'

Warwick said, 'It's the trussing of the body that's so significant. Marjorie maintains that Sophie couldn't have done it either.'

'She could be wrong there,' Lorton said. 'If

you hate a woman enough to kill her, would you have any qualms about tying her up? Hatred's stronger than compassion. We'll have a better idea when we meet her.'

Rumney, sitting to one side, silent until now—in fact once or twice his eyelids had drooped—asked out of the blue: 'Why did Michael lie about Sophie taking her car and driving to Ireland?'

'To protect himself of course.' Mackreth was too tired to be more than mildly surprised at the question. 'Because he knew she—' He stopped and gaped.

'Was dead.' Rumney nodded sagely. 'But he knew he hadn't killed her. He was innocent. So why lie?'

'Embarrassment,' Lorton said loudly. 'He felt humiliated. He's macho and couldn't take her firing at him and walking out so he invented the Irish trip.'

'Why dispose of the car?'

'Two Minis,' Warwick murmured. The car in the quarry pool had been recovered, the registration confirming it as Mary's. It contained only one object of significance and that was a padlock which Barbara Howard confirmed was the one from her lock-up garage. 'Two green Minis,' Warwick mused. 'Both disposed of. Does no one find that odd?'

'Not when you consider why they were dumped,' Lorton argued. 'Mary's had to be put in the quarry pool to delay finding the body. The body weighted, the car submerged: the assumption is Mary's gone off with a new fellow. As for Sophie's car, it had pellet marks on the boot: suspicious when there was a possibility that the owner had been murdered.'

'But she wasn't,' Mackreth insisted, nodding to Rumney, acknowledging his contribution, 'Michael knew he hadn't killed Sophie. Why abandon the car?'

'Because he thought someone else had?' Warwick suggested.

'Had what?' Mackreth knew his brain was closing down. Post-mortems shouldn't be held at the end of the day.

'That someone else had killed Sophie,' Warwick said patiently.

'No.' Lorton was becoming more feisty as her elders flagged. 'Sophie killed Mary and the car was disposed of because it was used to transport Mary's body—'

'Nothing was found—' Mackreth began but Lorton hadn't finished. She had a theory, she was going to expound it.

'Michael was protecting Sophie all along, saying she'd gone to Ireland, putting us—the police—on the wrong track.'

'He's turned on her now,' Rumney reminded her.

'Did Lambourne have any reason for accusing Michael of murder other than Michael had stolen his girl?' The question from Warwick fazed all of them.

'Lambourne?' Mackreth repeated weakly. 'You say he sent the text message.'

'Oh yes! I'm with you now. Weston told us that. Lambourne told him. It was useful at the time: made us look more closely at Michael.'

'But did Lambourne have anything more concrete than spite to back his accusation?'

Lorton was staring at her boss in bewilderment. 'Lambourne was accusing Michael of killing *Mary*? But no one was looking for Mary then surely; you thought you could be searching for Sophie's body.'

'That's right,' Mackreth said in wonder. 'We were investigating Sophie's disappearance.'

'Then why was Lambourne accusing Michael of killing Mary? No one at the time knew she was dead.'

'The killer did,' Warwick said. 'We'll have another word with young Lambourne tomorrow. And then there's Sophie—if she comes back. I think she will; she has to return to face her husband, or rather, his accusations.'

Chapter Fifteen

To Lorton, glancing into the dining room at the Station Hotel, Lambourne and Weston looked homely, as if they were related, father and son: eating breakfast, passing the toast but not conversing. They didn't see her and she retreated with Rumney to wait in the foyer, an unfriendly place with large pictures in tarnished frames and, on some kind of sideboard, a display of plastic flowers in shades of brown and yellow.

Weston and Lambourne were the first to finish eating. They emerged from the dining room, the big man hard-faced in close-up, intent, the youngster listless. Still in shock, thought Lorton, which should make him easier to deal with. The detectives approached their quarry, neatly separating them. Lorton introduced herself to Lambourne who was startled and resentful. Weston focused on her, ignoring Rumney who was asking if he could have a word, it wouldn't take a minute, trying to edge him away. The pair were reluctant to be parted but it was possible that Weston realized protest could be viewed with suspicion and he submitted to Rumney's demand, which it was, however discreetly disguised as a request. The two men went to another depressing place labelled 'Lounge' while Lorton took Lambourne to a television room.

There was a table and she sat at it, feeling she would lose authority in an easy chair. Lambourne sat opposite her, now wide-eyed and defiant. She wasted no time.

'You accused Michael Daynes of murder.'

'So? I got there before you. You should be grateful.'

208

'What made you suspect him?'

The defiance faded, he hadn't expected the question. After a moment's surprise he started to think. 'She was missing, and you—that is, Mackreth—made it plain he was looking for her. The first person the police suspect is the partner.'

'We didn't know Mary was missing.'

'Maybe not, but I did.' He remembered something. 'And she'd told me she was going away with Daynes but he denied it, see? And she had gone to the Boathouse although he said she was never there, and he *had* murdered her.'

She considered him and his response. After a long moment she said, 'When you sent the text message to the police people thought you were accusing him of murdering Sophie.'

He shrugged. 'It's immaterial. He's a killer and you've got him. Ends justify means. Probably it did occur to me that he'd killed his wife as well, but I don't know her, I wasn't interested. All I was thinking about was my girl.' He winced.

She tried again. 'Did you have anything more substantial to go on other than your concern for Mary, and the fact that she'd told you she was going away with him?'

'And disappearing immediately. Wasn't that enough?'

'I didn't know Mary.' Lorton was gentle. 'I do know that when young girls turn against a partner they say the first thing that comes into their heads. They twist the knife. She was winding you up; she could have been going away on her own, going back to Mum—or to her brother.'

'Half-brother. And her mother's in Thailand with her stepfather.' He shook his head angrily. 'No, she was speaking the truth—and anyway, what's happened confirmed it. She did go to him.'

'You didn't know that, Andrew! Not at the time.'

'His behaviour, his manner, everything; he was guilty as hell.'

'When did you meet?'

He swallowed, glaring at her, caught out.

'When, Andrew?'

'We didn't. I never met him.'

*　　　*　　　*

'We can strike him off the suspects' list,' she told Rumney as they walked back to the car park. 'He maintains that he knew Mary was dead and that Daynes had killed her several days before her body washed up, but it's all hindsight. He didn't know, he assumed it because Mary said she was going away with Daynes, and naturally he hated the man. My reading of it is he got caught up in the hysteria: missing woman, rumours of foul play, husband suspected. Lambourne just added Mary to the

210

list of Daynes' supposed victims. That lad's either innocent or a superb actor.'

They reached their car and stopped as Rumney searched his pockets for the keys. He said, 'Lambourne could have panicked: struck one blow in anger, realized she was dead . . .'

'OK,' Lorton said slowly. 'But even if he did tie her up, that puts him at the Boathouse because there's no question that the rope and stuff came from there. Well, I suppose he could have followed Mary . . .' She trailed off in her turn.

'He'll bear watching,' Rumney said. 'We can't rule him out. Weston neither, although there's his alibi. Now that's a tough character. We thought he was simple first time round—not an idiot, you know, but a bit of a peasant like, a country boy. If so, he's hardened up since the death of his sister. Mackreth thinks they could have had a thing going. Unhealthy if you ask me, makes you wonder.'

'Could be there was a relationship. Nothing illegal, they were only step-siblings, not even half-, although Lambourne made that mistake; he said Weston was Mary's half-brother.'

'Maybe he doesn't want to face the fact that Weston's another guy who was in love with her.'

She glanced at him over the roof of the car. 'If Weston was in love with Mary it puts him in the frame,' she pointed out. Rumney looked blank. 'Love and hate,' she went on, instructing him. 'Like Michael Daynes betraying his wife to save himself. He must have loved her at one time.'

'That man never loved anyone.'

They settled in the car, rolling down the windows. He made no move to start. She looked across at him.

'How did you make out with Weston?'

He shook his head as if denying a thought. 'The object was to give you time with Lambourne. We've established that Weston couldn't have killed Mary if she died that night—the night Sophie shot—shot at Daynes, and then walked out. That same night and for two days Weston was in Essex or on the way here.'

'But, if Mary was still alive after he reached the Lakes, he doesn't have an alibi, right?'

'We haven't been able to shake him so far. He never saw Mary alive after the family reunion down south at Christmas. Oh, he admits he was at the Boathouse but that was three days after the night in question; he went there to ask Daynes where Mary was—and got no joy, as we know. We passed him as he left so he has to admit he was there, although it was the natural thing to do: approach the man who his stepsister was having an affair with, according to her.'

'That girl was playing with fire: Daynes, Weston, Lambourne . . . what's with those two? Why have they joined forces? What are they doing here? Of course they have to stay for the inquest but why stay together?'

'Not much choice for the lad; he had nowhere to go after he left his job and no doubt Weston took him under his wing. After all, they both loved Mary, one way or another, and if she was ever a bone of contention, she's not any longer. Now, I suppose her death makes a sort of bond between them.'

She glanced sideways as he turned the ignition key. He could be right; she was surprised, she hadn't put him down as that imaginative.

*   *   *

At ten o'clock Marjorie phoned the station and was put through to Warwick. Marjorie asked if the DCI would be available at eleven to come to Losca adding, as if it were an afterthought, that her god-daughter would be present. Warwick accepted in kind but she was thoughtful as she replaced the receiver. She saw that Marjorie's intention (and that of Sophie?) was to keep the atmosphere of this interview informal and relaxed. Sophie was in an awkward position; she could be summoned to the station at least to help with their inquiries, and at most as a suspect for murder, indeed Mackreth was virtually demanding that she be brought in. But Mackreth was prejudiced; he bitterly resented the time spent investigating what had been viewed as a disappearance, possibly murder. The woman was guilty of wasting police time, he maintained, and should be interviewed and recorded like any common offender. But Warwick looked at the broader picture and pulled rank. They were after a murderer not a petty crook and they drove to Losca.

They were received in the shabby sitting room, Marjorie introducing a thin middle-aged woman in chinos and brown shirt, with gold at her throat and sandals on her feet. Fine eyes were set in deep sockets giving an impression of tension, and her clothes hung loosely as if she had lost weight since they were bought.

Marjorie went out leaving Sophie alone with the detectives.

'When did you get back?' Warwick asked as if this were the most normal social occasion.

'This morning.'

'Did you come far?'

'From Inverness.' Mackreth's eyes glazed as he calculated times and distance. 'I drove through the night,' she added.

So she hadn't had much sleep and might make mistakes. Warwick asked in the same tone of normality, 'Can you tell us what happened the night you left the Boathouse?'

Mackreth could have sworn Sophie's lips twitched in the semblance of a smile. 'Only what I know,' she said, and then she frowned. 'It's unpleasant.'

'We know.' Warwick was referring to murder but Sophie didn't react to the implication.

Marjorie came in carrying a tray and escorted by cats, worrying Mackreth who was concerned that the old lady might trip. Warwick's eyes came round to Sophie to find that the other woman was watching *her*. Mackreth, on his feet, fussed about their host and handed coffee round, cats weaving about his ankles. Warwick had the feeling that she and Sophie were apart, opponents sizing each other up. She placed her coffee on the table beside her chair and asked, 'How was it unpleasant, apart from the obvious?'

Again that ghost of a smile, like a tic, as if she couldn't restrain herself. 'The confrontation,' she explained. 'It was farcical—that is, until you remember the outcome. You know, I liked her; isn't that odd? I was sorry for her'—she gave a snort of angry amusement—'and we fought like alley cats.'

Warwick didn't turn a hair. 'How did it start?'

'How much do you know?'

'Think of us as totally ignorant. We know you left work early and came home . . .'

'Right.' Sophie composed herself. 'My husband was out so I came in,'—she looked away as if recalling images—'poured a drink—and that was when she phoned.'

'Who phoned?'

215

'Why, Mary of course. You didn't know that?'

'What did she say?'

'I can remember every word.' She smiled wryly. 'She thought it was Michael because I just grunted when I picked up the phone. Actually she didn't say much. She'd been trying to get Michael for ages, for days, and she was frantic to see him. She said she was coming to the Boathouse—she still thought she was talking to him—and then I put the phone down. And Michael was standing in the doorway—' She coughed, gulped some coffee, replaced the cup and saucer and sighed. 'After that everything fell apart.'

They waited, Marjorie regarding her fiercely.

'Who spoke first—when you saw him in the doorway?' Warwick prompted.

'What?' Sophie started; she'd been miles away. 'Oh, him probably—yes, he did. He asked who phoned. I told him. I was still holding my whisky—in Mother's crystal tumbler: something precious, something I loved. So I broke it.' She stopped as if this were adequate explanation for something unspecified.

'You threw it at him?' Warwick asked.

'At the cooker. It smashed, and then I took the gun down and he said it was loaded and I didn't believe him; you never keep a loaded gun in the house, never. I was livid! I was so wild I must have fantasized that it *was* loaded—wishful thinking—and I followed him out and pulled the trigger as he jumped in the car, and the bloody thing went off! I was astounded!' She shook her head. 'I'm still amazed although I know now that he'd loaded it for rats, the idiot, but that's Michael: typical, he has no more sense of responsibility than a child.'

'What happened after you fired?' Warwick asked.

Sophie thought about it. 'I went back in the house—no, first I went to look at the sets and sure enough there were pellets and flakes of green paint on them so I knew I hadn't imagined it. Then I came back to the kitchen, replaced the gun after I'd unloaded it, and Mary turned up. It was just one thing after another, although for a time we talked quite rationally, if you can credit that.' She looked round at their intent faces as if expecting contradiction but no one said a word. Marjorie's face was a wrinkled mask, her eyes fixed on her god-daughter. 'Mary,' Sophie resumed, 'was under the impression that my marriage was finished, that Michael owned a half-share in the Boathouse, that he would buy me out, then sell the place and relocate somewhere on the Mediterranean. She assured me that Michael wanted to do the right thing by me. Her words—or,' she added bitterly, 'his.'

'Stupid child,' Marjorie grated.

'Gullible and immature,' Sophie corrected. 'And Michael's a plausible liar.'

Marjorie's lips thinned.

'So,' Warwick put in, 'did you enlighten Mary as to the true state of affairs?'

'I started to but—oh, I remember what made me lose my rag—I was telling her that not only the house but everything in it belonged to me and—one gets worked up, you know? He'd spent my money on her, they'd slept in my bed . . . It's amusing now—not the events but my fury. I was raging and ranting and she was terrified, and we both made a move for the gun but I got there first. By then we were both over the top and she accused me of having shot him—I wonder, could she have heard the shot?—and she got terribly distressed because she thought he was wounded or dead. I told her how she'd been exploited by him and she retaliated: told me she was pregnant. I said the parentage had to be in question because Michael said she was a working girl. Not true, I made that up. Then—naturally—she came for me and I kicked a chair in her way and she fell over it and hit her head an awful crack on a corner of the dresser.'

There was dead silence in the room until Warwick prompted, 'And then?'

Sophie hesitated. 'She seemed all right,' she said doubtfully. 'She wasn't knocked out. She sat up almost immediately and I went to help her but she was still furious and wouldn't let me touch her, said I'd tried to kill her. Her head was bleeding and I wanted to put something on it, a bandage, plaster, anything, but she wouldn't have any, and she went outside under her own steam.' There was another long pause. 'That's it,' she said miserably. 'Nothing else. I suppose her skull was fractured.'

Marjorie said furiously, 'You didn't touch her. It was nothing to do with you. She tripped over a chair.'

'My godmother takes her duties seriously,' Sophie told Warwick.

'Why did you come back—from wherever you were?' Warwick asked.

'I've been with Marjorie's cousin. Nothing underhand about it. I came back because I'm responsible for her death. I didn't hit her certainly, but the fall killed her. And if I'd followed her out to her car I'd have seen she wasn't fit to drive. I should never have let her leave.'

'You think she left?'

'If she did she didn't go far. At some point she must have collapsed. I didn't go out in the yard again. I left the front way: packed a bag and came up here through the woods.'

'You must have looked out of the kitchen window and seen if her Mini was still there.'

She thought about it. 'I don't remember

219

seeing it. It couldn't have been there because if it had been I'd have realized she hadn't gone and I'd have done something about it. Where did she—What happened to her?'

'We'd expected you to tell us.'

'I can't tell you more than I know. How far could she have gone before she collapsed? Collapsed and died, presumably.' She was doleful.

'She didn't get far.' Mackreth took over. 'She was tied up in bin bags with rope from the stables at the Boathouse.'

Sophie nodded. 'He was protecting me.'

There was a sharp intake of breath from Marjorie.

'How did he know you were responsible?' Mackreth asked.

She was surprised. 'He knew Mary was coming to the Boathouse, I told him she said so when she phoned. He must have come back after I shot at him and he saw us through the kitchen window. Mary died as a result of the fall but Michael would have thought I hit her. He found her dead and got rid of the body.'

'Because . . .'

She raised her eyebrows. 'He's a Walter Mitty character: always dreaming of freedom but he'd never give up security. He's getting on: forty, that's a tricky age. Mary was an aberration, I think he found her rather tiring. He needs a home and someone to look after him. I fill the bill.' She smiled faintly. 'I'm reliable. By covering up what he thought was my murder he was protecting me.'

Warwick looked at Marjorie who remained stubbornly silent. If her thoughts were as hard as her expression body language was speaking volumes. She was no stranger to Sophie's rationalizing.

'The fall may not have killed her,' Warwick said. Sophie blinked. Marjorie looked wary. 'Her skull wasn't fractured,' she went on. 'She was probably concussed, could have collapsed, but we don't know the cause of death as yet.'

'You had the result of the autopsy!' Marjorie protested.

'Only a preliminary report.'

'No!' Sophie cried. 'If the fall didn't kill her you're saying she was alive when she was put in the water?'

'No.' Warwick was firm. 'She didn't drown. We know that much.' Her tone changed. 'Tell me, why did you leave the Boathouse?'

'I'd have thought that was obvious.' Sophie was resentful. 'My husband was having an affair with a girl half my age, who implied she was pregnant by him. The violence between us hadn't cleared the air. I was still raging.'

'You wanted to bandage her head.'

'Violence comes in waves.'

'How did you leave?'

Sophie glowered. 'I told you! I walked out the front—the lake side—and through the woods. I came here.'

'On foot?'

'How else? Michael had taken the car.'

'You could have phoned for a taxi—'

'To walk a couple of miles?'

'—or phoned Miss Neville.' Marjorie frowned and fidgeted. 'How long did you stay here?' Warwick asked.

'Only a day or two and then I went to Inverness.'

'And before you ask,' Marjorie put in, 'I lent her my car.'

Mackreth was grim, he'd been almost certain, on his first visit, that this house had been occupied by more than an old woman and her cats.

Warwick went on: 'What made you decide to go to Scotland?' She was like a bulldog. 'The Boathouse is your property, why leave your husband in possession?'

'I wasn't sure of him. I assumed—I thought Mary might join him there. The last thing I wanted was another fight. I hate scenes. Imagine, if I'd walked in on them keeping house in my own place after all the lies he'd told me! No, no way could I go back to the Boathouse to find them in possession.'

'You were afraid of his reaction.'

Sophie made to answer but checked herself. Tension was palpable on all sides. 'Why aren't you afraid of him any longer?' Warwick pressed. 'What changed?'

After a moment Sophie said quietly, 'Mary

died and I'm responsible. You can't be partly responsible for a death. My husband is weak and exploitive and a terrible liar. When he's backed into a corner he'll tell more lies, digging a deeper hole.' She went on, with only a trace of venom: 'Mary was exciting in the short term and I think, despite his lies, he had strong feelings for her. Certainly she adored him—and he always protested too much that she meant nothing to him. She must have died from the fall and he found her dead. The worst he's guilty of is disposing of a body.'

*   *   *

The police left and Warwick, driving, stopped in a lay-by on the shore road. They hadn't spoken since leaving Losca. Now she locked the car and they took a path through silver birches to the water where a log seat had been positioned before the stupendous view. They used the seat but the view was no more than something in front of them.

Mackreth spoke first. 'She's doing her best to get him off the hook. Do you believe her?'

Warwick said distantly, 'I can't see where she's lying. Are you a mountaineer?'

'Good God, no. Why?'

'There's a ridge on the Isle of Skye: lethal in bad weather because there are long drops on either side, and subsidiary spurs going off in all directions, many of them blind. So a compass

223

is essential. But in places the rock is magnetic and a compass reading can be anything up to 180 degrees in error. But one doesn't know where those places are so a compass is useless anywhere. Everywhere.'

He nodded glumly. 'Because you have no idea when a reading is correct. So it isn't that we don't know when she's lying but even if she *is* lying.'

'We don't know how clever she is.'

'Or whether they acted in collusion.'

'According to her they were—or rather, she puts forward this theory that the fall caused the death, and along comes Michael who disposes of the body. A kind of innocent collusion, more or less.'

The steamer appeared, chugging purposefully past, people waving from its deck. Warwick beamed and waved back. 'Alternatively,' she mused, 'collusion could have been criminal. She struck the blow, he dealt with the body.'

'And dumped the car.'

'Ah yes, Mary's car. Where is this quarry?'

He gestured to the south. 'Five miles or so that way, this side of the hause. They'd have needed two people and a second car.'

'Not necessarily, five miles isn't far to walk. But they had two cars. Two Minis.'

'You mentioned that before. It was the women we mixed up, not the cars. I mean, we confused the women, thinking one was dead but it was the other one.'

'You're tired. You were second-guessing Sophie all the time. I watched you.'

It was nice to know he had merited her attention, he thought petulantly. Aloud he demanded, '*Why* did she come back?'

But Warwick was watching the steamer, its wake like champagne on silk. 'Old sisal,' she murmured. 'It's organic, degradable; didn't stand a chance with those screws churning the water several times a day.' Mackreth said nothing. 'How vicious is Michael? Sophie's sketch of him could be the truth but not the whole truth. You could add viciousness to the picture without distorting it. What do you think?'

'Abused women often go back to their partners, which could account for her coming home. And the way she sees him: weak and exploited.'

'Exploitive, she said. It could be a pretty accurate picture, but abusive? Are you suggesting physical abuse?'

Mackreth's attention was caught by a flight of duck and when they splashed down he continued to stare but he was seeing something in his mind. Warwick was immobile, she could have been a tourist basking in a blissful summer's morning. In fact both were considering their experiences of domestic horrors, recalling battered faces.

'Those women are cowed,' he said.

225

'Even when the abuser isn't present.'

'Sophie's not afraid.'

'She doesn't show any sign of fear,' Warwick amended. 'And that night she walked out: listening to her, observing her as she describes it, she left because she couldn't bear to be in the same house where he'd—entertained the girl, even though it's her property. The situation was intolerable *because* it was her property. He'd soiled it, like a burglar defecating on a bed. That woman wasn't frightened of her husband, she was in a towering rage. No, not an abused woman.'

'Not physically, but she was humiliated.'

'Ah.' Warwick turned and regarded him with interest. 'Insulted?' she suggested.

He nodded. 'She's not a woman you'd want to be on the wrong side of if you were married to her. By her own admission she fired at him.'

'She didn't know the gun was loaded.'

'She says.'

'Ye-es.' Warwick was thoughtful. 'But he admits he loaded it. I wonder if those trespassers were a figment of his imagination. Sophie saw a deer, he said it could have been an intruder; it gave him an excuse for keeping a loaded gun in the house: waiting for an opportunity to devise an "accident" to his wife. Sophie isn't stupid and she knows the man. What are the odds she's wondered if the gun was loaded with that intention? It destroys the collusion theory. He'll be released this

226

morning. It'll be interesting to see what happens if they get together.'

*   *   *

'He's dangerous,' Marjorie told the Fairburns. 'She maintains he's protecting her. If he is, he has an ulterior motive, like putting her in a position where she's in his debt.'

'He's not that cunning.' Gerald was restrained in the face of his neighbour's concern.

'Could be blackmail,' Davina said brightly, topping up their sherry glasses. Marjorie had brought them a duckling for tonight and they had insisted she stay for lunch, Davina avid to hear the latest developments.

'Blackmail?' Marjorie was lost, flushed with sherry as much as anxiety for her goddaughter.

'If she injured Mary by accident and Michael covered up for her, he'd have a hold over her.'

'I told you what happened.' Marjorie was incensed. 'Sophie never touched the girl.'

'I wonder what Michael's story is.' Gerald made a clumsy attempt to divert her from Sophie's culpability.

'She says she has to talk to him.'

'Is that a good idea?'

'There'll be bloody murder,' Davina said, unaware of any irony.

227

'I forbade—I would have—' The old lady was flustered and furious. 'What can I do?' She appealed to them angrily as if they had accused her of dereliction of duty. 'She's a grown woman. She *can't* go to him. I told her she's mad, at least take me, I said; I'd even have him come to Losca, but she mustn't meet him on her own. I mean, that loaded gun!'

'Where's the ammo?' Gerald was sharp; this was something in his department. 'More to the point, where's the gun?'

'The police have it.' She glowered at him. 'There are other forms of violence besides shooting.'

'Sophie never parcelled that girl and put her in the water,' he said firmly.

'Of course she didn't.' Marjorie was dismissive. 'Michael did that.'

Davina was dubious. 'He's admitted it?'

'Not as far as I know, but Sophie couldn't have done it, so it had to be Michael. It'll be what she wants to talk to him about.' Marjorie's voice faded as if she were listening to her own words, doubting them.

'Tricky,' Gerald observed: 'asking your husband if he trussed his other lady like a fowl and put her in the water.'

'She's in two minds whether he could have done it.'

'It sounds as if she's protecting him,' Davina said. She turned to Marjorie. 'And yet you said she reckons Michael's protecting *her*. Are you sure she's told you everything?'

Marjorie hesitated and the pause lengthened. 'No,' she said with finality. 'In the ordinary way, yes; she used to confide in me, but that was no more than—' She shrugged and tried again: 'That was merely money difficulties, and Michael being unemployed and so on. The present situation's serious and maybe, where life and death are concerned, a life sentence anyway, she's being less communicative. It isn't that she distrusts me but she'll be thinking that the less I know the better.'

'The better for whom?' Gerald asked then, since she didn't respond: 'Where is she now?'

'At Losca.' Marjorie was suddenly alert. 'Why?'

He was silent, trying to think of an excuse to visit the Boathouse. Davina, more specifically, was wondering if Sophie were closer to Michael than they thought, at least since Mary died.

Marjorie said awkwardly, 'I won't stay for lunch after all. I have to go home. Another time . . .'

Neither Fairburn was surprised.

Chapter Sixteen

Sophie had walked down through the woods to the Boathouse. It had been her family's holiday retreat and now it was her home and she loved it. She felt safe here although the empty gun rack in the kitchen was a reminder of violence. She'd been at fault in not securing it and when it was returned it would be kept under lock and key. She needed it for the rabbits. Not rats, there were no rats at the Boathouse.

She was making out a shopping list when a car entered the yard: a battered Volks Polo which belonged to no one she knew. She was thinking that a reporter would be driving something better when Michael got out and came to the back door, which she'd left ajar. He was sure of himself; he showed no hesitation in approaching the house. Sophie remained seated at the kitchen table, tense but trying not to show it.

'Hi,' he announced from the doorway. 'How's it going?'

'Who owns the car?' She was having no truck with convention.

'It's mine.' There was a rising note as if he dared her to question it; he wasn't going to explain how he could afford to buy even an old banger.

'Are you out on bail?'

He tried to smother a gasp but she heard it. 'I was never charged,' he said, and his eyes hardened.

She said coldly, 'I have to know if she was alive when you came back.'

'She wasn't here.'

She leaned back in her chair and studied him. 'Sit down,' she ordered. 'I need to understand this. I know what happened but I have to understand how you—'

'Exactly,' he snapped. 'That's why I'm here. *I* want to know what happened, of course I do.' He sat down. A drink would have been welcome but neither made a move. Anyway it wasn't his house. He said, or rather stated, 'Mary came back.'

'Back,' she repeated. 'Had she been here that afternoon? No, when she spoke to me on the phone she'd been trying to contact you all day.'

'Figure of speech. She was accustomed to being here. She was here most days when you were out. So what?'

'That night: the night she died—'

'Was murdered.'

Her eyes widened. 'Was murdered,' she repeated. 'She came here after you left, and we talked.'

He sat like a stone man. After a while he said, 'So?'

'We talked about you, about our marriage,

231

about your half-share in this house.' She waited. He said nothing; his eyes didn't move, watching her. 'It was when she said she was pregnant that things got awkward.' She winced, remembering. 'I doubted the parentage of the baby and, naturally, she came for me. I kicked a chair into her path, she fell over it and hit her head on the corner of the dresser there.' Her eyes followed the action as she described it. His remained fixed on her.

'And then?'

Her attention returned to him. 'She wouldn't let me patch her up. She left . . .' Her voice trailed away.

'Go on.'

'That's it. That's my part in it. I'd assumed she drove off.'

'I'll stand by you.'

'You can't. You weren't here.'

'It makes no odds. I'll vouch for you.'

'What are you saying?'

'Exactly that. I'll stand by you. It's called a character reference. What you said is the truth, and all the rest.'

'There is no "rest".'

'Well, only putting her in the bin bags and tying her up and taking her down to the boat— oh yes, and the weight—what was that, part of an engine?—and rowing out because you couldn't risk the noise of the outboard, and heaving her over the side.'

'I see.' She sighed. 'Everyone assumed that

was how it was done.'

'It's your word against mine.' Only his lips moved. 'And you've admitted you fought with her. You were the one that had it in for her, not me. She was my girl, my lover; she was my whole life.' They were the sentiments of a man deeply in love but his eyes were without feeling. It could have been because he condemned and hated her for killing Mary but there was no hatred. Hatred is hot. Here there was only a chill emptiness.

As they confronted each other a Peugeot entered the yard and his attention shifted. He stood up but she remained seated knowing he was no longer dangerous.

He left the kitchen without a word. Marjorie flung herself out of the Peugeot as he crossed the yard to his car. 'What are you doing here?' she shouted. 'Sophie! *Sophie!*'

She opened the kitchen window. 'I'm here, Marjorie,' she called. 'Come in, I'll put the kettle on.' Anything to get the old lady away from him. She wanted to shout some kind of reassurance like 'He's harmless now,' but she kept quiet until he was out of earshot. She felt she'd lost touch with him, knew only that he was unpredictable. He might get away with one murder, in fact he was confident that he could, but not a second, and not with a witness. If he killed her he would have to kill Marjorie. She shuddered and moved to put the kettle on.

'So,' Marjorie said fiercely as they drank coffee and Martell in the sitting room, 'he's not only putting all the blame on you, but accusing you to your face! He's evil.'

'Following through,' Sophie said. 'He has to do that: makes the theory all the more convincing. Maybe he's starting to believe it himself.'

'What was his purpose in coming here?'

The confrontation had exhausted Sophie and the brandy was relaxing rather than stimulating. She lay back in her chair and tried to make sense of his behaviour. 'He had a purpose,' she admitted, 'but as to what it was, your guess is as good as mine.'

'How did he know you were back?'

'Wouldn't the police have told him? That was why he was released surely, because I'd confessed.'

'Not to murder, woman!' Marjorie was sidetracked. 'All you did was to kick a chair in her way. That detective, Warwick, would never think you capable of murder.'

'Everyone is capable and the police know it as well as anyone. But I thought I'd convinced her that Mary must have collapsed after she left the house, and all Michael did was dispose of the body. D'you know, Marjorie, he described that part of it to me; even said the boat was rowed out on the lake because the noise of the outboard would have attracted attention.'

'And he put you in his place. He substituted you. Is that why he came here: to accuse you?'

'He could have intended to steal something. He needs money, maybe he stole the car he was driving. But he still has some stuff of his own here: his typewriter, clothes and so on.'

'Throw them out and change the locks.'

'That's not foolproof; he could break in, he's only got to smash a window. He's changed, he—' She stopped, confused.

'He what?'

'I was going to say that he's cruel. Spiteful might be more appropriate. I wouldn't have said that before. Before Mary's death?' She was questioning her own statement.

'He's a sadist. What—' Someone had shouted from the back of the house. 'You stay here,' Marjorie ordered. 'I'll deal with this.'

They were thinking in terms of reporters but when she returned she had a big man with her who was a stranger to both of them. 'Mr Weston,' she announced, her eyes signalling caution. 'He's rather insistent—'

'It's an intrusion,' Weston told Sophie, 'but we had to meet sometime. I'm Mary's stepbrother. I'm afraid you've been put to a great deal of inconvenience.'

Sophie closed her eyes momentarily, feeling that she couldn't take much more of this.

'Sit down, Mr Weston,' Marjorie ordered. 'We're rather tired. Michael Daynes was here. You just missed him.'

'I heard a car go past.' He removed his cap and sat down. 'I didn't drive down here. I left my Land Rover at the same place Mary could have parked her car. There's tread marks on a track leading to an old ruin.'

Sophie smiled wanly. 'She'd hide her car in case I came home unexpectedly. If she was in the house she could get out by way of the deck—' She bit her lip as she realized that the image of his sister scrambling away from Michael's side must be excruciatingly painful for Weston.

He saw her concern. 'It's all right, you get hardened to shock. And she's not suffering any longer although—she did.' Suddenly his face was contorted. He tried to smile. 'They just gave me the autopsy report.'

'Oh God!' Sophie was stricken. 'She *was* pregnant.'

'No, not that. It's how she died.' His eyes had changed to slate. 'She was throttled.'

They were dumbfounded and they needed time to recover. It was Sophie who whispered, 'What does this mean?'

'You said he was here.' Weston saw that they needed reminding. 'Why did he come?'

'To collect something,' Sophie said dully, missing the undercurrent. 'Or steal something. I don't have much to steal,' she added, looking

236

round her sitting room distractedly, 'not that's portable. Even the gun's gone. The police have it.'

'A pity.' Marjorie was thinking of Mary. 'A pity you didn't hit him instead of the Mini that time.'

'She didn't know it was loaded.' Weston spoke as if Sophie were not present. He must have had the information from the police.

'He'd meant to kill her,' Marjorie said.

'Mary?'

'Sophie, of course. The man's mad. He's accusing her of killing Mary. He says he'll stand by her. He'd have loved saying that.' She glared at Sophie as if she were the sadist rather than his victim.

'He didn't accuse me of throttling her,' Sophie said in wonder.

'It isn't public knowledge yet,' Weston said. 'The police told me because I'm family. No one else knows.' His voice faded.

Marjorie grinned horribly, 'You're slipping. The killer knows.'

Weston turned to Sophie. 'You can't stay down here on your own—'

'She won't,' Marjorie cut in. 'Either she comes home with me or I stay here.'

Sophie would have agreed to anything. 'I'll come back to Losca for now. Until this business gets resolved.' She sounded as if no resolution could be found this side of the grave.

Weston said, 'How would you like me to stay here, to look after the place for a day or two?'

Marjorie gaped and turned to her god-daughter, unable to think of a response that would not be rude.

'Why not?' Sophie asked, at the end of her tether. 'You seem the kind of man who goes in for good deeds.' Besides, she owed him, she owed Mary. 'You'll need food, I was making out a shopping list.'

'Forget that.' The tone was kindly. 'You leave it to me. I'll take care of things.'

* * *

Back at Losca, sprawled on a sofa, Sophie said, 'Did you feel an undercurrent there? He'll take care of things. He didn't mean the Boathouse, did he?'

'You're shattered,' Marjorie chided. 'We're going to have a nice bowl of soup and then you'll sleep off that brandy and we'll talk when you wake up.'

'I never sleep in the daytime. You know that.'

But when Marjorie went back to say the soup was on the table, Sophie was curled on the sofa, Sharkey ensconced in the crook of an arm.

Two hours later she woke and washed, found the soup and drifted outside to discover

Marjorie hoeing spinach, accompanied by Patchouli. 'Good sleep?' she asked cheerily, determined on a fresh start, and that on an even keel. 'I'll put the soup on.'

'I've had it, thanks. We must talk, Marjorie.'

'Right.' She looked across the rows, considered the wisdom of protest and decided against it. Reluctantly she followed Sophie to the terrace.

They were silent for a while but the thoughts of both women were on the same lines. At last Sophie said, 'I don't think he did it.'

Marjorie wasn't surprised but she was curious. 'He could have done it but why do you think he didn't?'

'Because when he accused me he didn't mention her being throttled. That was obscene and he loathes me but he didn't taunt me with it. He didn't know about it.'

'He knew about the boat—'

'Simply because that's how it must have been done. Anyone'd know you couldn't use the outboard at that time of night.'

'All right—but if it wasn't him, who was it?'

Sophie was thoughtful. 'A stranger or a lover?'

'We haven't met the young boyfriend.'

'Andrew Lambourne. I spoke to him on the phone. He comes over very young and emotional.'

'And Weston? Sophie, what on earth made

239

you leave that man in charge of your house?'

'Guilt. I owe him. No—' as Marjorie threw up her hands in disbelief. 'You heard him say I'd been put to a great deal of inconvenience. That man was apologizing to me because his sister slept with my husband! And Weston loved the girl—he's devastated, you saw his face when he told us how she died. Think of one of the cats being throttled, Marjorie. I owe that man. I disabled Mary, and someone came along and found her—what? Crawling in the yard? Slumped in her Mini? And finished her off.'

'If someone intended to kill her they'd have found another opportunity. You weren't responsible.'

'Nor was Weston. I trust him to look after my house. I don't trust Michael. Would you? He could damage the place to hurt me. He's changed; there's a side to him, an underside, I didn't know existed. I find it appalling.' Sophie stopped and stared across the lake in bewilderment. 'He's implacable,' she went on, 'like a—like something inanimate. He looks at me with dead eyes.'

Marjorie, an unbeliever, prayed for inspiration. 'And yet you think he didn't kill Mary. You know who that leaves? The people who we thought were in the woods, who could have been after Coulter.' Seizing on the diversion, she galloped away with it—anything to distract the girl from thoughts of Michael.

'Warwick was involved in the Coulter case. She's a local woman and she's not stupid. She pointed out that there are no timber operations in the vicinity other than those in the spruce plantation above the village, and a stranger wouldn't know about those.'

'Marjorie! We were talking about Mary. What makes you go off on a tangent about Coulter?'

'The caravan door was wedged shut with a spruce log. It had been cut. There are no spruce in those woods.'

'OK, the caravan fire was arson and you're saying it was set by a local man. Where's the connection with Mary? There was a theory I ran into trouble because I saw intruders in the woods; now you're suggesting Mary did? She was in the wrong place at the wrong time?'

'We've eliminated all the obvious suspects.'

'I don't believe this. You're not only saying that a local man killed Coulter—'

'Or woman; they kill too. If Coulter had connections with an urban gang, it could be that there's someone else in this area with criminal connections, someone who could be hired to kill him.' After a moment Marjorie went on: 'A respected member of the community who lives here under cover, a kind of sleeper, who can be called on to do odd jobs, but one who has to preserve his double life at all costs. Even his wife wouldn't know. But Mary saw something—or discovered

241

something—and had to be silenced.'

Sophie was trying to follow. 'Does Michael come into this?'

'Oh, my dear, it's only a theory—although Warwick saw the significance of that spruce log. I wonder if she's seen a connection between Coulter and Mary?'

'Perhaps you should talk to her.' She wasn't serious but Marjorie took her at face value.

'I don't think so. We're not out of the wood yet. That scenario is wild enough that the police could think we dreamed it up to get you off the hook. Remember they wondered if you and Michael acted in collusion. I don't think your contention that he appears to be ignorant of how she died is likely to convince them of his innocence.'

'He's not innocent.'

'What does that mean?'

'I'm not sure. Maybe it's that the intention is there to kill but very coldly and carefully, and making damn sure he doesn't get caught.'

'You've changed,' Marjorie said.

Chapter Seventeen

'Daynes has got hold of an old Polo. He went to the Boathouse and stayed twenty minutes. Sophie was there on her own, then Marjorie arrived and Daynes left. About ten minutes later Weston turned down towards the Boathouse but he left his Land Rover at some old ruin nearer the road. We think you should go and look at that place. Someone else has parked there recently. There are tracks.'

Stokesley, a female DC, and the massive Heslop had been keeping surveillance on visitors to the Boathouse. It was a tricky assignment because a car parked in a lay-by on consecutive days could arouse suspicion. In fact, their presence was suspect at any time, the woods, being private, boasted no public footpaths, and there was no obvious reason for tourists to stop where there was no view. The DCs had done their best by simulating interest in a map when traffic passed.

'That ruin is the old Flass place,' Warwick mused. 'What's the significance of the tracks?'

'There seem to be only two vehicles involved and most of the tracks are made by one of them. We took photographs. One set was made by a Land Rover and the rest belong to a smaller car.'

Stokesley laid Polaroids on the desk. Warwick studied the smaller tyre print and looked up at Lorton. 'Do we have a photo of the treads on Sophie's car?'

'I'll find some. Right now?'

'Wait a minute.' Warwick stared at the Polaroids. 'Is Mary's Mini still here? Get pictures of hers as well. On second thoughts you stay here. Stokesley, this was good work;

now you go and do the photography job on the Minis and come back pronto. Polaroids will do quite well.'

The youngster left in an eager hurry. 'Which one are you thinking of?' Lorton asked, shuffling the prints.

'Which Mini? Yes, but who was driving? If we knew the answers a lot might fall into place.' Warwick shook her head, bemused. 'Of course there might be no connection, could be a so-called courting couple, local, one or both of them married, have to meet secretly. We'll know soon enough.'

'We can't tell just by Polaroids. Forensics will be able to but we need microscopic examination of those treads to prove a match.'

'For a court, yes, but I'm happy to go ahead on—bugger!'

'What?'

'Call Stokesley. Tell her to photograph the treads on Coulter's pick-up if it's still in the garage. If it's not, tell her to find it.'

'For God's sake! What about Marjorie's Peugeot? And her Land Rover. And Lambourne has a car, a Fiesta.'

Warwick looked at her in reproof. 'We'll go to Flass as soon as we have photos of the Minis' tyres. If we can't get a match then we'll photograph everyone's tyre treads including Lambourne's and Weston's.'

'Weston wasn't here when she died.'

'We're not sure when she died.'

They had to wait for the Polaroids, Lorton grumbling that they would be useless, not admissible evidence, Forensics should be brought in. 'Think of it as elimination,' Warwick said and when, later, she held the three new sets of photographs and compared them with those they had already, they had a match, at least as far as the naked eye was concerned. The car that had been parked a number of times at Flass was Mary's.

They drove to the Boathouse, or rather to the lay-by close to the end of its drive. Leaving the car they crossed the road and, after walking about a hundred yards, they came to an overgrown track on the left where dog's mercury and rushes had been crushed and there was a strong smell of sweet cicely. It was very quiet; birds dozed through the long afternoon, and the new foliage hung heavy without a breeze. Lorton, a townie, was intimidated in this lush woodland, uncertain what she might see or was expected to see, her eyes jumpy. Warwick trudged ahead, thinking that high summer suited at least one of the crimes that concerned them. Steamy heat bred hot passions; emotions cooled in winter.

There was little left of Flass except heaps of stones; lead, slates and timber had been removed, salvaged or stolen. There was shattered glass about the remains of cold frames in an open space that would have been a vegetable garden, now thigh-high in weeds and nettles. A sharp little face with boot button eyes studied them from a pile of old wood and bricks but when Lorton blinked and looked again it wasn't there. Startled she turned to Warwick.

'Stoat,' the DCI said. 'There'll be hosts of rabbits around. Ah, there's the place where people parked and turned.'

It was obvious. The level ground had once been tilled and vehicles had crushed rank vegetation into the soil. In one place a land drain must have been smashed and there in the damp earth were the tracks that corresponded to the tracks on Mary's car. There was no mistake; they had brought the Polaroids.

Lorton said, 'But did she park here, or did someone else, driving her car? And if it was her, did she leave the car and go down to the house on foot or did he come to her? And if it wasn't her, who could it have been?'

The thick woods muffled sound; if cars had passed on the road their engines had been inaudible but now they heard something go by, bumping and rattling down the drive.

'Michael?' Lorton wondered. 'He'll have seen our car. I wonder if anyone else is there.'

'Marjorie and Sophie were there, and Weston. Fortunately we have the shotgun.' But both were thinking that there were plenty of weapons available to determined people.

They approached the Boathouse walking

confidently, seeing a Land Rover and a Fiesta in the yard, the back door open.

'Weston's Land Rover,' Lorton said. She had numbers off by heart. 'And that could be Lambourne's Fiesta. Now what are they up to?'

'One way to find out.' And Lorton, knowing her boss, was aware that an inane remark indicated a high degree of watchfulness.

'Hello?' the DS called along the empty passage. 'Anyone at home?'

Weston's bulk identified him as he appeared against the light from the sitting room. Lorton introduced him to Warwick. 'Come in, come in!' he shouted amiably. 'I was just about to put the kettle on.' They could have been old friends.

They stood in the kitchen doorway as he filled a kettle and switched it on. A clutch of bulging carrier bags stood on the table. Lorton stared and went to speak but he forestalled her.

'Mrs Daynes is at Losca with Miss Neville; I'm by way of being a caretaker.'

'Whose is the Fiesta?'

'Andrew's.' He smiled, showing he was aware that she would know what model vehicle Lambourne drove, and probably that of everyone else.

'Is he caretaking too?'

'No, he's staying in town. He brought me some groceries.'

247

'Why isn't Mrs Daynes here?' Warwick asked in her beautifully modulated tones.

He turned to her. 'Miss Neville suggested she should go to Losca for the time being. I volunteered to move in; it didn't seem a good idea to leave the place empty.'

'Michael Daynes was here earlier.'

'So they told me.'

'We were at Flass,' Warwick said. He looked blank. 'The old ruin nearer the road,' she explained. 'That's Flass.'

'I didn't know its name. You would be interested in it.' It was a statement, not a question. 'I think Mary left her car there; I saw tracks this morning. I parked there myself, preferring to come down here on foot.' He smiled but it didn't reach his eyes. 'I didn't know what to expect.'

In the silence that followed Andrew appeared in the doorway and the kettle boiled. Andrew said harshly, 'Where did he attack her?'

As the women hesitated, Lorton leaving it to her superior, Warwick considering the question rather than her answer, Weston said calmly, in sharp contrast to Andrew's angry demand, 'Mrs Daynes told me about the part she played that night: how Mary came here and things got out of hand, about her striking her head on the dresser—this dresser.' They all looked at it, Andrew's features contorted in pain. 'Sophie thought Mary drove away,'

Weston went on, 'but Andrew asked the right question: where was she attacked?' Everyone knew he meant the fatal attack, not Sophie's kicking the chair. He was sparing Andrew's feelings, avoiding the words 'killed' or 'murdered'. Lorton warmed to him.

'She was probably attacked between this yard and—her car,' Warwick told him, looking out of the window. 'Is there a yard light?'

'Yes,' Lorton said, watching her. 'Over the door.'

'He came back,' Andrew said, and then, as they turned to him: 'Daynes. After she shot him—at him, more's the pity—afterwards he came back.'

'You have an alternative theory,' Weston told the DCI. 'She didn't go far because the bin bags came from the outbuildings here.'

'The sisal matches,' Warwick said cautiously. It had been easier to match dust on the rope and twine than on the bags.

'And the boat was used, the one from here.'

Andrew said bitterly, 'It was him, and you've let him go.'

'They'll have had good reason,' Weston said, watching Lorton.

'Like suspecting Mrs Daynes, or the Neville woman, or us?'

'Tea's brewed,' Weston announced, and started to busy himself with mugs. They noticed that he was quite at home in the kitchen.

'Your prints are on the shotgun,' Warwick observed chattily.

He nodded, unmoved. 'When I came here looking for Mary I took charge of it as I went over the house with Daynes.'

'Reasonable enough,' Warwick said.

*   *   *

'She's all in; I've sent her up to have a good sleep.' Marjorie passed tea to Warwick and then to Lorton.

They were on the terrace, the detectives lulled into somnolence, full of tea and tranquillized by the sun and scents of mown grass and lavender. Marjorie had put up hanging baskets that dripped fuchsias in shades of cream and rose and purple. Now she urged brownies on her guests and asked politely, 'What conclusion did you come to on the Coulter case?'

Lorton's jaw dropped. Had she heard correctly? She swallowed and glanced at Warwick but her boss showed no sign that she'd heard; she appeared to be savouring the brownie, eyes concealed behind Prada shades.

'Coulter?' Lorton repeated. 'I'd forgotten about him.'

'You *were* on the case?' Marjorie was diffident.

'We liaised with the Manchester force.' Lorton was stiff. Why the hell didn't Warwick

250

butt in? Evidently the DS was following the right line: just act dumb, if she made a mistake it was down to Warwick to emerge from what was surely simulated torpor. 'What's the connection between Coulter and Mary?' she asked, not suspecting that there was one, but curious as to why Marjorie should think there was.

'No direct connection. No one's suggesting they knew each other.' Marjorie paused and Warwick, about to take a sip of tea, checked, her raised hand immobile. Marjorie went on quickly, as if an idea had surfaced and been dismissed: 'Coulter was killed by a local man and Mary knew who it was. So she had to be eliminated. But why was Coulter killed?'

Lorton looked deliberately at Warwick. No way was she going to attempt to answer that one.

'Coulter was an informant,' the DCI said. 'He was into organized crime and was in custody for the shooting of a courier, who had been employed to deliver hot money to Glasgow. The courier absconded with the money, Coulter tracked him down, shot him and retrieved the cash. But then he was stopped for speeding on the motorway with a load of hot money in the boot. Manchester had him in the frame for other gangland shootings over the years but there was never adequate proof. The courier was different and they thought they had Coulter to rights this

251

time but he escaped from custody.' Warwick's face was bland as milk.

'You say he was an informant. He escaped after he'd informed, presumably on the people who employed him?'

'Presumably.'

'And someone was sent from Manchester—no, someone local was hired—to find Coulter and kill him.' Marjorie frowned. 'I wonder how his former associates discovered that he'd gone to earth in the Lake District.'

'Perhaps he was betrayed.'

'And he thought he was safe, up there in his caravan. What an unsavoury world.'

'The other half,' Warwick said. 'Your god-daughter was lucky. She thought there were strangers in the woods, didn't she? But Mary Spence must have seen them; maybe they were looking for signs of Coulter round the ruins of Flass and they ran into her when she parked there to go down to the Boathouse. And she recognized the person or persons involved.'

'Like someone from the village,' Marjorie said slowly.

*   *   *

The detectives left and she rushed upstairs. Sophie was in the guest room, sitting by the open window.

'You heard all that?' Marjorie breathed.

Sophie nodded. She looked alert and—not

252

pleased so much as elated. 'What is it?' Marjorie asked. 'What's going on?'

'It shifts suspicion from me.'

'There is that, I suppose. But Warwick's not thick. Can she really think there's a hit man in the village? Do you?'

'A hired hit man,' Sophie repeated. 'It sounds terribly melodramatic.'

'Of course, it does happen.' Marjorie was following her own train of thought. 'It's how gangs keep a hold on their members: death as the price of treachery.'

'You're right, but that's inner city stuff, sink estates; it couldn't happen here.'

*　　*　　*

The detectives were considering a connection between the two murders. 'The weak point,' Lorton said, 'is the possibility of a local man being a sleeper. That's espionage bull, not organized crime. And the only clue to the presence of a local at the site of the fire is that log. But that could have an innocent explanation: Coulter could have taken it up there himself.'

'What for?' Warwick asked. 'You don't have open fires in caravans.'

'A camp fire?'

'There was no sign he'd ever had one,' Mackreth put in.

'That log was used to wedge the door shut,'

Warwick mused: 'to stop Coulter getting out.'

'He'd been bludgeoned,' Rumney reminded them. 'Why wasn't he shot?'

'The wound would show at the autopsy.' Lorton was a little too arrogant for Rumney: townie to rural Plod.

Warwick was frowning. 'Organized crime doesn't bother to disguise executions; they like publicity. It encourages the others,' she added drily.

Lorton said, 'If it wasn't a gangland execution, what was it?'

'*Who* was it? Rumney muttered, as if making a correction.

Mackreth glanced at him sharply, a look that didn't escape Warwick. 'Well?' she demanded. 'You have something?'

Mackreth said haltingly, 'Suppose Michael really did have the hots for Mary, he'd never have acted in collusion with Sophie. But if you rule out Michael as Mary's killer, who's the most likely candidate?'

'Sophie,' Lorton suggested.

'Right, but did she do the packaging?'

Warwick looked wary; Rumney was bland but he knew what was coming. Lorton was merely bewildered. 'Weston wasn't here,' she murmured. 'And it wasn't Andrew, he was mad about the girl. So was Weston: not mad about her but she was his stepsister, maybe something more . . . So who does that leave?'

'Coulter,' Mackreth said.

254

'Sophie—and *Coulter*?' Lorton was so astounded that she retreated into silence.

Warwick said, 'Is there any evidence that they met?'

'There's none that they didn't,' Mackreth said staunchly.

'You've been discussing this.' The DCI included both men in what sounded like an accusation.

'She meets the qualifications.' Mackreth refused to back down. 'She's local, she would have told him where the bin bags and the rope were, the boat, the oars, she could have sent for him, by mobile, after she killed the girl. And she would know where to find a sawn log.'

'Hey!' Lorton erupted. 'That's Coulter's murder: the spruce log and firing the caravan!'

'She had to kill Coulter because he could blackmail her. She doesn't have much money and hit men come expensive.'

'Oh, come on!'

Warwick said quietly, 'Sophie isn't the kind of woman to hire someone else to kill, she'd do the job herself.' She raised a hand as Mackreth went to interrupt. 'If she attacked Mary it wasn't premeditated, it would be one blow: hard yes, in a red rage; even throttling her, but not the trussing up. That was obscene.'

'We've said that all along—' Lorton began, to be ridden down by Mackreth:

'That's why she'd send for Coulter to get rid of the body.'

255

Lorton bridled. 'You're suggesting she had a relationship with him?'

'They'd have to be close if he disposed of a corpse for her.'

'But if she was having an affair with him why should she care about her husband having an affair with Mary, and care enough to kill her?'

'It didn't have to be a sexual relationship with Coulter, merely a financial one. She hired him.'

'She has no money.'

'That's what I'm saying: she had to kill him because she couldn't pay up.'

Chapter Eighteen

After supper Weston told Andrew that he was going to have an early night and he sent the lad back to town. 'You need sleep yourself,' he said. 'You're looking fraught.' Andrew was too young and, indeed, too tired to argue and he drove away, leaving Weston alone in the quiet evening. It did strike him, as he left, that Weston was vulnerable all alone in the woods, no one to hear him if he shouted, and Daynes on the loose somewhere. He almost changed his mind, turned back, but there was such an air of authority about the big man, a determination, a resolve, that he kept driving. In the extremes of emotion and fatigue

256

Andrew had a moment of perceptiveness: Weston had set his course and even a passive presence would be a hindrance. The moment passed, leaving him vaguely puzzled. He had to admit he was in awe of the man, and whatever was intended it was beyond the boy's experience. Faced with the unknown Andrew had to acknowledge that he was only a boy.

Behind him Weston stood at the back door until he could no longer hear the Fiesta's engine, then he locked the Boathouse and walked up the drive as far as the Flass turn. As he went he sniffed the air. This wasn't his country but weather is weather, south or north, and the atmosphere had changed. The sun was less brilliant, the air holding a faint stickiness that denoted a shift in the wind although wind was a moot term, for the moment it was no more than a zephyr. Occasionally a chance breath caught fresh foliage and a rustle ran through the woods. Weston liked it; he was a countryman and the land was in need of rain.

He came to the space where the stables would have stood and a little further, the crushed vegetation where vehicles had been parked. He started to wander about the ruin, which could hardly be called that; there was only one chimney breast left standing.

In the old kitchen garden, that sea of weeds, he came on a large wicker basket, half full of nettle tops, and beside it, a pair of yellow gloves.

The lowering sun was in his eyes and it took him a little while to see her because she was in the shade, wearing a dull shirt and sitting quite still, watching him. When she saw he'd spotted her she gestured without speaking. He was to approach.

'We can talk,' Sophie said quietly as he came down to her. 'You've disturbed them but they'll come out to look at you. Nothing so curious as a stoat and it's their territory.'

'Is there a family?'

'Five young. They den down there in the old well bricks.'

'What kind of bricks are those?'

'They're what's left of the parapet of the well. I'll show you.'

He followed her to the pile of rubble; there was wood amongst it which, she said, was the remains of the windlass. There was a mass of blackberry stolons and a dog rose with furled pink buds. Sophie, in boots and coarse denim, nudged the brambles aside to reveal mossy timbers set in the ground.

'It must have been where they drew water for the vegetables,' she told him. 'When the house was abandoned the well was left uncovered. When my mother bought the Boathouse and I had the run of the place she had this cover made. The workmen must have demolished the parapet when they installed the lid.'

'It would have been safer to plug the shaft.'

She shrugged. 'No one comes here. Except you,' she added meaningly. 'Are you just exploring or did you have something definite in mind?'

'I might ask the same question. You're a long way from Losca.'

'It's my home ground. Actually I wanted nettles for soup and the best ones are here. They grow well in soil that's been tilled.'

She hadn't answered the question and evidently she had given up on the stoats. She led the way back to her basket and up a flight of cracked slate steps to what had once been a terrace. There was a low section of wall bounding grass-grown cobbles and the air was redolent with the scent of flowering currant. She sat on one end of the wall and he lowered himself to the top step to face her. Elbows on knees, her chin in her hands, she regarded him speculatively but without hostility. He felt comfortable; in different circumstances he would have found her more than likeable.

'Are you waiting for him?' she asked. 'Is that why you want to stay in my house?'

'I needed time to think, a space. Andrew crowds me. He's too intense.'

'Where is Andrew?'

'I sent him back to the hotel.'

'What makes you think that Michael will come here?'

'He won't go away because that would imply guilt. He'll stay, try to tough it out, act

259

normally. His typewriter is still in the house; he'll be needing that.'

'It's probably what he came for this morning but my godmother turned up and that's one formidable lady. He wouldn't want to tangle with her.'

'Did it occur to you that he could have come for you?'

'To see me? Only to accuse me of'—she hesitated—'of guilt.'

'You didn't kill Mary.'

'Thanks.' She couldn't quell the sarcasm.

He said quickly, 'Of course *you* know that you didn't; what I'm saying is that I don't think you did.'

'You said that already. Don't *think*? Are you suggesting that I could have done it after all?'

'Nothing's certain, but you're not a murderer. I know you better now. You could make a mistake but you wouldn't cover up.'

She said nothing. He thought it possible that she had it in her to cover up something more than a mistake but not for mean motives. She said slowly, 'The yard light was on when she walked out of the kitchen. She hadn't parked her car here that night—' She indicated the abandoned garden. 'She drove down to the Boathouse. She'd spoken to me on the phone, she'd exposed herself, she intended to have a confrontation with me. If Michael wouldn't leave me she was going to make me leave him. There was no reason to hide her car, she parked it in my yard. When she left, I left shortly afterwards and never gave a thought to whether she'd driven away. I'd switched off the yard light by then so I wouldn't have seen if her car was still there.'

'You didn't hear an engine start up?'

'I don't remember one and I'd have been listening out in case Michael came back, but as I said, I didn't stay long. I didn't want another scene with him. I didn't know how he'd behave when she told him I knew everything, like him lying about owning a half-share in the house.' She looked appalled. 'Is that what happened? She called him and he came back and she told him? Did he turn against her for exposing him?'

Weston said heavily, 'He did come back.'

She shook her head. 'He swears he's innocent, that she meant everything to him, that I did it: says so to my face—'

'He would; he's reinforcing—confirming the story he's telling the police.'

'The odd thing is that he doesn't know the details—' She stopped, she was talking about the murder of the man's stepsister, for heaven's sake! Unable to help herself she blurted, 'He never mentioned that she'd been . . .' Her voice faded, she couldn't go on.

'Throttled,' he supplied brutally. 'It's all part of the scenario: if he doesn't know the details of what happened, he wasn't there. He's a clever bastard. Sorry, he's your

261

husband.'

She made a helpless gesture. 'She was your family.'

*   *   *

'Weston said something odd. He said that this morning Michael could have come to the Boathouse for me.'

'For you?' Marjorie paused in the act of unscrewing a bottle of Bell's.

'I said he could have come for his typewriter. Weston said it could have been for me.'

'Meaning?'

'I didn't ask what he meant. I find that man intimidating. Attractive though.' Her tone changed. 'Why does he want to stay at the Boathouse? It's not to look after the place; he left it unguarded to come up to Flass.'

'You should never have gone to Flass yourself.' Marjorie advanced with a pad of cotton wool. 'Hold him tight.'

Sophie gripped Sharkey's scruff, the sheep tick on his nose a bloated monstrosity. Marjorie cupped his chin and applied the whisky-soaked pad. Sharkey submitted, ticks being the occupational hazard for country cats.

'Loading the gun was only a gesture,' Sophie said: 'a private action, convincing himself that he possessed the power if he cared to use it.'

'Rubbish. He was waiting for an opportunity. You're still in denial. Or are you making excuses for him: saying he killed Mary because she threatened his marriage?' She stood back. 'You can let him go.'

On the floor Sharkey staggered and fell over. Marjorie went out and returned, the tick disposed of.

Sophie said, 'Michael wanted to have his cake and eat it. He would have liked the affair to continue but to stay married to me. Mary blew the gaff.'

'So he killed her.'

Sophie said nothing. Sharkey had collapsed on the carpet, drunk on fumes. Patchouli, strolling in from the garden, paused, sniffed his face and backed off with a snarl. Sophie said, 'Could drink have played some part?'

'He throttled her in a drunken rage?'

'No. Coulter. I was leap-frogging. Sharkey picks up ticks in the woods—Coulter lived in the woods. I never met the man but if he was a gangster he'd surely have his wits about him, particularly if he was a wanted man. How did anyone get near enough to knock him out so he was trapped in that blazing caravan? He could have been drunk when he was hit. Which implies a drinking partner.'

'There was a bin bag full of lager cans and bottles when Gerald and I discovered the fire.'

'There'd be fingerprints.'

263

'Warwick would know.'

*   *   *

The morning dawned fresh and bright, too bright. The heat haze was gone and the fells stood up hard and high, individual trees on the shore shining like jewels in the brassy sunshine. The lake was a sheet of glass. In the Kelleth station all the windows were open to create draughts.

'What d'you make of that?' Warwick replaced the phone as Lorton entered the office. 'Marjorie Neville wants to know if there were fingerprints on the cans in the bin bag outside Coulter's caravan.'

'She would. It was a murder scene and she's a nosy old bat.'

'What does she think it has to do with her? Or Sophie?'

'They never found any prints,' Lorton muttered. 'Only Coulter's. I wonder if he crushed the cans and wiped the bottles deliberately to destroy prints made by visitors.'

'But then there'd be no prints at all, not even his own.'

They regarded each other. Lorton said slowly, 'If some cans had Coulter's prints and there were none on others, who wiped them?'

'The drinking pal.'

'Has Marjorie tumbled to this? What did you tell her?'

264

'Only that no prints were found other than Coulter's. I asked why she was interested and she said—she sounded hassled as if she hadn't expected me to ask—that any prints other than his could belong to his killer, and since it had been suggested that Sophie knew Coulter, she would be eliminated. Her words.'

'I don't believe it. No one here suggested to her that Sophie knew Coulter—did they?'

'I'm just repeating her words.'

'She's senile.'

'Oh no, just acting that way. She's thinking of a relationship between Coulter and someone else. Not Sophie.'

'Michael?'

'Yes, but why? To what end?'

Chapter Nineteen

The morning wore on, hot and heavy with no breath of a breeze. At Losca Marjorie panicked: 'With the Fairburns coming tonight we don't have enough couscous for Moroccan lamb. Could you run into town and get some? Oh yes, and while you're about it, we could do with another bottle of brandy.'

The errand suited Sophie down to the ground. Since the visit to Flass she'd known she'd be hard put to it to find another good reason to escape from Losca on her own.

She took the Peugeot and drove to the first empty lay-by on the shore road. She had bought a mobile in Scotland and she had Michael's number. To her surprise he was switched on and he answered.

'Michael, we have to talk.'

'Ah, great. I'd been meaning to call you.'

'I'm on my way to town. I'll meet you in the castle park in half an hour.'

'I'll be a bit pushed.'

'An hour then.' That would give her time to do the shopping. She wondered where he was. That was the problem with mobiles, they gave nothing away.

On the hour she entered the park by the back gate, guessing that he'd be watching the main entrance. It was a small park with the remains of the castle on a mound above the river. She emerged from the cover of rhododendrons to see him seated to her right, watching the main gate. He looked isolated and vulnerable; he would have preferred the anonymity of a rural car park but she needed the security of a public place.

Close to he appeared slovenly and it wasn't only his attitude, slumped on the bench, one arm along the back. He was smoking; she didn't know that he'd ever smoked. He must have heard her approach because he turned and stood up. If this was courtesy it was another surprise, but he made no move to touch her. He hadn't shaved and on this humid

266

morning he smelt rank. He must be living in his car.

'Did you bring my typewriter?'

'No.' She stopped herself from blurting that she wasn't staying at the Boathouse.

'Then I'll come down for it.' The way he looked at her was begging a question. Asking permission? 'Or I could come back,' he added gently.

'After everything that's happened?' She looked towards the river, as if the outlook were more interesting than this exchange.

'I've never hurt you,' he said. 'On the other hand, it was only luck that stopped you from wounding me badly.'

'I didn't know the gun was loaded!' Her voice shook. 'It was you loaded it!'

'For rats—'

'We don't have—'

'That was my excuse. I was worried about a break-in. You saw people in the woods. I was concerned for your safety.'

'Oh yes? So you told the police I killed Mary.'

'Nothing of the sort.' He was quite calm. 'They'd backed me into a corner, accused me of killing her. I flipped but I only implied it was you. Of course I knew it wasn't, but I'd have said anything to get them off my back. I was out of my mind. They break a guy with their questions, they're like the Gestapo, you'll confess to anything just to make the questions stop, to get some rest. Rather than confess I shifted the blame to the most likely suspect.'

'You told me. You accused me to my face.'

'That was a mistake—'

'And later,' she said coldly, 'you would have told the police you'd retracted.'

'No need. Everyone knows you didn't do it. Oh, you hit her, yes, but you'd never have tied her like it was done and put her in the lake.'

'You're saying I hit her?'

'You said there was a fight—'

'And throttled her?'

'No, I didn't say—' He stopped short. Until that moment he had been controlled; even when recalling police questioning he had the air of conducting the conversation. Now, as he fell silent, she saw that strange transformation when his features seemed to lose their humanity. Whether the emotion portrayed had been amusement, horror or malice, the indications faded and he regarded her without any trace of feeling at all.

'I didn't kill Mary,' he said.

'I know.'

'How do you know?' His eyes didn't change.

'Because you don't know how she died.'

'Go on.'

'You think I did it and you're in two minds whether it's an advantage to protect me, an advantage to you, that is.'

At last he looked away. He scratched his wrist. He said flatly, 'She was only a child:

immature, affectionate, like a kitten.'

'I know, and that's why you didn't kill her. And why I didn't. I might have wanted her dead but I could never have brought myself to kill her. I'd have got someone else to do it.'

His head came round to her slowly. Another sea change: he was angry and with him she related anger to fear. 'That's the police thinking,' she pointed out.

'That you hired someone? Who? I mean, is this what they're saying? Do they . . .'

'Name someone? Of course. Coulter.'

'Oh. You were having it off with Coulter?'

He rated the man more important as a lover than as a hired killer?

'They're going through his rubbish for prints.'

'His *what*? What in hell are you on about? What prints?'

'There was a sack full of lager cans and bottles outside his caravan. They're being tested for fingerprints to find out who drank with him.'

His parka was on the bench beside him. In the face of her intense glare he felt in a pocket and produced cigarettes and matches. She said nothing. He lit up, inhaled deeply and stretched his legs. The smoke reached her but she didn't move.

'I was sorry for him,' he said distantly. 'He was on the run. He'd got himself involved with some criminals in Manchester and informed on them. There was a contract out on him. He'd never be free of it, not as long as he lived. He knew they'd find him eventually, it was only a matter of time. He was a man under sentence of death. I met him by accident in the woods and a sort of friendship started. Yes, I drank with him. They'll find my prints.' He sighed. 'Poor old Coulter, to end like that. I just hope it was quick.'

'He was a hit man.'

'Oh, for God's sake! You and your melodramas! He was a petty crook and an informant and that's it.'

'He was suspected of several murders but he was clever, the police couldn't get proof. He was in custody for the last one, and he escaped.'

'Balls. Someone's spinning you a line.' His eyes sharpened. 'Did *he* tell you this?'

'Who?'

'Coulter. You knew him. That's it!' He was transformed: incredulous, triumphant. 'You did know him and the bastard never told me. That's why—It was a scam; you set me up between you. You're right, he was a professional, he once offered to get rid of—a man's wife—I think he said the going rate was five, ten thousand pounds, a lot of cash anyway. He talked like that when he was drunk, thought too much of himself, boasting, no way did I take him seriously. I'd forgotten until this moment.' He stopped and stared at her. 'Well, well.' He had returned to the gentle tone but now it held more than a thread of malice. 'You and him in collusion. He killed my girl and I was to be the fall guy, is that it?'

'You've lost the plot, Michael. If I'd hired Coulter to kill Mary, who killed Coulter?'

'You, his mates, who cares? I'm not bothered about him; he was pond life, he had it coming.'

A mobile was ringing and Sophie grabbed her bag. Michael was like a spring under pressure but he made no move to stop her; there were a number of people in the park, some quite close.

'I'm finished now,' Sophie said tensely, the phone clamped to her ear. 'Yes, everything you wanted. I'm in the castle park, with Michael.' She listened, smiling grimly. 'Chief Inspector Warwick? She's with you? Tell her I'm on my way.' She looked at Michael. 'The police want to talk to you.' She held out the phone. He stared at her, mute and furious. 'Give me twenty minutes,' she said into the mobile and switched off. 'I must go now,' she told him, deadly polite.

'What about us?'

'What would you suggest?'

'We have to meet. You said that when you called me. You wanted to talk.'

'Yes.' Tacitly acknowledging that in discussing past violence they had avoided the

271

question of their future relationship. This part was more difficult. 'What I needed to know—' She stopped and started again: 'I had to get at the truth.'

'I told you: I never had any intention of hurting you when I loaded that gun: the opposite in fact. OK, it was stupid bravado, posturing, whatever, but nothing to do with you basically. I need you, Sophie, there's no one else. Look at me, I'll go to pieces without you.' He was pathetic: the old abused cat, sore and wounded, crawling back to the only home that would take him in, the only woman who had cared for him.

'If we still had capital punishment you'd have seen me hanged.'

'I was terrified. I am still. Without you there's no point in going on.'

She stood up. 'I have to think about this. I have your number. I'll call you.'

'Don't leave it too long.' His eyes were fervent.

'I won't.' She smiled. 'That's a promise.'

*   *   *

Marjorie was on the terrace when she heard the Peugeot climbing through the woods. She was starting to feel crowded; here she was trying to calculate how long she had before the weather broke, should she pick the spinach now or wait till the last moment? And there

272

were the young chicks to get under cover, and the Fairburns arriving at six for drinks, so how soon should she start on the lamb? The sherbet could go in the freezer at one—and here was Sophie coming up the drive, surely alone. If she was crazy enough to meet Michael, could she be so demented as to bring him back for lunch? She threw a despairing glance at the sky and went indoors. In the passage she hung back until she saw that Sophie was alone then she retreated to the kitchen and was grating cheese when her god-daughter appeared.

'You haven't eaten?' she asked tightly.

'No, and I'm starving.' Sophie sounded surprised at herself.

'Welsh rarebit then. I gather that ploy of pretending the police were here was for his benefit. You weren't sure of him even in public?' Marjorie's voice had risen. 'Are you all right?'

'You can see I am. That's why I met him in the park. Too public for tantrums.'

'So that's what you call his temper. Are you going to tell me why you had to meet him?'

'I wanted to know the truth. It was essential.'

'What, whether he killed Mary Spence? You asked him!'

'I didn't ask him, but he didn't kill her. What I had to know was whether he'd intended to kill me.'

'He loaded the gun!'

Sophie sat down wearily and looked out at the sky. Marjorie was perplexed. 'He did load it?'

'Oh yes. It's less important.'

'Than what?'

She regarded her godmother helplessly. 'I don't want to talk about it.'

As always when she didn't understand people and their motives Marjorie turned cross and pushy. 'You talked to him but you don't want to talk to me.'

'I don't want to talk about him, about his behaviour.'

'Oh. You went to meet him because you had to know if he was intending harm to you—which is the most innocuous way of putting it—and you didn't find out after all. He's convinced you otherwise, is that it? Don't tell me: you're going to take him back. Did he threaten suicide? Said he couldn't go on without you—and you fell for it. Again.' Marjorie stopped, uneasy about her own vehemence, registering that Sophie's attitude was neither stubborn nor defiant, but attentive.

'It could be worse than you think,' she said.

'Jesus!' Marjorie pulled out a chair. 'Tell me.'

*　　　*　　　*

274

Lorton burst into Warwick's office sweating with excitement and heat. 'They've found a print,' she shouted: 'on one of the crushed lager cans. The bottles were all wiped but someone had the bright idea of teasing out the crinkles in a tin can and there's a thumbprint!'

'That's something, and we have Michael's, but do we have a match?'

Lorton's face fell. 'Sort of. It's a partial. What there is looks good.'

Warwick didn't swear but her silence was eloquent. 'What you mean is it's not enough.'

'We could tell him we've found a print.' Lorton perked up again.

'We could . . .' but it was drawn out. 'It's dodgy. His solicitor might question it.'

'You're bringing him in?'

'Chance would be a fine thing. He's disappeared again. Sophie was at Losca last night and she came into town this morning, shopped in Safeway's, put her stuff in the car, went back to the store and vanished for an hour or so. Michael's Polo was also parked at the store, Heslop saw it by accident when he was looking to see where Sophie had got to. But the couple didn't make contact—weren't seen to make contact, I should say.'

'Because our people were watching the cars—'

'Yes, and the drivers met elsewhere. That is, they could have met, but it's an odd coincidence otherwise that they should both park in the same place. The question is, are we concerned because here we have a husband and wife in collusion, or on opposite sides?'

'And if in opposition, how much does Sophie know about him?'

'If she did meet him this morning she may well know quite a bit—and that print on the lager can gives us a handle. Let's get out of this oven and take a drive in the country.'

Chapter Twenty

Two mobile phones were on the kitchen table. Marjorie was dicing potatoes while Sophie greased a baking sheet. Although they were preparing for the party, both women were considering the use to which the phones might be put. Neither spoke and sounds from outside were absorbed by air like blotting paper. The steamer passed, seeming to skim the tree tops below: a toy boat on a sheet of mercury. And then, through the heavy silence, came a murmur like the far rumble of a plane with a faulty engine. The women paused for a moment but they didn't speak; Sophie thought about Michael living rough in the woods, Marjorie wondered if an electric storm affected mobiles. Then they heard the steady note of an approaching car: a powerful engine, not a Polo, but they were apprehensive still, the occupants could present problems. They continued to prepare food: simple tasks that occupied their hands as they readied themselves for unknown hazards.

Warwick and Lorton appeared outside the window: jolly, summery, like neighbours looking in for a chat.

'You're busy—' Warwick in inane mode. 'Can we come in?'

As if anyone had a choice. 'You'll have to excuse us—' Marjorie trotting out a formula in her turn as they entered. 'A dinner party. We can talk at the same time. Sit. I'll make tea when I'm finished here.'

'What's this?' Lorton stared at a brimming bowl in the sink.

'Nettles.'

'For a dinner party?'

Warwick beamed fatuously. 'A trifle hot for soup?'

'That's why I'm starting now.' Marjorie was patient. 'Cream of nettle soup, iced.'

Lorton gaped. Warwick's gaze passed over the mobiles and focused on Sophie, barefoot, hard and tanned in a skimpy camisole and very short shorts: a young girl's outfit but she had the body for it.

'What's your contribution?' Lorton asked, nosy as a child.

Sophie stopped stirring dough. 'Cheese straws.' Lorton looked blank. 'For nibbles,' Sophie added kindly. 'Perhaps they'd like cold lager rather than tea,' she told Marjorie.

There was a moment of hesitation, the guests neither accepting nor declining, the query having been addressed to the host. 'Ideal,' she said. 'There are cans in the fridge.'

'There's a coincidence!' Warwick announced. 'We found a fingerprint on the cans at Coulter's place.'

Sophie didn't falter on her way to the fridge. Marjorie nodded smugly. 'It was obvious.'

'It was even more obvious when we knew the bottles had been wiped clean; obvious that someone needed to conceal the fact that he'd been drinking with Coulter.'

Sophie was taking tumblers out of a cupboard. 'Use a tray, dear,' Marjorie cooed. 'The sitting room's so much cooler.'

Thus manoeuvred out of the kitchen Warwick stopped in the doorway. 'Aren't you joining us?' she asked politely, meaning 'We need to talk to you too.'

'In a moment.' Marjorie pulled on rubber gloves and made a great clatter extracting a colander from pans under the sink. Her back warned that violence could result if there were further moves to distract her from the chore of straining stinging nettles. Cunning old bat, Warwick thought, following the others to the sitting room, escorted by cats who didn't like clattering noises.

Marjorie gave them a few moments to settle, then she slipped both mobiles into her apron pouch and went upstairs. Lorton saw her pass the door but thought nothing of it, people had to go to the lavatory.

They drank cold lager in a room which was only marginally cooler than the kitchen. 'The fingerprint matched your husband's,' Warwick began chummily: 'what we have of it—'

'I know.' Sophie was prepared for this, They waited. 'They were drinking pals,' she added.

'I was going to say that it's only a partial print but then it's superfluous if you say they knew each other. How long have you known that?'

'Only a few hours. We talked this morning.'

Warwick was silent, returning Patchouli's cool regard. Lorton came in smoothly: 'Where is he staying?'

'He's living in his car.'

'A bit rough in this weather.'

Automatically they looked out of the window to see thick clusters of cloud were starting to show above the fells.

'He's saving money,' Sophie said.

'How do you contact him?'

'I'—she checked for a millisecond—'don't. He called me.'

'You have his number?'

Warwick's glasses flashed as she turned from contemplation of the gathering weather. With two pairs of eyes on her Sophie made to lick her lips but she said steadily enough: 'No. It's a mobile.' As if one could have a land line in a car.

'Mobiles have numbers too.' Lorton grinned. It was a joke, sort of.

'Good God! I can't remember mobile numbers; I can't keep track of conventional ones, what with all the area codes.'

'You'll have it stored on your mobile.'

'Stored? What's that? I've only had a mobile a few days.'

'Like, programmed. You have a record of the numbers you call most frequently.' Sophie was frowning, trying to follow. Lorton sent out a silent plea for support and Warwick responded.

'When you have to get in touch with your husband how do you do it?'

'I leave it to him. He won't tell me where he is. I think he's afraid of you getting to know.'

Warwick abandoned the attempt and switched to something the woman might be prepared to talk about. 'How well did he know Coulter?'

Sophie relaxed visibly. 'Michael visited him occasionally but he thought the chap was just a petty crook and an informant, which was why he was keeping a low profile. He says Coulter shopped some people in Manchester and they were after him.'

'He told you that this morning? Why didn't he tell you before?'

'I didn't ask him.' She thought about that. 'It could be that he was forced to come clean

280

because he feels you're getting close, which is why he's gone into hiding—well, he's not really in hiding, he stays in the locality. I mean, if he did a runner it would look suspicious, so he hangs around. He's on hand as it were. You'd find him quite easily if you tried. *He* could hide in the woods but there's no way you can hide a car.'

Warwick ignored this, and the fact that there were isolated barns where a car could be concealed. She stayed with the original question: 'Could he have felt that you'd disapprove of his friendship with Coulter?'

'It wasn't friendship; he was sorry for the fellow.'

'And didn't know he was a killer.'

'Of course not. He'd have been scared stiff. Michael's not a courageous chap.'

'So he came clean about the—relationship—only this morning. After he knew about the fingerprint.'

Sophie hesitated and they saw her gulp. 'Must have been,' she said, uncomfortable before their concerted attention.

'How could he have known? Miss Neville called us about ten and then Lorton here phoned the lab asking them to look at those lager cans again. How did Michael know that was being done?'

'Why, I must have mentioned it!' Sophie was enlightened. 'Marjorie told me she was phoning you.'

'That explains it.' Warwick leaned back in her chair, giving every appearance of being satisfied with the answer, adding as an afterthought, 'So that's why you had to meet.'

'Not really. We needed to talk about the future. Our marriage.' She was prim.

'Ah, *you* needed to do that.' The emphasis was slight but there.

'Naturally.'

'So you told him to park at Safeway's'— Sophie's eyes widened—'and you talked about your marriage.'

'We talked.' She was starting to clam up.

'He made no objection about meeting you?'

'No, why should he?'

'Because when a demand comes out of the blue from the person who you maintain was responsible for your lover's death it seems odd to acquiesce and agree to meet.'

'Actually he needed to—get things straight.' She ended limply. She'd seen the trap.

'He came at your bidding,' Warwick said. 'You phoned him. Now you give us his number.'

Sophie's face hardened. 'I don't have it in my head. I have it jotted down somewhere. I can find it for you.'

She got to her feet and Lorton stood up as if invited to accompany her.

In the kitchen Marjorie was washing her hands at the sink, nettles still steeping in the bowl. The mobiles were on the table, seeming almost animate in their significance. Sophie went to a cagoule on the back of a door and started to rummage through the pockets. Lorton studied the mobiles.

'Which is yours?'

'They're both mine,' Marjorie said loudly, turning, wiping her hands on her apron. 'Why?'

'Both yours?' Lorton's heart sank. Couldn't they win *anything*?

'Only one works,' Marjorie said as if apologizing for inefficiency. 'The other's on the blink, I mean to try to charge it once I can lay my hands on the charger thing.'

'Where's yours?' Lorton asked sharply of Sophie who turned, red-faced.

'My what? My mobile?' She looked round the kitchen distractedly. 'Now where did I leave it? In the car? In my room? Look, what d'you want: my mobile or Michael's number? I can't find the bloody piece of paper it was on. Really, we're preparing for a formal dinner party and how long—I'm sorry, it's just that we've rather a lot on today, we do have a social life, you know, and with the storm coming and the chicks—Christ, Marjorie, shouldn't we get the chicks in before the rain?'

Lorton said viciously, 'Rinsing nettles takes for ever, doesn't it?'

'Not at all.' Marjorie was at her most serene. 'I had to go to the lavatory. That's the problem with old age: incontinence.'

*   *   *

'She used the phone,' Warwick said as Lorton started down the drive. 'That's why she wanted us out of the kitchen. I didn't hear her phoning, did you?'

'She went upstairs. Nothing we could have done; you can't stop an old woman going to the loo.'

'Particularly if she's incontinent, the wily old fox. Who did she phone? Not Michael, not to warn him we were closing in; she's too fond of Sophie, she *wants* him to go down.'

'Her solicitor?'

'Why? Are we a threat to her—or to Sophie?'

'Actually, yes. Sophie's protecting Michael. Obviously she has his number. She may not know where he is but she's able to contact him, no doubt about that.'

'If one of those mobiles was Sophie's—no, Marjorie's too cunning for that. What happened was that when she went upstairs she swapped Sophie's for an old phone that's useless, dead. Sophie's, with his number stored on it, she left upstairs. Marjorie isn't protecting Michael but concealing the fact that Sophie is. Sophie could be following some line of her own that her godmother disapproves of. Does she strike you as an abused wife?'

'She doesn't show any sign of—'

284

'No, no. Abused in the widest sense: betrayed several times over. The affair with Mary, and then Michael accusing Sophie of murdering the girl, if only by implication. Of course that was abuse.'

'So?'

'Some abused women take their partners back.'

'You reckon Sophie's considering taking Michael back? That's what the meeting was about this morning? After the way he's treated her? And will in the future,' she added darkly. 'That leopard's never going to change his spots.'

'Abused women. We see it all the time.'

They returned to the station to find Mackreth and Rumney snatching a tea break, eager to acquaint the women with an update on the print on the lager can, now almost certainly Michael's.

'We knew,' Lorton said. 'He's admitted that he visited Coulter and drank with him.'

'You found him?'

'No, we've talked to Sophie.'

They gathered in Warwick's office and the men were briefed on the interview with Sophie at Losca and the significance of the mobile phones.

Mackreth said, 'I'm sure we have Michael's number.'

Lorton was incredulous. She turned to Warwick. 'Why didn't we think of that? Here

285

we've spent hours trying to prise it out of Sophie.'

'I thought of it.' Warwick was cool. 'But it wasn't the objective of the interview, only the excuse. We needed to find out what Sophie isn't telling us.'

Mackreth was startled. 'Did you?'

'I worded that badly. We needed to know if Sophie was keeping something from us.'

'Collusion,' Rumney put in.

She considered this, pursing her lips. 'Possibly—but, more interesting, if not collusion, then what? Could she be following some kind of programme on her own?'

'What would be the point?' Lorton asked. 'If she suspects Michael—or Coulter . . . I mean, you're thinking in terms of Mary's murder, aren't you?' Warwick nodded assent. Lorton continued, 'If she knew something that implicated Michael—'

'Or exonerated him.'

Lorton checked for a moment but she stuck to her theme: 'Then she'd tell us, wouldn't she? Like Marjorie calling to suggest we check those cans again for prints.'

'Marjorie and Sophie could be working in opposition,' Warwick pointed out. 'Or rather, they need not be in full agreement. Or'—she looked surprised at herself—'they're not coming clean with each other.'

'But she's—'

'Marjorie would never—'

286

'There's no way that—'

While the three of them argued and remonstrated Warwick sat quietly, seemingly mesmerized by the light in her Caithness paperweights, the one in dusky pinks, the other in shades of green. She murmured something. Lorton, running out of steam, glanced aside. 'What was that?'

'I said: two green Minis.'

In the sudden silence the room darkened and a paper lifted on the desk, caught by a waft of air.

'They both had the same car,' Mackreth agreed. 'The same model: Mary and Sophie. What are you saying?'

'You could confuse the cars,' Lorton was trying to follow the boss's thinking, 'but not the women. Mary was slight, Sophie's muscular.'

'If Michael is speaking the truth,' Warwick began, and seeing Lorton open her mouth, forestalled her: 'as he did on occasions—although we agree that makes him more complicated—but if he was in love with Mary he's unlikely to have killed her. And, as you say, no husband could mistake his lover for his wife as he was throttling her, even in the dark—'

'There's a light in the yard,' Mackreth interrupted.

'Sophie put it out after Mary left the house. Mary,' Warwick said slowly, 'had suffered a hard blow to the head. She walked outside. Did she get in her car and collapse, or get out of it again and fall? Sophie had fired a shot earlier. Did someone else hear that shot and come to see what was going on? And he finds a woman, in the dark, in or beside a Mini. And he knows Sophie drives a Mini.'

'Coulter,' Lorton stated with finality. 'And he throttled her and put her in the bin bags. Why was she trussed up? Has anyone thought of that?

'To implicate Michael!' Mackreth cried. 'Coulter was setting him up. Michael was speaking the truth when he said he was the fall guy: stuff from his outbuildings, his boat used—'

'But Michael didn't want Mary killed! You just said—' Lorton turned on Warwick and stopped, enlightened.

'Exactly,' Warwick nodded approval. 'Coulter was meant to kill Sophie. He got the wrong woman.'

'And when Michael found out, he killed Coulter: a revenge killing?'

'No. Coulter was killed four days before anyone knew that Mary was a victim. Everyone thought—and that surely included Michael— that although you were looking for a missing woman who could be dead, that woman was Sophie. If Coulter killed the wrong woman he never knew it, and if he killed for a fee, as he would, being the man he was, he demanded payment.'

'But Michael had no money,' Lorton protested. 'Oh, I've got it: both guys thought it was Sophie who was dead, and she had the money and Michael would inherit and could pay Coulter . . . after he sold the Boathouse. Would Coulter agree to wait that long?'

'Maybe Michael tricked him,' Mackreth said doubtfully. 'They fought—but Michael's not young, he'd be no match for a professional killer.'

'He's charming and devious,' Warwick reminded him. 'And they drank together. He'd have opportunities to get behind Coulter particularly if he stayed sober. If you're drinking in the open air, possibly at dusk, nothing's easier than to pour your drink on the ground.'

'It's all circumstantial,' Mackreth muttered.

'It fits.' Lorton was backing Warwick.

'He'd break if we was to feed it to him bit by bit,' Rumney put in. 'He'd lie like mad but he could well lie himself into a corner: the more you tell, the more you got to remember. He'll break, mark my words.'

'We'll bring him in,' Warwick decided, and glanced at the window. The sky above the town was plum-coloured and lights were coming on in buildings. It was only five o'clock. 'Let's have his number.'

It was found and rung but Michael's mobile was switched off.

'Perhaps he's bothered about a lightning strike,' Lorton said. 'Do you think Sophie has reached the same conclusions as we have: that Mary was killed in mistake for herself, that Michael actually hired a hit man to throttle his own wife and put her in the lake? It's diabolical.'

'It happens.' Warwick was expressionless.

'If she did know—or suspect—I wouldn't want to be in Michael's shoes.'

'Perhaps that's why she's protecting him.'

'You're joking.'

'Think about it.'

'What? Taking things into her own hands? Why, only an hour ago you were considering her as an abused wife, at least in the sense of humiliated.'

'Quite, and that's one reason why I want him brought in: out of her reach. For tonight we'll keep a watch on Losca, assuming she'll stay there for this party. And if she goes anywhere—to the Boathouse or anywhere else—we follow, make sure they don't meet, that is, if we haven't already found Michael.'

Chapter Twenty-One

The sky darkened further but there was a strong wind at altitude tearing the clouds apart, and through the gaps shafts of sunlight came streaming to paint new foliage an aching green against the shadowed fells. Here and there the surface of the lake was roughened by a vagrant breeze. At Losca Marjorie fastened the door on the hen house and dusted her hands.

'That's the lot,' she announced. 'The garden's going to take a beating but that can't be helped.'

'All the birds are safe anyway—' Sophie began, and at that moment there was a piercing flash throwing all the world into relief: trees, water, mountains. The women gaped, waiting, and then came the crash, followed by fading drumbeats as the echoes, trapped, rolled up and down the valley—and all the ducks and hens erupted in a cacophony of alarm.

'I'll close the windows,' Marjorie said. 'You call the Fairburns, tell them to come up now, while it's still dry. Tell them to bring wellies.' Summer storms never lasted long but trees could be brought down, blocking the guests' return by car, which could mean a wet tramp home through the woods.

The storm advanced, night arriving before its time; lights showed along the far shore to be lost in the magnificent flares of lightning. Thunder exploded and growled, prowling round the headwalls of the corries and, in the charged silence between, Fairburn's dogs could be heard baying defiance. The cats were silent, burrowed deep under bed covers.

The rain didn't come in showers as with customary lakeland weather; one moment flagstones on the terrace were dry, and patches of soil were cracked like desert laterite, the next, a big dark spot appeared, and another; then below the lawn the canopy rustled and bowed, and the heavens opened.

The Fairburns came stumbling in at the back door, laughing and shouting as Sophie appeared in the passage, all behaving like children now that they'd shut up their animals and could revel in the storm from the sanctuary of the shabby sitting room.

'There's a car in your woods,' Gerald told Marjorie. 'We saw it gleaming in our headlights: quite obvious but I took its number, not sure whether it might belong to a friend of yours or tourists. 'Fact, I've seen it somewhere before. How about reporting it?'

'Would it be a police car?'

'Unmarked, but it could be. Better find out what it's doing there, eh?'

Marjorie called Warwick and wasn't surprised to find the DCI still at the station at close on six o'clock; in a storm you never knew what shape an emergency might take. Warwick was apologetic: yes, there were police in Losca's woods, they were maintaining surveillance, nothing to do with the residents or their guests, a police presence just, in view of the ongoing situation.

'Shouldn't we have been informed?' Marjorie's tone was dry.

'It would worry you,' Warwick said mendaciously. 'They shouldn't have shown themselves, they had orders to be discreet.'

'How long will they stay there?'

There was hesitation at the other end. 'They will accompany Mrs Daynes back to the Boathouse,' Warwick said formally, as if she were arranging precedence at a funeral.

'She'll be sleeping here tonight.'

'Ah.' That sounded like relief. 'Then they'll stay until your guests leave and you've locked up—unless you'd like us to—'

'That will do,' Marjorie put in quickly. 'I mean, she's not going to come to any harm with someone else in the house, is she?' She sighed heavily. 'I do hope you—trace him soon. I didn't realize, I'm sure she doesn't . . . you think he actually intends . . .' She trailed off.

Warwick said, 'We'll find him tomorrow. We have his number.'

'You have? Sophie couldn't find it.'

'Mackreth had it back here at the station.'

'Has he talked to you?'

'Michael? Not yet. His phone is switched off.'

Marjorie returned to her guests to acquaint them with the gist of the exchange. Rain lashed the windows but the storm had moved north and now, in the lessening gloom, the pale light revealed white horses running across the lake.

Marjorie and Sophie were lavish with the drinks, tacitly trying to get the party going. Conversation was stilted as it must be with the awareness of surveillance and the presumed motivation behind it. Any subject appeared contrived when the Fairburns viewed Sophie as a potential murder victim. And of course everyone was wondering where Michael was. As the storm passed Gerald stood up and went to the window. He turned to his host.

'All right if I draw your curtains, m'dear?'

'Not at all.' Marjorie was equable. Sophie slid her a glance. Curtains were never drawn at Losca.

Out in the woods DC Stokesley stretched her cramped legs and reached for the second Thermos. 'What do we do if he does come?' she asked resentfully. 'He'll be past here before we have a chance to stop him. Anyway, he's not about to try anything with a house full of guests.'

'Only two of them—and the two of us. He's supposed to see us, we're a deterrent like:

keeping a high profile.'

Heslop accepted coffee in a plastic mug, placed it on the dashboard and reached for his cigarettes.

'Not unless you open a window,' Stokesley growled.

'How can I? It's pissing down.'

'Then get out. You can coat your own lungs with tar but no way do you damage mine.'

'Women!'

'There are as many men have given up as women.'

They bickered while the rain turned to drizzle and the becks swelled. By ten o'clock the drizzle had stopped although the woods were full of the sound of water. The Fairburns left, easing down the drive past the police car ('They'll be lucky not to be mired,' Gerald chuckled. 'They're protecting Sophie,' Davina said reprovingly.) The DCs emerged gingerly and plodded up the slope to the house. There were lights in upper bedroom windows and they were inspected by prowling cats but there was no sign of anything untoward, neither of people approaching Losca, nor of either occupant leaving. They returned to the car, reported, and Warwick called them in. He wouldn't come tonight, she averred, moreover Marjorie had a shotgun and, if Sophie were to be believed, Michael wasn't a courageous man.

*   *   *

The day after the storm dawned bright and fresh, and all road patrols were on the watch for him, first in the county and then the region. There was no result until the public were alerted by an item on the News regarding his importance to the investigation into Mary's death. The make and number of his car was broadcast and two days after the storm hikers reported it, unlocked and empty, at the end of the road that served the lighthouse on the great sandstone cliffs of St Bees Head. There was no sign of Michael and no note. A sea and ground search was launched.

The Polo was traced to a Thomas Lewthwaite, a garage owner in Lancaster who, at the request of his son, had lent the car to Michael against a cheque for five hundred pounds. Interviewed, his son, Sam, told how he'd acceded to his friend's anguished pleas for transport. Michael's story was one of domestic trouble and his wife's appropriating his own car. His solicitor had things in hand, he said, but for the moment he was without wheels and desperate for the loan of any old vehicle just for a week or two. Sam passed him on to his father. In the event Michael's cheque bounced but Lewthwaite Senior kept quiet about it. Everyone thought Sophie was a widow and anyway he had the Polo back.

After several days the official search for Michael's body was abandoned. People remained on the alert round the Cumbrian coast and the Solway Firth but nothing was found.

Sophie, encouraged by Marjorie, moved back to the Boathouse and set about rebuilding her life. She found evening work at the Lurcher and for the rest of the time she laboured happily to become more or less self-sufficient. Marjorie supplied her with pullets, a clutch of eggs and a broody hen, and two kittens came from the rescue centre who would, in time, keep rabbits out of the vegetable plot. Meanwhile she had her gun, the police having returned it with the shot-up Mini. She sold the Mini and bought a Land Rover, making up the cost by selling what remained of her mother's jewellery. She wasn't surprised to find some of it missing, any more than she questioned the odd item of a hundred pounds on her next bank statement. She'd always known that Michael was a thief.

As for Weston, he took Andrew back home with him to Essex where he helped out in the nursery until they returned for the resumed inquest on Mary—but not for that on Coulter. In both cases the verdict was murder by person or persons unknown. Ralph Fisher's brother-in-law was curiously vague as to the identity of the perpetrators) because, of course, everyone knew that the verdict was a fudge. No one could be sure who had murdered Coulter, nor how to apportion the blame for Mary's death—not that it mattered, ran the grapevine, they were both killers, and both got their deserts even if Michael's end smacked of divine justice, tumbling down the cliffs into the sea. Actually he must have been very careful in choosing the point where he went over because in many places the high tide line was some distance out from the foot of the cliffs.

After the inquest on Mary, Weston returned to his business and Andrew departed for the Seychelles to take up a post managing a five-star hotel.

With Flass lying derelict and abandoned Marjorie put in an offer for the ruins and grounds, and a ten-acre parcel of woodland that comprised all that was left of the estate. It made an ideal nature reserve. There were some rare ferns and liverworts apart from the kind of lakeland fauna that haunted private woods: red squirrels and green woodpeckers, the roe deer and those stoats by the well. At some point the well was plugged; the cover had been removed and all the rubbish that was the remains of the parapet and the windlass was dumped in the shaft. The cover had been replaced and topsoil laid down. Sophie didn't notice it for a few weeks when, surveying the property with Marjorie prior to the purchase, she remarked on the absence of lumber and bricks at the site of the old well and she remembered that Weston had mentioned plugging the shaft.

'He must have done it while he was staying at the Boathouse,' she said. 'Thoughtful of him. You'd never know there had once been a well here. And the young stoats were full grown so they wouldn't come to harm. They can den elsewhere. I just hope he filled the shaft to the top, otherwise someone could fall in; presumably the old cover is underneath all that new vegetation.'

'I'm sure he did,' Marjorie said comfortably. 'He wasn't a man who left anything to chance.'

They climbed the slate steps and found seats on the broken wall of the terrace.

'He's there, isn't he?' Sophie indicated the place where the well had been. 'Michael would never commit suicide—and jumping off the top of a cliff? No way.'

'He could be there, yes.'

'It was Weston? But Michael didn't kill Mary. And Coulter was meant to kill me, not her. It was a mistake.'

'Weston wouldn't make allowances for that kind of mistake.'

'How was it done? *You* were involved? This is why you're buying Flass. It's why you told me to come home. You knew it was safe because Michael was dead. St Bees was a false trail, but it wasn't laid by him. What happened?'

'I called Weston on the day of the storm, when the police were interviewing you in the sitting room and I took the mobiles upstairs. I told him to text Michael and tell him to come to the Boathouse. The message purported to come from you.'

'The poor sod.'

'He had aimed to have you killed.'

Sophie inhaled deeply. 'So he came to the Boathouse . . . and now he's there, in the well shaft. And Weston drove the Polo to St Bees Head. How did he get back? Ah, Andrew followed in his Fiesta, and now Andrew's been sent to the Seychelles, out of the way.' She frowned. 'Somewhere there's a mobile with a message on it from me telling Michael to come to the Boathouse. No, there isn't. It's in the sea.'

'It would have been smashed first.'

'Weston thought of everything. Thank God he's on the side of the angels; what an opportunity to blackmail me if he'd kept that mobile. Blackmail. Didn't someone say, was it Michael himself, that he was a fall guy, that wrapping Mary's body in stuff from our outbuildings set him up as the killer? Sometimes he spoke the truth. Coulter could have blackmailed him, which was why Michael had to kill him. Not much to choose between them in the end, both of them motivated by money, although Coulter was the honest one: killing for a fee. Who am I to talk? I was working out how to—disable Michael myself. Trouble was I couldn't think how to do it

300

without getting caught and no way was I going to go to prison for life.'

'I know,' Marjorie said. 'You would kill but you'd never get away with it. Guilt would be your problem.'

'You knew what I had in mind? You got in first! You *used* Weston.'

'Not at all. We knew where we stood and we each—all, actually, Andrew included—all played a part. It's called collusion, dear: a more refined form of civilized behaviour. Not cynical, just practical.'

Chivers Large Print Direct

If you have enjoyed this Large Print book and would like to build up your own collection of Large Print books and have them delivered direct to your door, please contact **Chivers Large Print Direct**.

Chivers Large Print Direct offers you a full service:

✧ **Created to support your local library**

✧ **Delivery direct to your door**

✧ **Easy-to-read type and attractively bound**

✧ **The very best authors**

✧ **Special low prices**

For further details either call Customer Services on 01225 443400 or write to us at

Chivers Large Print Direct
FREEPOST (BA 1686/1)
Bath
BA1 3QZ